**Nicholas Hogg** was born in Leices̶~~~~~~~~~~
ating from ̶he U ̶rsity of ̶ ̶on ̶ ̶w ̶
̶̶̶̶, he travelled widely, living in Japan, Fiji and the
United States. He won the 2005 New Writing Ventures award
for fiction and was a prizewinner in the London Writers
contest. His first novel, *Show Me the Sky*, was published in
2008. He is currently in Asia working on his third novel.

# THE HUMMINGBIRD AND THE BEAR

NICHOLAS HOGG

corsair

Constable & Robinson Ltd
55–56 Russell Square
London WC1B 4HP
www.constablerobinson.com

First published in the UK by Corsair,
an imprint of Constable & Robinson Ltd, 2011

This paperback edition published by Corsair, 2012

A copy of the British Library Cataloguing in Publication
Data is available from the British Library

ISBN 978-1-78033-219-2

Printed and bound in the UK

1 3 5 7 9 10 8 6 4 2

MIX
Paper from
responsible sources
FSC
www.fsc.org    FSC® C018072

A love story is not about those who lose their heart but about those who find that sullen inhabitant who, when it is stumbled upon, means the body can fool no one, can fool nothing – not the wisdom of sleep or the habit of social graces. It is a consuming of oneself ...

Michael Ondaatje, *The English Patient*

Before us, stands yesterday.

Ted Hughes, handwritten in a signed
copy of *Birthday Letters*

# I

WITH THOUGHTS OF OUR own fairy-tale wedding on the banks of the Thames, booked for the first week of May next year, Jenni and I watched the radiant bride float down the aisle.

'My God,' she whispered. 'Look at that dress.'

It was a meringue piled upon another meringue, in my opinion. But at that point in my life the thought of a grand church wedding was still romantic theatre, not pantomime. Together we watched the bride and the bridesmaids and the pageboy walk the aisle of a church dating back to the eleventh century, the huge stone font covered in carvings of the apostles, no doubt baptising newborns and observing weddings since Norman times.

From Monday to Friday, Jenni was an assertive PA who shooed brokers around billion-dollar investment banks. Tall and slim, willowy I'd heard people say, and long blond hair with a Scandinavian lustre inherited from the Norwegian blood in her mother. Jealous men would've worried about the chat-up lines of testosterone-fuelled traders, the leering suits ogling her in a mirrored lift. But her slender figure belied a taut strength of body and mind, a sharp wit ready to cut down the barrow boys dealing millions. And her boss knew this too. Her rising status meant she could be doing anything from arranging a conference call to actually being the representative sitting before the screen.

Now she wiped a tear away with a handkerchief that matched her dress. And she cried some more during the ceremony, as did other guests, many whispering it was good luck that a tiny sparrow had flown into the church and fluttered over the vows.

'I pronounce thee man and wife,' intoned the priest. 'You may kiss the bride.'

They embraced, and for that moment all the dreams of love and marriage were true.

On the church steps Jenni scanned the brooding weather. 'Friendly clouds, friendly clouds,' she repeated. 'We just need sun for the photos, then it can pour down.'

I looked at the swirl of thunderstorms, the patches of blue sky bruised by rain showers sweeping across the Cotswold hills. Jenni looped her arm through my elbow as we stood clutching confetti, waiting in the shrinking sunshine, unaware that the timing of a shower could alter a life so drastically.

What if the rain had fallen on a different field, or blown over ten minutes earlier, or later?

Waiting on those church steps, on stone worn by centuries of guests attending ceremonies joining one to the other, if you'd asked me to tell you what it means to love, to give your body and soul to someone else, I'd tell you about Jenni.

Then the bride and groom appeared.

We threw confetti and rice, regaled them with cheers, our own hopes of happily ever after. The photographer was keen to get the shots in before the rain, and hurried the various groups of guests into position, shepherding different sides of the families on to the church steps.

In one photo the groom holds the bride, as if carrying her over the threshold of their new home, laughing, blissful, their hair and faces speckled with bits of brightly coloured paper. I remember this photo in particular, because it was the snap Jenni ordered from *Mark and Briony's Wedding Album*. 'Are you going to pick me up like that?' she'd asked, setting the photo on the bookshelf in our Maida Vale flat, a red-brick apartment with an ironwork balcony we'd bought with my first six-figure salary last year. This mortgage was a statement, I believed, not only of success to myself, but to Jenni of my intentions, that I was serious about our future together.

Hundreds of guests had been invited to the reception, and as the quaint Gloucestershire village had no venue bigger than a scout hut available Briony's father had erected a gleaming marquee the size of a big top in a nearby field.

Like a procession of worshippers following two deities, the guests followed the horse and carriage through the narrow village streets. Local children ran and jumped and threw bunches of second-hand confetti picked up off the church steps. Hooves clip-clopped and so did our own heels and shoes. Bewitched by the romance of the occasion, Jenni was practically skipping along, ignoring my snickering comments about someone's gaudy dress or fruit bowl hat. When the first spits of rain dotted the road she snapped, 'No, no. Not yet.'

'There might be a rainbow,' I ventured.

If there was I never saw it. When the shower fell it flashed from the sun like streaks of mercury. Those that had umbrellas popped them open.

'Shit,' swore Jenni, grabbing my arm and pulling herself closer for some shelter. 'My hair.'

'You're the one who said an umbrella would bring bad luck.'

I took off my jacket and held it over her head until we got to the marquee. Other guests without umbrellas scuttled under the awning or back to cars parked just beyond the guy ropes.

'I could do with some lipstick,' said Jenni. 'Let's make a run for the car.'

We ran through the rain, Jenni now holding my jacket above her head until we slid inside and slammed the doors.

'Good timing.'

'Only just.' Her hair was wet. She flicked down the visor mirror. 'Fuck. It'll be frizzy later.'

'We'll all be pissed by then.' Buses had been laid on to take us from the reception to the nearest hotel, then back again in the morning to pick up the cars.

'Is that still the plan, then?' She was asking about my dawn exit.

'You know it is.' I had to be in London by noon to meet a senior analyst, and would be leaving Jenni to catch a lift later on.

'Fancy scheduling a meeting the day after a wedding.'

'Blame the Germans.'

'You always do.'

'He's flying in from Frankfurt.'

'You make it sound like an air raid,' she laughed, fiddling with her hair.

'It could be if he's firing people.'

'Not you?' she asked, a mild concern.

'Nein. I'm the star of the firm.'

'Big head.' Jenni playfully slapped my arm, again. A part of our relationship that had developed into an unuttered, habitual *I love you*. 'How perfect was the horse and carriage?'

'A bit Disney.'

'True.' She had the lipstick in her hand, readied. Then she turned, a spark in her pale blue eyes. 'Are you going to smudge my lips if I put this on now?'

'My advice is to let me kiss you first.'

And she did. I leant across the seats and kissed her hard until she abruptly drew away.

'So weddings get you horny. That's good to know.'

'Must be the thought of all that fancy underwear.'

She kissed me back, and I wanted all of her, in the rush of the raindrops on the car roof, behind windows steamed with breath. I put my hand up her dress.

'Not now, Sam.'

She was right. It was hardly the best spot to have sex.

But if we had made love there and then it would've been the last time I'd think only about her and not someone else.

I NEVER UNDERSTOOD WHY men went to war, why men would die in the corner of a muddy field for the colour of a flag, until I saw her at the wedding. She wore a yellow dress and no shoes, a woman lit by electric cloud running through a storm with a pair of high heels dangled in her hands.

It was Jenni who called out for her to shelter with us.

'You sure?' she replied, ducking under the umbrella.

'At least keep your hair dry.'

As simple as that. There she was against my shoulder.

I was standing between the two of them, raising the umbrella high over the three of us. I inhaled the aroma of some exotic perfume lifting off her bare shoulders. I was that close. I could have leaned forward and kissed her neck.

Or bitten her.

That close before we'd even said hello.

'I'm Kay.'

She was American. We introduced ourselves, Jenni doing the 'who invited you' bit. Which was good, as I doubt I could have pulled myself together to make the necessary small talk. In that briefest of greetings, before she turned back to look where she was stepping, we were face to face, all eyes, lips and mouth. Too quick for any details, yet long enough for me to wonder what makes one person fall into another.

And fall is the right verb. We don't walk, shuffle, or decide. We *fall*, some further than others. Some without warning.

'Hey,' said Jenni, breaking step. 'Be a gentleman and keep *both* the ladies dry.'

I was holding the umbrella further towards Kay, letting the rain fall on Jenni's hat and dress.

'Sorry, sorry.' I laughed nervously.

The rain smacked down on the umbrella, harder, and the three of us pressed closer as we walked, bumping hips, bodies. We high-stepped the puddles and runnels, and then ran like frightened children when lightning forked into the next field.

'Oh my God,' screamed Jenni.

The thunderclap crackled about the valley, and I ushered us all into the marquee. Drenched guests stood about in shock. Soaked hats and limp flowers, outfits ruined.

Then Kay waltzed in with muddy feet.

'Not quite the entrance I was hoping to make,' she laughed.

Jenni laughed too. And so did the nearly drowned others, glad of distraction from their bedraggled hair and running make-up, happy to let this American woman steal the show, which she did.

I stood back and shook the umbrella. I was looking, but I wasn't. Not looking at her copper skin wet with rain, how she cheekily lifted a glass of water from a passing waiter and poured it over her slender feet, a private moment public, the thought of her preening in a scented bath.

I took a towel from one of the caterers and stepped forward. Jenni was there, I know that. Otherwise I might have bent and dried her feet. Not because I wanted to, but because it was the thing to do. She thanked me, smiled. By not looking her in the eye, I was looking. Again. Looking at her painted toes, the way her black hair shone like wet coal.

I quickly slipped back to the circle of onlookers, watching as Jenni helped her balance into her shoes.

THE WEDDING RECEPTION WAS the usual orchestrated procession of thank yous and toasts, glasses of pink champagne cordially raised in appreciation of fathers, mothers and brides. On rows of tables bedecked with flowers and attended by a legion of uniformed waiters, we sat and politely listened to the parents' gentle anecdotes. Until the speech of the best man, a rugby-playing currency trader I knew via a friend in the City. Perhaps he was already a little drunk, perhaps he was a stand-up comic trapped in a suit and tie, but it was one of those rip-roaring performances that rock a wedding with laughter, inspiring guests to knock back drinks with merry abandonment.

I heard, and laughed, at most of the jokes, but not all.

She sat two tables away. A yellow flame burning at the corner of my vision. I took wide, sweeping looks of the marquee to hide my stares.

Of course she was with someone else. I was hardly surprised by this. But neither did it mean anything.

So was I.

I was drunk before the end of the meal. I can't recall what was on the menu, what food I ate. Possibly duck? Some stringy game bird I chewed without tasting. My senses had been overloaded, burned out. And I know this sounds fanciful. If I'd heard something similar from a friend, that he or she had been sitting with the one they'd pledged to marry, consumed not by thoughts of a rosy future with their betrothed, but of whether a woman across a crowded room was seated next to her husband, I'd have passed it off as juvenile, wanton lust.

He looked a little older than her, silver in his hair, early forties. He looked like a man who'd made money, a man who usually got what he wanted.

From where I sat, I couldn't see if she wore a ring or not. Though I could certainly see the engagement ring flashing on Jenni's finger, the brilliant cut diamond I'd bought in a Bond Street jewellers.

'Don't get too pissed,' she leant over and whispered, resting her hand on my thigh. 'I want a dance with you later.'

She also reminded me that I had to be on the road at seven o'clock in the morning.

'I'll have a couple of coffees.'

'You'll need the whole pot at this rate.'

The bride and groom took the floor for the first dance. He twirled her a little awkwardly to begin, and they quickly gave up the pretence of knowing any choreographed steps as she nestled her cheek against his. Jenni leant into the crook of my shoulder. 'That's better than them learning some crowd-pleasing tango.'

Watching the newly-weds hug and sway, I forgot about Kay and thought of Jenni. I forgot the heat of Kay's body, her bare shoulders, her silky hair over the back of my hand. I was free, content with my future, the woman pressed against my chest, *Jenni's* scent, *Jenni's* hair. This was how she slept, how we fitted together in bed, arms curled around each other till morning.

But then again that flicker of her yellow dress at the corner of my vision. The way a flame might catch the corner of a piece of paper, or a photo, and burn its way into the centre of the picture.

'CHRIS SEGUR.' HE PUT out his hand to be shaken. He had the tanned skin of a weekend sailor, broad shoulders and a heavy frame. A man who probably played golf on a workday and closed business deals over lunches of smoked salmon. 'Kay told me you kept her dress dry.'

We gripped hard and vigorously shook, alpha males. I bumbled something about there being plenty of space for the three of us. Jenni, flushed with champagne, launched into chatter with Kay about her outfit, while Segur and I did the obligatory intros.

'Mark's my guy in London.' Segur pointed his glass towards the groom. 'Now he's got a wife to slave for, I've really got him pinned.'

I faked a laugh for the comment, and noted the offhand tilt of his glass to point out a man across the room. He bragged about hedge funds and profits, an American show of money where we British would hide. But still, a blowhard's introduction.

'She's quite a catch, too.' He nodded towards Jenni. 'You tied the knot yet?'

'Next year,' I replied. 'And already planning.'

'You've got that right.'

'Planning', I'd said. Yes, perhaps I already was. When he launched into a monologue on the predictions of an oncoming

15

financial crisis, I focused on Jenni, standing chatting with Kay at such an angle that when I looked over Segur's shoulder, and then over Jenni's, we stared past our partners and directly into each other's eyes.

And when she immediately dropped her gaze, her sparkle, I felt caught out, a fool. And rejected. We'd passed no more than a greeting and I'd been hurt by a woman who was talking to my fiancée.

I knew I was behaving like a schoolboy in raptures over his teacher, or any other fanciful, ridiculous and unrequited attraction. Resolved to take back command of my own body, I apologized to Segur and slipped my arm round Jenni's waist. 'Let's dance.'

She laughed to Kay. 'Whisked off my feet.'

I danced with my wife to be, a woman I'd been waking up next to for the last three years. Below the glitzy disco lights I kissed her neck and told her I wished our own wedding was tomorrow. And I really did. I was afraid of the schism Kay had so suddenly caused, and hugged Jenni tighter, pushing my pelvis against her hips. We were one again until a change of song and Jenni made a run to the Ladies.

I headed to the bar despite promising I wouldn't.

A broken promise.

Broken promises.

I was drunk. I felt heavy, as if walking across the surface of a planet with stronger gravity.

I looked around for Kay. And Segur. But I was too pissed to see much further than my own nose. So when he appeared in the mirror behind the bar, I thought I might turn round and find him gone. One moment I was poking in my wallet, the next moment he was there, as if beamed down by a spot-light in the roof, a stark light, that for the briefest second seemed to reveal a crueller being before the amiable busi-nessman held out a note and paid for our rum and Cokes.

'Still standing, then?' he joked as we clinked glasses.

Guests were drifting away. Buses had begun ferrying those worse for wear back to the hotel. When I asked him if Kay had already left I thought I'd revealed myself, but he replied, smiling, 'Early night. She's got a flight to New York tomorrow, and I hear you might be able to help me out?'

'Help you out?'

'I have to be in Glasgow Monday. And I know I should be the gentleman and drive her to the airport, but what's with the trains in this country? I book a first class ticket from Stroud to Marylebone and then find out they want to put her on a bus.'

'Sunday is repairs day.'

'Track replacement, or something. Sounds like a goddamn train set.'

I asked if she was flying from Heathrow.

'That close to where you're heading?'

I said it was, and felt a sharp jolt along my spine.

'Be great if she could jump in. I have a car service, but I hardly trust the shmucks to find this place by tomorrow morning.'

'Not a problem,' I said. 'I'd be glad to.'

When he shook my hand I could smell her perfume on him.

'I owe you one.' He reached into his blazer and pulled out a silver case filled with business cards. 'Here. You get across the pond much?'

17

I told him I did. 'New York's a happening city.'

'Can't compare. Next time you're in town be sure to look me up. You like football?'

'Not soccer?'

'No, no. American football.'

'Great game,' I said. 'But not as good as rugby.'

He laughed, and, as bigger men often do, affirmed some higher status by manfully slapping my shoulders with his bear paw hands.

'We tackle *without* pads and helmets,' I added, contesting the hierarchy.

'Hell, call me if you hit New York and I'll take you to a Giants game.' He shook his head. 'Not as good as rugby, my ass.'

We arranged that I'd drop by their room in the morning. 'I owe you one,' he repeated. 'I mean it.' He then opened his leather wallet and pulled out a thick roll of notes. 'At least let me get your gas and lunch.'

Of course I refused the money.

'Don't say I didn't offer.'

Perhaps a little perturbed because I hadn't accepted the cash, he slipped the notes back into his wallet and again patted me on the shoulder. 'Maybe I can throw some business your way.' Then he shook my hand and wished me good-night. As he walked off I imagined nailing him with a rugby tackle, clattering him across the dance floor.

I also wondered if he'd touch his wife's naked body with the same palm that had just shaken my hand.

By the time Jenni came back I'd drunk both our rum and Cokes.

'Your alarm,' mumbled Jenni. 'Switch off your alarm.' I swore. Sunrise hit the hotel curtains. It seemed that only minutes ago I was standing with a drink in the bustle of the reception.

'Do you have time for a shower?' Jenni addressed me from beneath the sheets. 'You smell like a brewery.'

I sleepwalked into the cubicle, scrubbed and scoured. Once I'd towelled myself dry I looked at my puffy face in the mirror. 'Fuck.'

'You're still pissed, aren't you?'

'Tell me about it.' Whisky and rum seeped from my pores. 'If I wasn't on taxi duty I wouldn't have even got up.' And that wasn't a lie, either. If I wasn't due outside Kay's room I'd have cancelled the London meeting.

Jenni was sitting up against the headboard, watching me dress. 'For God's sake don't get pulled over. You'll lose your licence.'

'That would be handy,' I said sarcastically. 'Imagine me handing accounts a receipt for a year-long taxi service.'

'Exactly.'

I leant forward and kissed her forehead. 'I'll drive carefully.'

'You do that.'

19

I brushed the hair from her face and kissed her again, on the cheek. 'I'll call you later.'

Before I closed the door she said, 'Tell Kay it was nice to meet her.'

I walked the empty corridors of the hotel. Floated might be a better word as I felt drunker than I'd been when falling into bed, floating past the room numbers until I found theirs. Just before I rapped on the door I heard Segur's voice, sharp and curt. Then Kay, muffled, playing something down before Segur snapped, 'How the fuck do you lose an airplane ticket? Get yourself together.'

And I felt a relic of hate when I heard his anger, a boy again, hearing the threats of a drunken stepfather towards my mother.

I quickly knocked again.

'See,' said Kay. 'I knew you had them.'

Then Segur opened the door. 'Good man.' He checked his watch. 'Six forty-five on the nose.' He was dressed in his shirt and trousers, as if he hadn't even gone to bed. Or just sworn at his wife. He didn't invite me into the room, but I could see Kay zipping up her suitcase.

'You got everything, hon?'

'Ready for the off?' I added, awkwardly English in my own country.

'*Ready for the off*,' repeated Segur, mimicking my accent, smiling.

'Whatever you want to call it,' said Kay, 'I'm ready.' She bumped her cases against the wall as she walked out. She still looked good, great even, considering the time of the morning. She wore a skirt and boots with a maroon jacket over a black top. Stylish, feminine, strong. Yet, and perhaps it was the dulling effects of the hangover, or simply the presence of Segur, the woman who'd entranced me beneath the umbrella had faded. And she vanished when he kissed her.

'Call me in a while,' were his parting words.

Segur had kissed his wife goodbye on the lips, whilst I'd kissed Jenni goodbye on the cheek and forehead. And how significant this daily act that particular morning. Now I'm like the engineer sifting through the wreckage of a plane crash, reconsidering the hairline cracks in the wings that he once ignored.

After their kiss we walked through the bland, quiet corridors of the hotel into bright morning sunshine. I put her luggage in the boot and we opened and closed the doors.

II

Two months after that wedding in the Cotswolds, riding the taxi from JFK into Manhattan, my jet-lagged ghost floating somewhere above the leather seats, I watched downtown rise in a bug-smeared screen. The highway was a fibre optic of blipped light streamed into the city, sun bouncing off glinting mirrors and nuclear glass. But instead of thinking about the work ahead, the task of telling two banks how they were going to become one, the deals brokered on the strength of a handshake, the stats and graphs to justify job losses and pay cuts, I was consumed by different thoughts.

My first kiss.

Her name was Debbie Western. She ferried notes to the one I thought I loved, Hannah Stillman. Because, aged ten, I was too afraid to speak to a girl I fancied. Instead I passed on letters and whispered sweet nothings to her best friend, Debbie.

I even sent Hannah a Valentine's card, posting it on my morning paper round before school. When I got to class they were both walking the tables asking the boys to spell 'guess'. And once I wrote down my attempt, my anonymity was stripped. I was the only boy who'd signed his Valentine *Geuss who?* My spelling was honestly better than that. It was just the pressure of writing in a card from the newsagents which had cost me a week's pay.

And anyway, all my romance was in vain. That night on the way home from school we went to the park and played on vandalized slides and swings with their chains wrapped around the frames. Although Hannah let me hold her hand, she wouldn't let me put my arm round her shoulder. We fooled around on the see-saw for a while before she went home for tea.

That left me and Debbie with the graffiti and broken bottles, the rusting roundabout. So we explored the brook, taking the path along the water's edge to the cow fields and the building site. To cross over to the fallen tree, a huge oak felled by lightning, you had to take the stepping stones. It had rained the night before, and the high water flooded over the bricks. I skipped across before Debbie followed. I remember she wore one of those long skirts that were fashionable at the time, and she had to lift the hem to stop it getting wet. It was this concern that put her off where she was stepping.

She tripped. She didn't fall in, but she dipped her foot enough to lose her shoe, a white PVC slip-on that bobbed along the current like a toy canoe.

'My shoe,' she screamed. 'My mum'll kill me.'

I ran along the bank, watched the current whisk that little boat towards the weir, saw the grates it would sink between. Where a branch leant over the water I swung out low enough to reach down and pluck her shoe from drowning.

I ran back along the path holding it aloft, triumphant. I was her knight in shining armour, her hero. I was Prince Charming himself when I knelt to slip it back on to her outstretched foot.

'Stand up,' she ordered. We were face to face on the riverbank, late summer sun skimming the hedgerows. 'Here,' she said, pointing to her cheek.

I leant forward and kissed her. My soul melted like ice cream.

Then she kissed me.

And whatever shape I thought the world was when I was ten, I was wrong. Because by the time I got home it had changed for good. I walked across the park, the sweet taste of her still in my mouth. I was dizzy with a baffling joy, for I had no reference point against which to compare what a boy and girl could become when they touched lips.

That was my thought on arriving in New York, a very real *then*, and a dreamlike ride along the Van Wyck Expressway in a yellow cab.

I COULD HAVE ASKED the consultancy for a larger apartment, more luxurious, with wooden floors and a view, the golden Trump or the silver Chrysler. Not a tired block wedged between the Port Authority bus station and a homeless hostel where tramps dressed for the post-apocalypse in ripped jackets and trousers tied with strips of plastic bags. Whatever I thought about the state of my own life was ridiculed by these men, building shelters from cardboard boxes and begging for change to buy dollar pizza slices. That first morning I watched two drunks in torn ski jackets hugging and bawling. It should have been pitiful and saddening. Yet there I was in my suit and polished shoes, the jet-setting business analyst, envious, and somehow exhilarated, that they had each other to hold against the world.

As I was there on a mission to streamline systems and cut costs, asking the US management for plusher accommodation might not have gone down too well. And from past New York projects I also knew that time spent in my room would be minimal. Whether seated behind a desk, at a restaurant table courting clients or knocking back beers with drunken co-workers, I had to give the company their pound of flesh. So a bed and a TV were all that I required. With a month to go till the election, Obama versus McCain,

28

the news channels buzzed with mud slinging and polls, blue bars higher than red. Unless of course it was a financial bulletin where the red graphics dominated, accompanied by words from commentators like *meltdown, record fall*, and *the Great Depression*.

Once in my apartment, the opened, unpacked suitcase on the bed, the windows wide to the blaring traffic massed at the crossroads after rising up out of the Lincoln Tunnel, I tried to read the paper in an effort to switch off from what I'd done.

Or perhaps not what I'd done, but what I was capable of doing.

Beyond the articles 'Campaigns Shift to Attack Mode on Eve of Debate' and 'Transgender Candidate Who Ran as Woman Did Not Mislead Voters', the columns of the *New York Times* didn't grab my attention. I never read further than the headlines: QUAKE KILLS AT LEAST 72 IN KYRGYZSTAN, ISLAMIC GROUP GAINS POWER IN INDONESIA, and 1 IN 4 MAMMALS THREATENED WITH EXTINCTION.

I could have looked at some stats from work. Scheduled meetings with stakeholders and devised workshops to get IT guys talking the same language as their managers. A business analyst riding the landslide of a financial crash hardly had time to sit and read the paper, ponder a personal life that needed restructuring as much as the banking industry. Yet I found my focus for spreadsheets and diagrams wanting.

But this was nothing new.

Long before the field and the rain, the wedding, her yellow dress and bare feet, my life had become a simulation I'd constructed, what I believed I wanted. A job earning silly money, a flat that I owned and a loving fiancée. From the outside I had a good thing that was only getting better.

Two years ago I'd graduated from the London Business School, armed with an MBA and ambition, though the real achievement wasn't a curled scroll or a mortarboard and gown, the job offers from Shanghai to Boston. No, it was meeting Jenni. From the day we first kissed, on a sunlit bend of the Thames I'd planned to make my move on for weeks, I'd made a promise to myself. To be better. To be worthy of this woman with her lean and courtly grace. She was as beautiful first thing in the morning as she was in that fine summer dress, her body glowing in diaphanous gold.

Within a month I was deemed suitor enough to meet her mother and father, Freya and Philip, a doting couple in semi-retirement who had a full life behind them and time to dedicate to their daughter and a future son in-law.

If we stayed the weekend at Marlow I'd play cricket with Philip, impressing with brisk outswingers and flashing cover drives. One evening, after I'd clipped a fifty to claw back a match he thought we'd lost, we were driving back to their quiet house, both fuzzed with a couple of pints of cider, when he cried, 'You've done bloody well, considering.'

He could have been considering any number of afflictions inherited from my dysfunctional family. While the steady-going Philip certainly qualified as a good man, I doubt my own father did. But now, well, now my father has retrial. Because if he's guilty then I certainly am. Though if my mother was appointed judge I doubt the verdict would change. The fact remains he left her when she was eight months pregnant with my younger sister. In his defence my father might argue that it wasn't some tawdry affair as he married and stayed with the woman he left my mother for. And that was nearly thirty years ago. But does this redeem him? Not in my mother's eyes, I'm sure. She'd say she was the one who lived with the remains of the divorce, the ruins, a two-bedroomed house on an estate where half the kids, including my sister and me, were on free school dinners. Well, until we moved into my stepfather's when I was ten.

He was a man who wanted no more to do with me and my sister than he did with our cat, who soon decided there were better homes to frequent for saucers of milk.

I can still see the plastic sheet covering the discarded furniture we left at my mother's house. We only moved one town over, but I vividly recall a wet day when I preferred to shelter in *our* garden, riding my bike to the old house and crawling under the kitchen table next to the tatty sofa, listening to raindrops strike the tarpaulin.

At first my stepfather, Les, tried to buy our loyalty with what money he got from his welding job, believing an army of Stars Wars figures would win me over, a mansion-size doll's house for my sister. For a while they did. I was a boy benefiting from a man about the house, sport and discipline, a helping hand fixing a puncture. Then he realized two kids were an unwanted part of the deal of having my mother, a woman I now understand needed him as much as if not more than she needed us, her children.

But as much as she loved him, I hated him. Soon the feeling was quietly mutual. He became the model of every-thing I didn't want to be. A second-hand dealer of racist jokes, the caveman football fan who bragged about beating up policemen in his hooligan youth.

For the next six years I'd rather be outside than in his home, whatever the weather. And a housing estate bordered by farmland, coal pits and derelict factories was an adventure

31

playground. Train tracks and a landfill, building sites and canal locks. Watching the Inter-City flash past on sunlit rails, then vanish in the heat wobble of distance, spawned my first dreams of travel, escape.

Nothing at all like Jenni's upbringing, her loving parents.

'I'd be proud to have you in the family.'

That's what Philip said when I asked him for his daughter's hand in marriage. Perhaps I was hoping to be part of a family I'd never had, to inherit Jenni's wholesome upbringing in a house with a pond and a manicured lawn, the riding club round the corner where one day she dreamed of taking her own daughters. *Our* daughters.

Her mother used to hug me goodbye on Sunday evenings, before the drive back to London, and I'd feel the charity and empathy for my bereft past pressed against my chest. The hearty welcome into their huge house felt like coming in from the cold after ten years of rented flats and friends' floors, a decade of drifting after the night I was kicked out of home by my stepfather.

I was sixteen. My mum was taking my sister to a dance contest in London. The older and closer I got to her, the more estranged and jealous Les became. He'd down bottles of Pils, get drunk, and boss my mother about as if she were a mangy dog. And hit me. Though we both knew the day was coming when he'd get one back.

'Who the hell does that?' Philip had asked angrily, driving back from the cricket match. 'Throw a boy on to the streets.'

What he said next, his knuckles white on the steering wheel, was one of the few times I ever heard him swear.

Philip had brought up the subject because it was the night after a cricket game that I last walked through my front door. I'd been playing at a picturesque oval in the next village, its trickling brook and stone cottages in direct contrast to the scruffy factories and estates of my own town. After matches I'd have beers at the local, already drinking with the 'men', an eclectic mix of farmers' sons, factory workers, businessmen and millionaires. Fellow cricketers about to become my surrogate fathers. I had a curfew of eleven o'clock, a choice of either the mickey-taking of my team-mates for leaving the pub early, or the ire of Les, usually sitting up surrounded by full ashtrays and empty bottles.

It was just gone eleven when I put my key in the front door. He was in the bedroom watching TV. Before I even had my foot on the bottom step he called out, 'Start looking for somewhere else to live.'

I hesitated, then began climbing the creaky stairs.

'Start looking now.'

A clinical order shouted through a closed door. I turned and walked back into the night.

After years dreaming about running away, the Oedipal fantasies of his murder, pushing him down the stairs, the flashing knives, I had finally come to the moment of leaving. Not fighting. Now I was old enough he hardly seemed worth the effort. With my cricket bag slung over my shoulder I headed back to the park and sat under the slide. I planned to sleep there, but when headlights swung across the grass I slipped beneath the hedgerow at the back of school. I dossed down in a spot I'd played in as a boy, beneath the very bush where I'd once built a den. That I actually slept there, wearing my cricket whites over the top of my clothes to keep warm, was a boyhood dream of a night in the wilderness come true. Though I'd never pictured the stray dog that came sniffing me in the dark, my fist on its hollow flank when I woke up terrified, lashing out.

'And you never cried?' Jenni had asked when I first told her.

I'd shrugged my shoulders. 'Cry at what?'

'That's not healthy,' she'd argued. 'I swear the way you break into tears at films and the Olympics is a way of letting it out.'

What was 'it'? Being homeless, adrift? My mother?

'More than that,' she'd contended. 'How about the fact you never talk about being kicked out, or the distance from your father?'

She was right. She knew parts of me better than I'd ever admit.

'But especially your mother.'

I'd shrink into the protection of my shell at this point, avoid the personality surgery. I needed Jenni to love the person I wanted to be, a good fiancé, the dashing business analyst designing slick new systems, not the person I had been, a boy tramping the streets because he had no bed.

In the end I stayed with my cricket captain and his wife. I had their boxroom for two weeks before the government put me in a council flat and I moved what possessions I had into a bedsit on the edge of an industrial estate.

Whoever I am now, started then. That cell of a home. The dawn shifts in a plastics factory. That season playing for Nottinghamshire at cricket and rugby, yet drinking and taking drugs. Out every night because I had no one telling me what time to go to bed.

But I also had boundless energy. Driven by what I couldn't say. Anger? Relief? I'd never wanted to move into Les's house anyway.

Not one of my classmates had thoughts of university, but from what I could see of my future I'd be condemned to my old pit town if I didn't get away to study. The following years I fitted in about five different lives. College, being a rugby and cricket star, the borderline alcoholic.

And my first girlfriend, Siobhan, the damage of what one heart could do to another.

O N THE SECOND DAY in New York, after a hellish afternoon explaining to the vice-presidents that without rapid changes to the job structure there would be no bank, neither the acquired nor the acquiring, and therefore no jobs to restructure, I walked through Union Square. Between flitting about market stalls helping myself to free slices of apple, trying to think about nothing but the tart, crisp bites, I came across the kittens in cages. Kept outside a pet shop, six or seven bundles of fur rolled, played and mewled for the passers-by, myself included, stopping to stare at two tabbies curled up asleep despite the sidewalk throng.

Of course, I thought about our own cats.

A fortnight after the wedding Jenni and I walked the river path from Chelsea and crossed the Thames. A warm, blue September day. The four-pronged stack of Battersea power station like an upturned plug, barges unzipping the water below, Jenni clutching my hand that bit firmer than usual.

And the knot in my stomach tightening, Kay strolling alongside us like a ghost.

'Does the colour really matter?' She was asking about the two kittens we'd decided to take in from the cattery.

'A pair of tabbies, a ginger tom, I don't mind.'

'Aren't tabbies always girls?'

'Is that a problem?'

'I don't know,' she replied, her furrowed brow giving it some serious thought. 'Only if you're a girl.' She laughed.

Subconsciously, we knew getting two cats was a test for having children. If we could look after a couple of mewling kittens then surely a baby would be a natural progression.

'Can we manage them in the flat?' asked Jenni as we got to the Battersea Dogs and Cats home. 'We did say we were going to wait until after Christmas.'

Since the wedding I needed as much distraction from my thoughts as possible. Two kittens tearing around a cramped flat suddenly seemed a brilliant idea. 'We'll manage,' I assured her. 'How hard is it to stroke a cat and put some food in a bowl?'

'For someone who loves cats, you make it sound very clinical. You'll soon be cooing over them like the big softie you are.'

She was right. I was nearly thirty years old, a rugby-playing flyer in the City, and the sight of a kitten could turn me into a doting mess.

They always had done. Once my sister and I had found a pregnant stray in a skip at the back of the supermarket, taken her home and hidden her in the garage. I crept downstairs each morning, poured out a saucer of milk and stole a strip of bacon from the fridge. Luckily, when Les discovered them it was too late. The kittens had come out in translucent sacs, gasped and cried into life. He immediately put an ad in the paper and sold them for five pounds each.

Jenni's theory was that my affinity with cats was with their fierce independence, because a cat belonged to no one but itself. 'Just like you on a bad day,' she'd needle, using my 'cat association' as the incision point for dissecting a part of my personality she said I guarded. 'And if there's anything that worries me about us, it's that.'

'That' was my reluctance to talk about my childhood, an upbringing very different from Jenni's. Not the fact I lived on an estate where friends went to prison instead of Cambridge or Oxford, or that we went on holiday to Butlins while Jenni took ski trips to Val d'Isère, but the sudden flight from home, the abusive stepfather. My mother.

And if this makes us seem a mismatched couple, I should remark on how we were attracted to not only the foreignness in each other, but also the drive to assert ourselves as individuals. Jenni's determination to overcome a privileged past, her battle to become a woman beyond the chequebook of her father, was similar to my need to be a man beyond a deadbeat estate, the runaway child.

Anyway, differences or not, on the subject of cats we were equal.

'Oh my God.' Jenni had pointed through the window in the cattery. 'Look at those. It's like they're wearing gloves.'

'They're polydactyls,' said the teenage volunteer. 'Six fingers.'

We picked the two fluffiest from the litter and saved them from the cattery. 'Mittens,' Jenni named the slightly larger one. 'And what about the other?' she asked in the taxi, poking a finger through the carrier. 'You should name her.'

For a week the other had no moniker. I had some strange blockage on choosing the right name. On finding out that Hemingway had kept dozens of polydactyls I looked around for something fitting, but despite having read several of his novels could only recall a single heroine, the nurse, Catherine, in *A Farewell to Arms*.

'Catherine,' repeated Jenni, cradling the kitten as if it was her very own unnamed baby. '*Catherine!*' She tested how it would sound as a call.

I practised, too. '*Catherine!*'

The kitten fidgeted in her arms. 'Then her nickname would be Cat.' She laughed.

'I guess that's a no, then?'

'Well, not necessarily.' She put Catherine down on the rug, rolled her over and rubbed her tummy until she purred like an old-fashioned dialling tone. 'What happens to Catherine in the book?'

'I remember them rowing across a lake to escape the Germans, then something about hiding in a Swiss chalet cocooned in snow.'

All that fortnight Jenni had woken earlier than me, calling me a lazybones and not knowing I'd been sitting at the kitchen table until dawn, pacing about the flat in the dark and standing at the window watching taxis trundle over the speed bumps, the revellers coming home from clubs. Or, like a prisoner working out in solitary, done dozens of sit-ups and press-ups. Anything to take my mind from the wedding, the woman I'd given a lift to the airport.

Waking on those mornings, before my mind assembled, and my conscience stretched off enough to start beating up my soul, I'd steal a few minutes of bliss when the kittens jumped in bed, purring, tumbling over each other.

Then getting up, the routine of breakfast, ironing shirts and choosing ties, thoughts of that humid day in August like an elephant in the room that only I could see.

I WATCHED HER PAINTED nails trace a route to Heathrow across the map. And my God I inhaled her perfume. So suddenly I was thinking about the smallest details, the skin on the back of her hands, the neat scar under her eyebrow.

Kay pressed her finger to the page. 'We're right here.'

The emptiness I felt when she averted her eyes at the reception, or at the moment she kissed Segur goodbye in the hotel, was filled once she sat in my car.

'Okay,' I said. 'Left out of the entrance, I think.'

'Looks good from this angle.' She had the atlas splayed across her lap. We drove from the car park. She wore sunglasses against the dazzle of the morning sun, as did I, hidden from each other behind darkened lenses and functional conversation about which turns to take. My first comments beyond the directions were about the beautiful weather and the journey time dependent on the traffic into London.

'I'd better not get us lost, then.'

And I was still drunk, focusing hard on the road, narrow country lanes lined by hedgerows and stone walls.

'Shoot,' said Kay, as the trees and fields sped past, the car handling like a hovercraft. 'We should have taken the right back there.'

I pulled into a gateway facing swaying cornfields. Blades of grass glittered with drops of silver dew.

'How beautiful.'

It was. I swear if I opened up that same page in the road atlas now I could point to that very gateway, perhaps see our miniature selves sitting in the car above the billowing fields, watching the wind sweep across the wheat like a wave through an ocean.

And if I could, would I lean in and advise that man in the gateway? Would I counsel him, as I often do clients in my line of work, on the outcomes of bad decisions, that the choices one makes in a split second may have repercussions for years?

Yes. Yes, I would.

But a road atlas is no more than a map of where, not who and when. Certainly not *why*.

We were pointed away from the rising sun. Kay took off her sunglasses, revealed her eyes and returned my stare, held it long enough to make me afraid of her. Afraid of myself.

Deliberately, I believe, she broke the moment. 'How's your wife with a map?'

'Not bad,' I replied, before correcting her that Jenni was my fiancée.

'When's the big day?'

I swiftly put the car into reverse. 'May next year.'

As I pulled into that narrow lane we returned to basic conversation, how far to the next turn, where I should get petrol. We were pretending to ourselves that we hadn't just stared at one another for so long.

And when I glanced down at the junction she was pointing to on the map, I should have been looking at the road, ready for the flock of geese waiting just around the bend.

Like the timing of the shower on the wedding day, if those geese had grazed a different stretch of tarmac at a different hour, that stare between Kay and me might have been the end of something that had yet to start.

That was about to.

I COULD SEE A bat with the head of a dog, eagles carved from stone. From my balcony over Manhattan I studied gargoyles on the building below.

Sober, I felt hungover. Not with alcohol, but from the buzz and flutter of data. Faces and names I had to remember. It was the morning after a meet and greet with the bank managers we were being paid to fire, the teams of staff we could cull or save. I'd spent a long day in a walnut-panelled office suite in a snapped together tower, spaced out in another continent. Empty-headed boy from the Midlands in a New York boardroom.

Watching the minutes tick past until I had to get dressed and go to work, listening to the street sounds flowing like a rushing river, as if a great flood gushed down the avenues, I felt so detached from my body that I could have been washed into the Atlantic.

I was jet-lagged, but at least I was sleeping.

For weeks after the wedding the insomnia continued, as if an invisible hand would shake me awake if I managed to drop off. Getting into bed with Jenni and knowing that I was going to lie there and stare at the ceiling was torturous. She had no idea that I paced the flat, exercised on the kitchen floor, or simply sat on the rug and let the kittens jump over me while she dreamed the night away.

Luckily, work was hectic. In fact, hectic was being kind to the state of the banks, the economy. I liked to compare the financial system to a rickety plane flying above the Alps, losing engine power, rock face looming and the crew desperately throwing overboard what they could to keep altitude. While it struggled over those mountains, the rising, falling peaks like the zigzag progress of the stock exchange, the crew knew there weren't enough parachutes to go round. If the plane, *the banks*, went down, some of them would float to earth while others would burn in the fiery wreckage.

For the US economy I preferred the analogy of a busted drug lord. From the brokers selling shoddy mortgages like corner boys peddling deals to the syndicate bosses at the top, rich, untouchable. And all the big banks getting their cut, then all the big banks missing their cut when the homeowners stopped paying and started defaulting.

But I was glad of the panic, the overtime. I believe the crash kept me sane, allowing me downtime from my own existence. I hid in numbers, streams of data, cold, exact facts, the same maths that make sense of the universe itself.

I began to numb the memory, although not entirely. The guilt I felt thinking of Kay during sex with Jenni ensured she occupied those spaces I thought were ours.

But when September skies blew over, fresh and gleaned of cloud, the season of change, I'd relegated what happened between Kay and me, the detour from that lift to Heathrow, to no more than a pre-wedding panic. I convinced myself it was a reaction to seeing friends tie the knot. And the vows, *till death us do part*, the solemn oath of commitment.

I was sleeping again, managing to wake without Kay as my first thought. For a month I'd flitted in and out of dreams sensing her very presence, as if she'd stood at the foot of our bed the entire night.

So back to the morning routine, not that Jenni knew of any break. I usually showered first, jumped out for Jenni to jump in, then browned the toast and brewed the coffee. If we were lucky enough for the postman to arrive before we left for work I'd grab the mail and sift through the bills and flyers, ads for takeaways and increasingly desperate estate agents.

'Hey!' sparked Jenni, coming from the bathroom, her wet hair bundled in a white towel. 'Who's got the purple envelope?'

I took it from behind a gas bill. It was a thick, decorated envelope addressed to us both.

'The wedding photos!' she guessed, correctly, before I slit the paper to find a CD titled *Mark and Briony's Wedding Album.*

'Do you want to pop it in your laptop while I get dressed?'

I mumbled I didn't have time.

'Time to put a CD into a computer?'

Of course I did. I just wasn't ready for who I might see floating across my screen.

When she came back into the kitchen, suited and perfumed, brushing her bright blond hair, I had the photos scrolling on a slideshow.

'Any good ones?' she asked, yanking loose strands from her brush and dropping them into the bin.

'I haven't looked yet.'

'Haven't looked?' She sounded annoyed. Annoyed that I was washing up instead of being whisked into Neverland by the thousand or so wedding snaps flashing into the kitchen.

'I've been playing housemaid.'

'I know, I know. Mr Poppins.' She poured her coffee. 'Five minutes, let's have a quick look.'

Impatient with the slideshow, the repetitive snaps of guests we didn't know, couldn't remember seeing at the wedding or the reception, and would most likely never see again, Jenni, thankfully, clicked the 'Church' folder. In these photos I knew I was safe. Safe from an image of Kay, of once again seeing her standing between Jenni and me. Because I knew she hadn't attended the service. Not that anyone told me she didn't attend, simply that I'd have remembered, had it hard-wired into my synapses as was the image of her running through the rain.

'How sweet,' cooed Jenni over a sweeping shot of the train being carried up the church steps by the bridesmaids. 'And wasn't he a cutie.' She pointed at the pageboy, a waistcoated toddler with curly blond locks. 'He nearly stole the show.'

I made the expected sounds of agreement, nodded. Then the shots of the ceremony, the austere priest and the grey stone contrasted with the beaming bride, that huge font with twelve apostles carved into it. Except Judas, I noticed, who was represented by a blank figure.

'She lost about a stone, you know?'

And not forgetting the wedding dress, how it illuminated the dim church.

When Jenni got to the close-ups of Mark slipping the ring on Briony's finger, the gold band of marriage, I thought back to our own engagement, Christmas at Jenni's.

If snow had fallen that year, and a robin redbreast had perched on the windowsill to peer in on the open fire crackling in the hearth, I'd have believed in a man climbing down chimneys with sacks of toys. I thought Christmases like that,

46

the roaring fire and tipsy uncles, cousins in new dresses and ironed shirts, only existed on Hallmark cards. Growing up I was hardly celebrating Yuletide with a bowl of gruel, but watching the Bond film with my sister while my mum and Les snored the afternoon away was a world apart from vintage port and a roasted turkey the size of a hippo. After a few drinks chatting with her uncle, her cousin and other ruddy-faced men warmed with alcohol and the satisfaction of their gathered families, we sat around a table in the conservatory.

'Raise your glasses,' swayed her father. 'First toast to the cook.'

We touched drinks. Jenni, ecstatic that I was 'fitting in', kissed me on the cheek. Her father saw the exchange. 'And you two,' he joked. 'Keep your hands off each other.'

Embarrassed, I apologized, and ingratiatingly thanked him for inviting me to spend Christmas Day in such warm company.

'Don't be silly. It's a treat to have you here. All I can say is that Jenni seems to have inherited her mother's fine taste in men.'

'Philip!' Freya scolded. 'Get on with carving the turkey.'

We sat, Jenni and I holding hands beneath the table. She was in love. I was in love. I have no doubt about that, however you want to define love. I was in love with it all, the decorations, the fireplace, the pine trees in the garden dusted with frost, Philip's cricket bat signed by Ian Botham, Jenni. I wanted every last part of it.

When I pulled a cracker with her uncle, and a plastic ring fell into my lap, I slipped it away into my pocket. Later, once the rest of the family had boozily bid us goodnight, I led Jenni into the top bedroom.

'I don't think so,' she whispered, pulling me back. 'We're not shagging in my mum and dad's house.' She was giggly, a little drunk. 'What are you up to, Sam?'

I led her into the centre of the room and turned out the light. I opened the curtains to the starry sky, got down on my knees and proposed.

For MONTHS I TALKED Jenni out of trips back to Nottingham, not wanting her to see the warren I'd played down as a boy, the rusting pit heads of the barren coalfields, the bush I'd slept in as the homeless teen. That was no longer me. Now I had a life in a suit and tie, marching to work with a million others along the medieval streets of the Square Mile. Entranced by the city, the chance to be born again in a metropolis that had risen from plague, fire and blitz to become the powerhouse of the financial world, I revelled in my reinvention. Give me the gleaming towers of banking, Lloyds and the Gherkin, the steel-tipped peak of Canary Wharf. I stood beneath the painted beams of Leadenhall and had my shoes shined, walked a circuit of the Roman amphitheatre that Guildhall was built upon and watched as the Lord Mayor in all his finery paraded the ancient courtyard. I thought I was part of it all. That we were part of it all, Jenni and I, the young lovers, the City flyers from a renowned business school making strides in blue chip companies, buying flats on bonuses and cracking open bottles of champagne in buzzing wine bars.

But if I sat and thought for a moment, perhaps on a lunch break in a park, or the bombed-out church near Cheapside with its roof bared to the sky and garden filled with flowers, I thought about my mother, and wished she'd lived long enough to see her son transformed into the man.

After the night I was kicked from home, I didn't speak to her for years. Nearly five, I realize now, too late. I refused to see her. Letters to my flat went unopened into the bin. Why did I need a mother who'd chosen a drunken thug over her son, the boy who loved her?

Our peace treaty had been my graduation from university. The invite, then an awkward coffee in a supermarket cafe. We hugged, that day in the rainy car park, and a week later at my graduation ceremony. In the photo you can see that what I thought was age was her illness. The rogue cells that were wrecking her organs.

It all happened so quickly. One weekend we were reminiscing about our old estate, friends and neighbours, games of tennis over the garden fence, the street party for Charles and Di's wedding. The next I was at a funeral with my sister, standing directly across from him, the man who'd kicked me from her world. We listened to a dolorous priest offer a final prayer, and watched the woman who'd fed, dressed and *loved us* lowered into that rectangular hole. I walked away from the shovels of soil, the bouquets of flowers that would wither on her grave.

This is what Jenni wanted to know about, what I kept in my locked heart. I dodged and parried her attempts at finding out who I was, leaving an enigma she loved even more.

YOU COULD HIKE MANHATTAN every day for the rest of your life and never take the same route twice. When I wasn't standing before flip charts or rooms full of men and women wondering if my strategies for merging their banks would slash their jobs, I locked myself in this grid, walking the graphed and numbered blocks, containing myself, my thoughts, to simple decisions of what turn to make, whether to cross at a certain intersection or not.

On a walk through Midtown, stepping away from the pulse of the crowd to bend and tie a lace come undone, I'd watched a scrap of paper pick itself up from the gutter and lift to the breeze, past the hats and coats, the signs and wires, aiming at the height of clouds but giving up where King Kong carried on, falling back to the multitudes flowing along the streets, the tourists, tramps and cops, the rich and poor, a frail old couple in Times Square wavering in the brute force of a city.

I walked to erase my conscience. I walked to avoid thinking about what I'd left. Who I'd left. But it wasn't easy. For the first three days not a cloud appeared on the blue, as if the cirrus and cumulus had massed on the US border awaiting a customs entry stamp. And this clear sky was a blank screen on which to project my thoughts. My guilt. Only by watching the frenetic streets, listening to the bark and song of New Yorkers hurrying about their day, the vendors singing out their wares, the peanut sellers and hawkers of fake brand handbags, and contemplating the dollar stalls selling hats and gloves within feet of men and women trading companies, could I forget myself.

But when I stopped it was all me. Beating heart and memories.

THE GEESE EXPLODED INTO flight, panicked wings flapping on the windscreen. I saw bright orange beaks, abandoned feathers and webbed feet, fishing line tangled about a leg.

But I didn't see them early enough to stop.

I hit the brake and missed the geese. The back wheels locked and slid. The rear end snaked out and I heard my expletive as if on a time delay, grabbing the wheel and over-steering so as not to spin or flip.

Instead we carved up the verge and bounced over a culvert before clattering into a junction sign.

Kay screamed. We bounced off the airbags, yanked back by our belts and thrown to a sudden halt.

We both swore, staring at the balloons which had burst from the dashboard. I asked if she was okay, and was checking she wasn't hurt when something under the bonnet thrashed and clunked.

'The engine,' she shouted. 'Turn off the engine.'

Pistons squealed then stopped when I yanked the keys from the ignition. Through gritted teeth I swore again, before apologizing half a dozen times.

'We're all right,' she said. 'You okay?'

It was very quiet after the crash, after the honking geese and screeching tyres, the racing engine and crumpling metal and the shocking pop of the airbags. Then, and I can't recall who was first, we both erupted into laughter. Maybe it was fear, the spike of adrenalin. Maybe other people would have cried. We laughed.

'Geese,' exclaimed Kay. I watched her laugh, saw how her cheeks dimpled.

We climbed out to inspect the damage as a car rounded the bend I'd just slewed from.

'The cavalry's here,' said Kay.

'A tow truck would be handy.'

It would have been, but instead a primly dressed woman in her fifties put down the window. Before asking either of us if we were okay, she said through pursed lips, 'You're not the first to come a cropper zooming these lanes.'

'I was hardly speeding,' I said, defending myself, and told her about the geese.

'Geese?' she repeated, a scowl of disbelief on her pinched face.

I had my hand on her car roof, and leant in closer to the open window, explaining how I swerved to avoid the birds. When I smelled her lavender air freshener I realized she could probably smell the whisky and the rum.

'Well,' she remarked sharply, drawing back from the window. 'You might find your reaction time a little sharper when you're sober.' And with that she scornfully looked Kay up and down, no doubt wondering what kind of woman would get into a car with such a man, before driving away.

'Bollocks,' I said, watching her turn the bend. 'We'd better get a move on. You've got a plane to catch, and I don't want to be breathalyzed.' As I said this I realized it was an admission of guilt, and started apologizing again.

'Hey, hey,' Kay cut in. 'I knew you'd been partying.'

With Jenni carless, Segur was the obvious man to ring. 'You better give Chris the bad news and call him.'

She deflated with this thought, shrunk with a sigh. 'He'll be mad,' she said, biting her lip. 'But not at you.' She stood with her phone to her ear, eyes on the empty road, but glazed, perhaps focused on where Segur was picking up his mobile.

At the time I missed this subtle hint, the anger her husband was capable of. Or perhaps I was aware, but knew there was nothing I could do about it, then. She was a woman married to another man, and I was a man about to marry another woman.

I pulled my phone from my pocket, ready to call Jenni. 'Have you got a signal?' I asked, noting the flat bars on my screen.

'Nothing,' she confirmed.

'I'm a great chauffeur.'

She shook her head and smiled. She should be angry, worried about missing a flight, but instead she beamed. 'And where the hell are we?'

'Somewhere between here and there.'

On the right of the road more cornfields sloped towards a shallow valley. Through the haze I could make out a church steeple, house roofs. To the left a cow field rose up to a small copse of trees. The cows lazily chewed grass and eyed us, standing by a wrecked car, surveying the yellow crops and a distant village hovering on the mist.

'Well,' said Kay, 'we couldn't be stranded in a more beautiful place. It's like I'm stuck in a postcard.'

'It's not as if hungry wolves are circling the fire.' In fact things were pretty calm considering I'd just written off my car and Kay was in danger of missing her flight. 'We might have to hitch.'

'I could lift my skirt,' she laughed, raising her knee and tugging up her hem to reveal a bronzed thigh.

'You'll cause a ten-car pile-up doing that.'

'Ten cars?' She smiled. 'That's optimistic.'

She was right. It was as if the road had been closed. I stood on the verge to look over the hedgerows and across the cornfields towards the village. I could make out the car of the woman who'd just stopped and tutted at our misfortune. I pictured her chatting with a bored local bobby, gladly informing him of drunk drivers joyriding their peaceful lanes, running down flocks of geese. I thought I was joking to myself with this scene, but my stomach tumbled when I imagined blowing a lungful of rum into a breathalyzer.

'Shit.' I panicked. 'We've got to get out of here.'

'I kinda guessed that.'

'I mean soon, now.' I looked past her to the wood on the hill. 'I'll pay for another flight if you miss this one.'

Perplexed, she asked what I was talking about. 'Won't the first car that drives by see us stuck and take us to the next village?'

'If that good Samaritan is a policeman I'll lose my licence.'

'They'll charge you with a DUI?'

I was definitely 'under the influence'. Physiologically the alcohol, and certainly my treacherous hormones, but I'd venture that far more profound forces were dictating my actions. Even fate, though not the kind found in newspaper horoscopes. Rather a destination in the future we were always travelling towards, yet would only recognize once we arrived there.

'If that old bat calls the police, and they drive up here and make me blow in a bag, I'm fucked. But if we sit it out for an hour or so, I should be okay.'

'I don't see a pub.'

'How about the trees?'

She looked to the copse, leaves turning in the light breeze. 'It'd be a picnic if we had a basket.'

Her acceptance of our situation was in stark contrast to how Jenni would have reacted, believing that her adroit PA skills of organization should have a godly control of events beyond the boardroom. Increasingly of late, in proportion to the amount of power she was garnering from the execs, any inefficiency, from London transport to our own arrangements, including weekend breaks and shopping trips that were planned with military precision, would be tutted at and noted for improvement. But the annoyance that came with the suggestions seemed to run deeper than logistics and common sense. Now I know the train delays and hotel complaints were proxy targets for her frustrations about us.

The chat between Kay and me, my cock-eyed plan of hiding on the hill accepted, told me that if we met such minor calamities with humour we were . . . well, how dare I put it? Connected? But did I really think that then? No. Perhaps my hormones did, but my conscience was still present. Just.

'I'd better get your case out of the boot.'

'So the police don't find the evidence of my abduction?'

I apologized again, but she waved it off as a bad joke. 'As long as I don't have to tip you for carrying it up the hill.'

Over the gate, and then between the startled cows, we hiked to the wood like trudging holidaymakers willing the hotel to be round the corner. Or people fleeing a crime, a country, immigrants on the threshold of a new world.

Yet if my previous life did exist – because on that morning it seemed more fiction than fact – I'd have to find another. Kay had seen the blueprints of my future with Jenni and set them on fire, sent that cosy home in Marlow, the church and a wedding dress up in flames.

And I was pouring on the petrol.

THE WEATHER CHANGED OVERNIGHT, as if someone had turned down the Manhattan thermostat. 'Uh-oh,' the Fox News forecaster warned. 'Looks like a drop into the forties for New York City.' Not that I've ever been able to work out what exactly Fahrenheit figures mean. I can do the calculations, of course, but the sense of actual temperature is somehow missing from the numbers.

Perhaps in the same way my sense of life had been missing from my sums of system analysis, the bank mergers and right-sizing, turning two jobs into one and not thinking of the individual at the temp agency, the unemployment office.

And from the calculations worked on my own affairs, Jenni, a marriage.

Yes, I'd made plans for the big day, booked the cars with my best man, written out the guest list with my mother-in-law. But I felt like a stand-in for my own body, organizing someone else's future, not mine. Though I analyse this at some remove from that day in Manhattan. And how very wise the fortune-teller looking into the past.

All I knew that morning as I stepped from my apartment was the cold wind slicing through my jacket and chilling my bones before I'd even walked a block. I quickly noticed that

New Yorkers had forgone style, turning up collars and pulling on hats, picking up the pace.

As I was about to do myself.

First I bought one of those hats with the furry ear flaps that dangle down, then a thick woolly scarf and a pair of sunglasses. Warm, protected from the sun dazzle bouncing off the storeys of mirrored skyscrapers.

And disguised.

Only four days in a city thousands of miles from Jenni, and, without her physically there to keep my thoughts in check, I was again inhabited by another woman.

It was time to find out where Kay lived. I hardly felt as if I actually made this decision to find her, rather that I was drawn to the pursuit in the same way men are compelled to scale deadly peaks.

All I had was the business card passed by Segur at the reception. If I couldn't get hold of her, that was surely the end of my infatuation. Wasn't it? Back in London, by the time October had come round, I was thinking of Jenni far more than I was of Kay. Even when my thoughts did turn to that hillside, the geese and the crashed car, it seemed a work of fantasy.

However, a month into the rugby season, mid-game and feeling the effects of a heavy night out after a bankruptcy party at one of the first restaurants to feel the squeeze, I was catching my breath as the fly half lined up a kick when Kay flashed into my head. Usually, once I was on that rectangle of muddy field nothing existed but an oval ball. A thought beyond a tackle or a pass was a first in my career, and I was glad when the league started, the lower divisions filled with thugs whose fists and studs needed keeping an eye on if you were to survive a game intact. Again, I could lose myself in the match, the skill and the violence. For eighty minutes a week I could forget the wooded hillside, a haunting woman.

Then a combination of the credit crunch and the Statue of Liberty brought her back into my life.

I was requesting overtime to make sure I wasn't one of the culled, one of the screwed-up faces of anguish from the Square Mile accompanying an apocalyptic headline. Number punching and schmoozing. If the consultancy stayed in one piece, then so would I. My job as an analyst was to streamline, improve efficiency and save money. I was needed. My focus on Jenni and work was once again honed.

Then broken. All by a postcard of the lady in the harbour. Signed very simply with the letter K and a kiss.

She must have found the business card I gave to Segur. No return address. I quickly slipped it into my desk drawer. The last thing I needed was one of the 'boys' in my department to start winding me up about mysterious mail from New York. But it burned beneath the files I'd hidden it between.

At lunch I grabbed a wrap from the Pret on Cannon Street, briefly wondering if the line at Tesco's for cheaper sandwiches was growing each day the economy shrank, then came back to my desk and looked at the postcard again. A buzz. Goosebumps from tracing the outline of that one letter.

'Quick word, Sam.' I still had it in my hand when Charlie Fanshaw, the co-director, called across the wall of computer screens, inviting me into his office to ask if I wanted a two-week transfer.

'Frankfurt again?'

He shook his head. 'Bail out the Yanks.'

'New York?' I asked, hearing a slight shake to my voice.

'That's where the action is. A change management project for you. Bank merger. Big fish eats the little one, and you have to throw out the bones. Well, give them a price for what it's going to cost to fire half their staff and kick out the contractors.'

There and then I declined. I made excuses to do with Jenni, something about her father and a weekend away. Charlie understood, said he had single men he could despatch instead. I walked proudly back to my desk, worked away the afternoon. When the clock struck seven and I decided to call it a night I thought I'd better throw out the postcard.

The mistake I made was turning over the picture, seeing the swirl of her handwriting.

Then telling Charlie I'd get on that plane. 'Do you a favour.'

'Good man,' he'd replied. 'I'll get on the phone.'

Of the many decisions I made that could be compared to a bomb disposal technician's cutting either the red or the blue wire, that was one. Lives detonated, showered in broken glass, promises. Blown from my office on Cannon Street, a suit and tie, to Wall Street, a disguise, Segur's business card clutched firmly in my hand.

WE SAT AT THE foot of a creaking oak swaying in the breeze. It sounded like the mast of a wooden ship bound for uncharted shores. We'd chosen a spot far enough under the canopy of trees to spy on the road without being seen. On sitting I'd performed a Walter Raleigh flourish by laying my jacket on the ground for Kay.

'Umbrellas and coats,' she'd remarked. 'How chivalrous.'

With my unuttered replies rattling around my head I'd felt like a lunatic. Right there and then, I wanted to give her everything I did and didn't have. Money and a house, my flesh and blood. These I possessed. But I couldn't offer my mind, at least not what I thought it was. How could I be sane and thinking such thoughts so soon?

Regardless of what I wanted to say, the intimacy of sitting in a secluded and shady spot beneath a tree had reduced us to the shy strangers who'd first got in the car an hour ago. We were awkward again, passing stilted comments on the scenery, the ridiculousness of the predicament. Until Kay reached into her bag and pulled out a bottle. 'Water?'

'You better drink before me,' I warned, catching a waft of the whisky-infused sweat rising from my body after hauling her suitcase up the hill. 'It'll taste like Jack Daniel's if I go first.'

She laughed. 'If only this were a Coke.' Then she twisted off the cap and drank. I was wired to the smallest details. The pop of her lips from the bottle top, her gulping, the throb of her throat as she swallowed, her neck, shining with perspiration. And finally, when I drank, the very taste of her in the water.

I then took a breath, a chance. 'Do you want to hear a story?'

'What kind?'

I told her about the Valentine's card and the floating shoe, my first kiss.

Kay said nothing when I'd done, and for a moment I thought I'd made a terrible misjudgement. She just looked out through the leaves, beyond the cows and a wrecked car to the glowing fields and a clear blue sky.

Then she said, 'When I was little, I loved to climb trees. As high as I could. I'd climb into the top branches and swing with the wind. And then I'd sit for hours, feeling the sway of that big old tree, imagining I was riding on the shoulder of a giant.'

I watched her talk. The very dark eyes, all pupil when she turned and held me in her steady gaze. And just like the boy standing on the bank of that little brook, my ice cream soul was melting.

'Is that it?' she suddenly asked. 'We've slipped into some fairy tale and have to get back to the real world.'

'Shall we slay a dragon?'

'Save the princess in the tower.'

I could have continued, but a car appeared on the lane, slowed, and then briefly stopped alongside the wreck.

One of us should have run down the hill and hailed a lift into the village. Would that have broken the spell?

Instead we sat and watched as the driver pulled away.

'You're still betting on that police car coming by?'

I apologized, once again, for our predicament. 'It's not worth the gamble. I'm a wanted man till I sober up.'

Kay was sitting with her legs crossed, reaching out and twisting bunches of grass. She was letting the broken blades drop from her hand, tipping her face to the morning sun that angled under the branches of the oak. She closed her eyes, and when she did I stared at her unabashedly, as though at a canvas illuminated for my private viewing.

She said, 'How we need the sun today.'

I studied her flaws, that nick across her eyebrow, a tiny scar puncture in her nose from an old piercing. I read these as marks of a life once very different from being the partner of a Wall Street millionaire, a jet-setting wife attending weddings in palatial marquees where the bride arrives in a horse and carriage. A wedding where guests at the reception talk about yachts and which schools to send their children to, boys and girls with flaxen hair and perfect skin running around the tables.

I had no idea I was going to ask what I next did. 'Do you ever feel like an actor reading lines?'

She opened her eyes and turned to me.

'Reading lines for the part of you, but written by someone else.'

'Where did you get that from?'

'Me.'

She smiled wryly. 'Not right now.'

I laughed, perhaps a little nervously. 'Does that mean you've hidden from the police before?'

'Now this is what you English do with sarcasm.' She shook her head. 'You pretend you don't mean what you're saying, but you do. You just disguise it in a joke.'

'Not at all,' I lied.

'Come on, admit it. I'm right.'

'I'm not saying you've been on the run or anything.'

'A fugitive. Hunted down by US marshals.'

She was playing with my embarrassment, making me squirm for suggesting, albeit humorously, previous run-ins with the police.

'Put it this way,' she said. 'I've been in worse scrapes than this.'

And now she studied me as I'd studied her moments before, but I had my eyes open, frightened by the force of her gaze, a serious focus.

'Are we baring souls here?' she asked, the jokey tone replaced by a sharper, almost angry voice. 'Because I can tell you what I think if you want to hear it. Why not? We're sitting here in our own little fairy-tale land, and, well, fairy tales end, don't they?'

I was stunned by her directness, the fearless turn in the conversation.

'Sorry,' she said, guessing my pause was a withdrawal from what she wanted to say.

'You've not told me what I don't want to hear yet.'

'Nothing. It's nothing. What do I know about these things? Who does? Some rock falls to earth and scientists tell us it's from Mars and so are we. They can look at dinosaur footprints in Arizona and say when they were there and what they were doing.' She picked up a twig and threw it against the trunk. 'But what do they know about this?'

I buzzed at the word 'this'. I let it hang in that August morning, what turned out to be the last true day of summer.

Kay opened the bottle and shook the last few drops of water into her mouth. When she angled her head back I noticed a slight cut on her neck, a smear of blood.

'Hey, you got cut.'

'Where?'

I pointed. 'Just under your ear.'

She rubbed the cut, looked at the red smudge on her fingertip before delving into her handbag and pulling out a tissue.

'Here.' I took it from her hand and told her to keep still. Then, in the same gentle manner in which I might sweep back Jenni's hair to kiss her neck, I pushed the hair from Kay's ear, and gently cleaned the cut.

I reached down for another tissue. I looked away, but kept her hair held back with my hand. She was turned away so I could get to the cut, but when I looked up she faced me. I kept my hand against the side of her head, felt the heat of her ear on my palm, her cheek on the inside of my wrist.

My whole self pulsed. I was all beating heart. I thought my skin might not be enough to contain me. I reached out with my other hand, pushed it back into her hair and cupped the sides of her head.

This was how I first held her, very delicately, as though if I let go she could break into a million pieces. Or I could.

She breathed hard. I gripped harder, almost clawing.

She said, 'Go on.'

She said, 'Do it.'

I pulled us together. We bit lips and forced tongues into mouths. We had fistfuls of each other's hair. We made two into one. I had no idea who was who, which hand was where. I wanted to see her, I had to see her, and drew back and held her cheeks, framed her face. And then I kissed her eyelids and her temple and the hollow between her jaw and her ear.

When I kissed her cut she whispered something I didn't hear.

Then she said it again.

'You fucker.'

WEARING MY RIDICULOUS HAT and thick scarf, I stood next to a stall selling cut-price headphones for iPods and phones. I let the ear flaps dangle on my cheeks and wore the sunglasses even though scattered cloud cast shadows over Wall Street.

'Bargain price. Best price,' called the West African stall holder. 'Times tough. Jobs cut. Houses lost. I save you money. This not expensive Sony. This a China bargain.' He chattered away at passing pedestrians, paraded his wares and warned, 'Hard times a' coming. Next year gonna make the Great Depression look like a vacation.'

I hoped he wasn't right. And I hoped that by standing next to him I'd be less obvious, less recognizable, should Segur walk from his office and look across the road.

I watched the revolving doors deposit the first workers on the sidewalk. Men and women who'd earned an early run home, keen staff at their desk hours before their colleagues, their managers, the ambitious sleeping an hour less to get ahead. As I once had myself, knowing that to rise above the privileged with school tie connections I had to excel by twirling data twice as fast as the twits with calculators. And I did, passing through the ranks of mid-management, the self-proclaimed big guns. With a natural common sense that some of the better educated seemed to lack, and certainly a better idea of thrift and cost cutting because I'd lived a life that had required these skills, I'd applied the lessons learned from the personal counting of pennies to big business with little effort.

While I waited on the sidewalk I thought about my earlier jobs, shovelling stone on building sites, selling double glazing, a whole career path of petty employment before I'd even met Jenni. Not including teenage girlfriends, or Debbie Western and that first kiss, Jenni was the second, and I truly hoped the last, woman I'd been in love with.

Siobhan was the first.

The day I knocked on her door the man on the news said it was officially the most depressing day of the year. It was hard to disagree. That was the winter after I finished university and moved back to Nottingham. The winter I watched my mother lowered into the earth. I drove around council estates selling windows to families too poor to pay gas bills, taking the job for the company car, a red Escort with a radio but no heater.

Graduate or not, this was the only work I'd found after a summer mixing cement. I'd already spent the cash made from selling a rental van then reporting it as stolen. My fellow doorknockers were much like me. Men in their twenties, either student dropouts or fiddling the dole. And desperate. Whether they were making money or not. This desperation ranged from Class A drug habits to those black-listed by employment agencies for turning down night shifts stacking pallets or loading lorries.

In a good week I'd make a couple of hundred, not including the dole I picked up every second Thursday, my doorknocking partner Jeff pulling round the back of the job centre while I whipped off my tie and declared I wasn't earning any money. And I believed it. Talking people into buying plastic windows wasn't earning in the same way hauling bricks up a ladder was.

That morning in the office, a converted garage off the back of a showroom displaying patio doors and conservatories that had roofs which opened with remote controls, was no different from any other. Cigarette smoke and coffee, cheap aftershave.

'Shit,' said Jeff, searching his jacket for some change for the vending machine.

'What's the act with your hand in your pocket?' I asked. 'We both know you're skint.'

Jeff borrowed some money from a guy he'd worked with at an abattoir, an agency job before selling windows. A minibus collected them at dawn and drove them out to a huge shed where hooded slaughtermen crashed through metal doors in aprons spattered with blood. Jeff suited up in a back room then stood at a conveyor belt where steaming cuts of meat rattled past. 'Still warm,' he grimaced. His job was to bag them up. 'And they had the radio going full blast so you couldn't hear the cows scream.'

The first toilet break he ran across the fields and hitched back to town. He had recurring dreams where blood seeped up through lawns in the next village.

But this was the kind of job waiting for us if we quit knocking doors. Not that there wasn't money to be made. The Indians in telesales were legends. Guys called Mukesh and Gurdip going by names like Sid Thompson and John Roberts, culturing accents of white boys from good families

71

that never lied. I envied their powers of disguise. Mukesh averaged a thousand pounds a week. His record was a three grand bonanza, armed with a contact list burgled from the offices of a rival company.

So with this promise of riches we flapped letterboxes and rang doorbells, occasionally sold a window, but more often than not got told to piss off. We parked in cul-de-sacs and crescents, streets on estates named after what was razed to make way for the red-brick homes: Plumtree Way, Oak Drive, Field Avenue.

I shaved and shined my boots, created discounts for pensioners, families, birthdays and Fridays. Security was a big selling point. 'Anyone could break this window,' I'd state, casually waving at the porch glass. 'But double glaze it and you can go to bed knowing that burglar isn't creeping around your kitchen, rummaging in the knife drawer.'

With a list of streets where homes were being fitted with new windows to lend credibility to our pitch, the housewife, shift worker or man on the dole could look across the road and see what we were selling.

But the first address that day was in Lenton, a studentville near the university. 'I'm renting,' was the standard reply. 'It's not my house.'

'Let's fuck it off,' decided Jeff. 'Get a bag of chips and drive out to where people pay mortgages.'

We looked along the terraced street, the sky and slate roofs merging into the same grey.

'It's freezing.' Jeff rubbed his hands together.

At each door I took my gloves off to knock. I felt like a serial killer when I knocked with gloves on. The few houses I got an answer from were dully predictable. Students.

Renting. I looked into the room of a guy who'd paused a computer game. Something was in mid-explosion.

'You'd better get back to your books.'

Halfway down the street, Jeff shouted, 'Fuck it.' He was hunched inside his jacket, trying to shrink into the warmth.

'I'm finishing this row,' I told him, then turned to the next front door, took off my gloves and knocked.

And when she opened that door she practically opened up another universe.

'Well go on then,' she said.

But I was speechless. She kept her very dark hair bundled up with a pencil. She wore a blue dress patterned with tiny white flowers.

'Sorry?'

'You're selling something.'

I was. Me.

'And you don't look like a Jehovah's Witness.'

Perhaps I looked like a man in an art gallery. The doorway framed her like a painting. I began the pitch then started laughing. Maybe it was the pressure of what was for sale.

'A free estimate for what?' she asked, smiling.

At that moment I wanted nothing to do with selling windows ever again. So instead of talking about glass, I asked where in Ireland she was from.

'Armagh.'

I could see goosebumps on her arms. She was cold. How long did I have before she closed that door? I needed an in. But I hadn't been to Ireland. North or south. I could hear music in the back of the house, a man singing about tea and oranges from China.

'That's Leonard Cohen,' I said.

She said it was.

'What would you bring me from China?'

She laughed, looked at me long and hard, then said she had the tea but not the biscuits.

'A brew would be fantastic.'

I followed her through the lounge. I tried not to stare at her swaying hips. Manuscripts scattered her coffee table. A Van Morrison LP with dog-eared corners.

I sat on a wooden chair in her narrow kitchen. She said I could have coffee, but I said tea was fine. She pulled the pencil from her hair, then again bundled those very black curls. I had to look away. It was too much. Postcards, ticket stubs and movie reviews covered the walls. She was working at the Theatre Royal, 'putting on plays'.

'It's a small city,' I said. 'I must have seen you before?'

'But you're not sure?'

I watched her pouring water from the kettle. I looked her up and down. 'Actually, I am sure. I'd have remembered.'

She asked if I wanted sugar. I was trying to play things cool, but saw that my hand was shaking when I stirred my tea. I told her I was selling windows because it was better than working in a factory.

'But you've been to university.'

It wasn't a question, and I asked how she knew.

'I guessed.'

'Is that a compliment?'

We talked over 'Famous Blue Raincoat', lyrics about a frozen New York.

I told her the first time I heard Leonard Cohen I fell in love. 'But I got the wrong person. I went out with the girl who played me his record, when it was really his music I wanted.'

She laughed. She liked that one. And I say that because she next said we should meet for a drink later.

'Or do you think I'm being a bit forward?'

'Not at all.'

I drank tea from a cup with no handles. There were a lot of empty bottles on top of her cupboards. Whisky, vodka and beer. But for all I knew she might have lived there for years.

'Snow's forecast tonight,' I said.

'I hope it does,' she said. 'I love the snow, getting a fire on and cooking up some mulled wine. You like mulled wine?'

I wanted to tell her how Jeff and I stole a crate of red from the back of an off-licence and slowly warmed it for days on a little camping stove. But she might not approve, so I just said, 'I love it.'

But we were getting too comfortable. Maybe she was conscious the mulled wine comment had come out like an invite to stay.

'Guess you've got some windows to sell.'

I finished my tea. 'Tell me about it.'

I stood and said thank you. We walked back through the lounge. Leonard Cohen was still singing, asking his darling over to the window.

At the door I turned and told her she was a Samaritan.

'Well, it's in exchange for that drink later.' She then gave me a little wave goodbye, and for a moment I swear I'd lived in that house all my life.


We drove out to Annesley, one of the pit towns that time forgot when the coal ran out, and parked on a rise over-looking fields of frost. The sun set behind leafless trees, as if the black branches were stencilled on its very surface. I told Jeff about my date.

'Spawny bastard. What's her name?'

'Shit.' I hadn't asked, and neither had she mine.

Jeff laughed. 'Don't hold your breath.'

'What do you know?'

While Jeff smoked down his cigarette, I watched crows hop around a scattering of breadcrumbs thrown on to a lawn. A lilac haze to the sky flashed their wings with violet, and I was thinking how beautiful the world had become since that cup of tea when Jeff threw his butt from the window. 'Anyway, you've got fuck all to buy her a drink with.'

The crows took flight.

'Better get your beer money.'

We knocked that whole estate. I got lucky on the first street, a new back door. 'Said he was sick of snails coming under the gap and sliming up his lino.'

Jeff got nothing. 'Another skint weekend.'

He was trying too hard. On the estates you needed to be more charity worker than salesman, make out that you're somehow doing the customer a favour. But I was thinking about the evening, how I wanted to buy her drinks all night.

We sat in the corner of the Western. Her name was Siobhan. I bought her two drinks. When she told me her name she bet I couldn't spell it. But I took out a pen and wrote it on the back of a beer mat. We swapped CV type biographies for the first drink. Then we broke from the formalities.

'I've been thinking about you all day.' This is what I told her. Her hair was down, framing her dark eyes.

'I should hope so.' She smiled. 'I've not come out in the cold for nothing.'

I was tingling with that remark. I felt drunk, and I hadn't even finished my pint. I tried making her laugh some more just so I could gather myself. I told her that I had to go because I needed energy for my Saturday job as a male prostitute. She laughed again, then asked how much I charged.

'About a thousand pounds an hour,' I joked.

'Well,' she said. 'Will you offer me a discount if I buy us a couple more drinks?'

I said I would. And she might have thought she had a bargain. But on that particular night of my life, I'd say the price was about right.

We walked from one pub to another, across the park, my hands pulled inside my sleeves because I'd given Siobhan my gloves. It started snowing as we crossed the bridge over the canal, and we stopped for a while, watching the flakes waft down from the blackness, meeting their own feathery reflections on that very dark water.

When we kissed I was young enough to still dream about the future. Houses, cats and children. Happily ever after.

Not stalking a man on Wall Street.

NAKED. TWO EARTH CHILDREN scrabbling in the dirt under an oak tree, hands and fingers interwoven, her thighs squeezing my pelvis as I came deep inside her.

This is how I picture what never happened on that Cotswolds hillside.

When the police car came we were tangled. Arm in arm, tangled in our clothes, the future.

'Shit,' said Kay, looking past my shoulder to the road. 'Your cop just arrived.'

I was kissing the top of her breasts. The shining patch of skin contained all my focus.

Until the police turned up.

'Can he see us from down there?'

I turned and looked to the lane. Whether he could or not, the moment was stolen.

'He's getting out.'

Perhaps the officer, plump and bearded, switched the beacon on out of habit. I doubt he knew we were the only other people who could see it, a sharp flash of electric blue above the hedgerows.

'He's interrupted us,' said Kay.

Or saved us. Saved a marriage, or two. That's what I thought but didn't say. Instead I suggested we hide in the bushes. Like predators, or prey, we watched him walk around the wreck a couple of times, note down the number plate, talk into his radio then briefly scan the fields and the trees before driving away.

I looked at Kay, sitting with her tanned legs stretched out, skirt pushed to the top of her thighs.

'You know we have to go,' she said.

"Should or have to?"

'We should at least move.' She straightened her clothes. 'That cop might come back.'

The moment had cooled. I didn't want to say gone. We walked down the hill from our fairy-tale dell across the bright green fields. From the dappled shade to the stark light, a broken spell.

'We should hike a little,' I said, helping her over the gate.

I pulled along her wheeled suitcase, a strange sight, I'm sure, as if a honeymooning couple had chosen this Cotswolds lane as their dream vacation. Conversation returned to the fundamentals, which direction to head, guesses how long until we caught a ride.

Did she feel guilt, right then, for what we'd just done? Guilt for being unfaithful to her husband, guilt for kissing another woman's man? I don't know, I never asked her. But I did ask myself, and fleetingly condemned my act as we waited for a lift, convicted myself of a crime against Jenni. But not Segur. My thoughts fluctuated madly between remorse and thrill, a squirm at the bottom of my stomach that was probably the same reaction to both feelings.

We'd only been walking for ten minutes when a car pulled over. A guy no older than eighteen, sporting gelled hair and gold hoop earrings, wound down his window.

'Guessing that's your mess in the ditch back there?'

We got in his Golf GTI. He turned down a pulsing house track then told us he was on his way to football practice. 'But I can drop you off somewhere.'

'That's lucky,' I said flatly. 'We could've been hiking all morning.'

I'd have been happy to hike all day, but once we got within a mobile signal I googled a car rental place on my phone while Kay called Chris.

'Cirencester, I think. Hertz?' our driver guessed correctly. 'I thought so. I go past it when I see my gran.' He rattled on about which bypass it was, which exit to take, while I was trying, and failing, to tune into what Kay was saying to Chris.

'We all good with the car?' she shouted from the back seat, her mobile pressed to her ear.

'I'll find out.'

Once I phoned and booked the car Kay confirmed with Chris, ending the call, 'I'll talk to you about it later, okay?'

'No problem,' answered our Samaritan when I asked if he could possibly drop us there. 'It's my good deed for the day.'

'Looks like you'll make your flight after all,' I said to Kay in the back seat.

'I guess,' she replied, her voice faltering.

Then I looked at her in the rear view mirror. I have to admit I was happy she looked sad. She was staring out of the window, watching the yellow fields flash past. I noticed her hands on her lap, how hard they gripped each other.

FROM THE SPINNING DOORS Segur appeared, smiling, shaking hands with two other men in tailored suits before turning and walking up Wall Street, away from the East River and towards the church.

Finally, my man. My heart thumped in my chest.

I gave him a fifty-metre head start, then followed. It was just before four o'clock and he'd beaten the rush hour. Though I'd been standing there since three, I didn't really expect to see him so early. Or even at all. I felt like a private investigator, a professional. Or just a man getting lucky on his first ever stakeout.

So far. Because it wasn't easy to follow him without getting too close. How well did he remember me from that day in August? If the lights at a crossing changed and I carried on walking I was in danger of standing next to him on the kerb. Instead I stopped, tried not to look too conspicuous tying a shoelace that wasn't undone, then quickly stood and followed once the walk sign illuminated.

His head bobbed above the other pedestrians, his broad shoulders cutting a swathe through a gaggle of German tourists pointing cameras at the Stock Exchange, a gum-chewing police officer posing in front of his squad car.

I nearly lost him in the melee, a squabble of hiking jackets and backpacks, before I saw him going through the doors of the plaza entrance to the subway.

I followed him across a marble court, beneath a glass atrium where homeless men sheltered from the cold around fake palm trees. Then down the escalators into the Wall Street station where I got a little too close when he fumbled in his pockets for his Metro card.

The deeper I followed him into the subway, the more I felt like his assassin rather than the detective I'd imagined myself.

He turned left on to the platform. I couldn't hear the grind of an oncoming train so let him go out of view before descending, feeling very conspicuous with shades on and no sun in sight. Not that I should have worried about looking a little freakish in New York, considering the anomalies that wander this city.

From the middle of the platform I leant against a girder and watched him pace, head down in thought, until the scrape of the 2 train broke his reverie.

I took the end door of his carriage. Strip lights and empty seats threatened my masquerade, and for the briefest second he did look at me, or the man I was, hat, scarf and shades. I angled my face away, watched him in the window reflection, his mirrored phantom fading in and out with the stuttering bulbs. From his foot-tapping stance I guessed he wasn't going far, unsurprised when he jumped out at 14th Street.

Up the steps and out on to Seventh Avenue. I trailed him as he walked north, keeping about half a block behind until he crossed at 18th Street and went into the Chelsea Organic Flower Shop.

I stood in a doorway until he emerged with a fancy bouquet of assorted blooms. And my heart sank when I saw this gift, a present, I presumed, for Kay.

When he came back across the intersection I had to turn against the wall and hide. He passed within feet of where I waited. To shield my face I mimicked lighting a cigarette, cupping my hands around the imaginary flame.

Then I followed again, this man with a bunch of flowers, over to Sixth Avenue where he crossed and briskly walked five blocks up to 23rd Street before turning into a flash apartment building called the Caroline. On seeing him nod to the top-hatted doorman I realized I couldn't trail him any further and walked on, my thoughts following him into the elevator, to his door, to Kay, her face on receiving the flowers.

'**Y**OU'RE JOKING?' I'D PHONED Jenni from the car hire office in Cirencester, waiting for Kay to run to the Ladies so I could talk alone.

No, not talk. So I could *lie* alone.

'Shit, you're both okay?' She was in the hotel restaurant. I could hear the breakfast clatter of plates and cutlery.

'As long as the traffic's not too bad on the motorway, we should be fine.'

'I bet Kay's not too happy about it. She could miss her flight.'

'She's taking it in her stride, actually.'

Jenni hesitated, very slightly, but long enough for me to think about what I was saying and how I was saying it.

'Well, that's good,' she went on. 'But you need to get her on the plane.'

I agreed. I didn't tell her that I'd promised to pay for a later flight if I didn't get her on board her scheduled one. Or how we'd hidden out in the wood from the police.

Or how I'd tended her cut, pulled her lips to mine.

'Give me a call from Heathrow, let me know how it went.'

'Fingers crossed.'

Fingers crossed for what, I wasn't sure.

Air-freshened and immaculate, the rental car was wiped clean of any personality. Mine, Kay's, or the previous drivers'. Like the ground beneath the tree, it was another space cleared of our history, a fiancée, a husband.

'No crashes this time.'

'Tell that to the geese,' I replied, swinging us through roundabouts where a wrong exit might get us lost in the Gloucestershire countryside for days.

'Cerney Wick.' Kay read signposts for tiny hamlets tucked in the Cotswold vales. 'Think you could live in Cerney Wick? What a name. Or how about Cricklade? You want to move to little old Cricklade?'

'Are you doing an impression of English sarcasm?' I asked, truly not sure what she meant by such questions.

'Isn't that a dream life? A house with one of those straw roofs by some babbling brook. Is that what you say? A "babbling" brook? With ducks. A village green where immaculate mothers have picnics and cut the crusts off sandwiches.'

'You've got the wrong Englishman.'

'Sorry,' she said, offhand. 'That's the impression. Beautiful fiancée, handsome man, both doing well in the City. You know, why not aspire to that quaint cottage and a nice life, kids and a couple of dogs?'

'I'm a cat man.'

'Well, I'm a cat woman.' She reached into the bag of snacks we'd picked up outside the car hire place and pulled out a pack of crisps. 'I never have chips.'

'Crisps.'

'Tomato, potato. And all those other pronunciations you Brits complain about.'

Kay drank a Coke and put back the crisps. Sun glimmered off cars on the bypass. Patchwork fields and more cows. I scooted along the outer edge of Swindon and turned on to the M4.

'We should be there in an hour and a half.' I looked across at her profile.

'That's good,' she said coldly. 'I wouldn't want to miss that plane.'

How quickly the atmosphere in the car had darkened. I glanced across again.

'You should look at the road,' she scolded. 'That's how we crashed this morning.'

We were quiet for a while after this, Kay putting her sunglasses back on, fiddling with the radio in an effort to find some music to fit the mood. Whatever the mood was. The picturesque countryside slipped from the windscreen to the rear view mirrors and we went past the suburban, low level sprawl of Reading and Slough.

I broke the silence. 'It's not all castles and quaint villages.'

'Same way we're not all hot dogs and burgers.' Kay looked at her watch. 'We're making good time.'

'Touch wood.'

She sighed, impatiently tapped her knee with her fingers. 'So?'

'So,' I repeated, but my intonation dropping on the 'o'.

'Are we pretending it never happened? Is that it?'

'It happened, I know that.'

'Does that mean you're afraid to talk about it?'

Perhaps I was. Before I answered she went on, an impatience in her voice. 'Maybe I've got you all wrong.' I could feel her eyes burn into the side of my head as I drove. 'That's it. You're just another player, cruising around behind your wife's back.'

'No,' I said sharply. 'It's not like that.'

'No? You didn't see this American chick in her yellow dress? Not quite as sweet as your sugar and spice Jenni, but a little different, dirty even. The sort of girl who might fuck you in a field.'

'Come on, really.'

'What am I supposed to think? I don't do this every day, you know.'

'Remember it was your husband who asked me to give you the lift.'

'How convenient.'

When I looked over to her, the traffic ahead drew up sharply. I braked hard and we jerked against our belts.

She steadied herself with the dashboard. 'Two crashes in one day?'

'Sorry,' I apologized. 'And not a goose in sight.'

I slowed down, hung back from the snarl of cars jostling towards Heathrow. I felt hot, my hands heavy on the steering wheel. Then I told her that if I could kiss her again, if I could crash without endangering her, I'd write the car off that very moment.

She shook her head and seemed to study her fingers, perhaps her wedding ring. And she didn't answer. Though what was she supposed to say?

On the winding roads into Terminal 3, beneath the concrete overpasses and manicured traffic islands, she suddenly said, or rather threatened, 'Don't even think of dropping me off like you're some taxi driver.'

'Look.' I pointed at the sign directing us to the main car park.

And I drove on, crunched gears exiting an island, still unfamiliar with the feel of the rental car, unfamiliar with my very own self.

Between following the maze of lane changes, I kept looking at the digital time display on the steering wheel, counting down her flight, working out what the clock would leave us before she disappeared through passport control.

She saw me looking. 'I did the online check-in. I just have to dump my bag an hour before take-off.' She paused as I reversed into a tight space, allowing me the concentration, or not wanting to compete with it, before asking, 'Does it scare you? That in under two hours I'll be gone?'

Planes thundered above us, rattled fittings of the plastic dashboard, thrummed in my ribs.

'Yes,' I said. 'Yes, it does.'

'Good.'

I looked at her. I looked at the planes angling in to land, the planes roaring into the sky. And then, just as I had with Jenni the day before, I leant across the seats and kissed her.

Was kissed by her.

CONSIDER THE SIZE OF the planet and the number of people on it, two people twenty streets from one another on the same island seems very close. The night after the day I discovered where Segur lived, Kay slept twenty blocks from where I did.

Except there was a husband between us, an obstacle equivalent to a continent.

And did omitting Jenni from this geography mean I'd already banished her from my world? No, I told myself. No. Or was this denial my conscience, convincing me that by searching for Kay I was just investigating a feeling, an enigma? *Yes*, I argued, that was it. *This infatuation is a test, galvanizing my love for Jenni.*

And thinking back on this counsel I offered the plotting adulterer, I'd contend that the greatest lies told to the most gullible people are the lies we tell our fallible selves. Because after I'd watched Segur waltz past his doorman with that bouquet of flowers I'd immediately set about scheming my way into the building and finding out which was his apartment. Which apartment he shared with Kay. Once my plan hatched I walked over to the East Village and hunted down a courier's shirt and matching cap. In Kinkos I bought a large brown envelope and printed off a label for a Mrs Kay Segur. After

Chris had gone to work I'd stride past the doorman and ask the receptionist for Kay's apartment number, blaming some jerk in the post room for not typing out the full address.

Before going to bed that night I stood facing my reflection in the bathroom mirror, my baseball cap and brown work shirt. I looked like a courier. I practised my shtick. 'How are ya? Letter for a Kay Segur. I need it signed, though. Do you have an apartment number?'

No 'please' or 'thank you' seemed suitably New York, but I was still an Englishman. This time I repeated my lines, changing 'Do you have' into a 'You got' and turning the 't's into 'd's. It sounded authentic enough, but when I looked in the mirror I didn't see an American. Walking Manhattan I could spot fellow countrymen and women before they even opened their mouths to ask directions for Times Square or the Empire State Building. Language, food, genetics, our general attitude, shape of faces and bodies. Pronunciation sculpts jawlines, different muscles for different sounds. And here, in the fructose corn syrup society, where a false smile and gleaming teeth are essential make-up, I was an alien. We may share a common, or thereabouts, tongue, but ultimately we're foreigners, the 'special relationship' akin to the good friend from school whose life took a tangent in the opposite direction.

Yet Kay seemed countryless. As I've always felt, too. I might cheer at a rugby international, boo the Aussies during an Ashes series, but I'm not weeping to 'God Save the Queen' or draping myself in a St George's Cross for a World Cup.

I rehearsed my lines one last time, aware of how ridiculous I looked and no doubt sounded. But not aware of how askew these very actions were, of what I was actually doing.

WITHIN A MONTH OF meeting on her doorstep, Siobhan and I were fighting as often as we were having sex. She'd drink a bottle of Buckfast before we went out, then match me pint for pint the rest of the evening. We made love in pub toilets, on a train to Coventry. On a central reservation wooded with sapling trees snagged with rubbish.

When Siobhan talked about Armagh, I thought Nottingham was some kind of urban paradise. Beatings, bombs and shootings. Executions. I was never quite sure if I believed the story about a murder in her street. 'My first memory,' she swore. 'I was out playing with my sister when three men pulled up in a car. One of them says, "Get inside, girls." Och, we should have listened. They dragged our neighbour on to the lawn and shot him. Right there. In his own garden.'

But I had no doubt she was a quarter Moroccan.

'That's for Mammy to tell, not me.' That's what she said when I asked about her grandfather. 'Good things can come from terrible men, put it that way.'

While Jenni passed off my university girlfriends as no more than flings, Siobhan grated on her, perhaps challenged her.

'Why did you fall out?' she'd ask.

91

I didn't help her irritation by shrugging my shoulders. 'I don't know, it just came to a natural end.'

'You got bored of wild sex?'

It was powerfully physical magnetism, I couldn't deny that, but contended it was an older woman fling at just the time I needed one. Mid-twenties and lost. My mother gone.

And what Siobhan also said about good things coming from terrible men. Not that I was such a bad man. Then.

The first thing I did was quit selling windows. Siobhan said that with every pane of glass I tricked someone into buying I lost a part of my soul.

What would she think if she knew that I designed systems for banks who evicted defaulting homeowners? Banks that kicked families on to streets?

But then, degree or not, jobs in Nottingham were rare. I was lucky to be moving radiators in a plumbing supplies warehouse. Eight hours a day at minimum wage. Break times I sat in the car park with a guy named Tegsy, a lanky stonehead who talked conspiracy theories and UFOs. Alien intervention, he believed, was the only reason a fuel card he stole from a van driving job a year ago still worked.

'Fucking year,' he said with disbelief, cannabis smoke fogging his car. 'And I'm still getting free petrol. I'll fill you a can for a fiver.'

I told him I didn't have any wheels, not since losing the Escort. Luckily my commute was twenty minutes along the canal to Siobhan's. I'd walk the bridle path over the weir thinking about what she'd have planned for that evening. Because she worked at the theatre she had access to the costumes. I didn't know what scene or period drama we'd be re-enacting until she answered the door. The bone corsets looked fantastic, but all the unlacing could get a bit tedious. If she left them on she'd have to explain the sweat marks and the stains. One night she dressed as an American police-woman, and when she put that plastic gun to the back of my head and cuffed me to the bedpost, I was genuinely a little nervous. Until she climbed on top. She'd tell me to try to fuck her off, and I'd thrust until the neighbours hammered on the walls and Siobhan would crouch down and bite my neck to muffle her screams.

If I'd known then that a good thing could be as damaging as something bad, I might have finished it all there and then. I definitely should have finished it when she said, 'You know I've kissed girls before.'

I told her I didn't doubt it.

'You're not shocked?' She was getting dressed, stepping into her jeans, no underwear.

'You love coming too much to be selective about who's pushing your buttons.' I thought I was being clever, but she didn't like my saying that. She thought I was calling her a slag.

'There's a difference,' she nearly shouted, 'between being horny and fucking around.'

'I know,' I said. 'Believe me.'

'I like to work on someone, get inside them.' She was sitting on the floor thinking about putting her socks on.

'You're inside me,' I told her.

She looked very serious, those nearly black eyes. Loosely she dropped her mouth open, the way she would, like a cat scenting the room. Then she lifted her bare feet up and told me to pull her jeans off.

'Now hold my ankles.'

I did.

'And push my legs as far apart as you can.'

We'd have sex, throw ourselves at each other, then drink and usually have a 'wee smoke', as Siobhan would say. I'd wake an hour before I had to get up for work, and slip inside her, the two of us drifting in and out of dreams, each other.

After her special breakfast of French toast and tomato sauce, I'd walk back along the canal to the warehouse, past the swans and ducks, the occasional heron creaking through the sky like a pterodactyl.

If I was sly about it I'd catch a nap in the stockroom, curling up in one of the bubble-wrapped baths for an hour before Tegsy would rouse me to load another lorry with radiators and bidets, faux gold taps and shower heads. At lunch I'd sit in his car trying to resist getting stoned. I watched him exhale smoke so long and hard that I wondered if he'd actually set fire to something in his lungs. It was after a particularly dragon-like plume of breath that I decided not to tell him about how Siobhan was on a mission to set up a threesome.

She'd slink the dance floor, looping her arms round the waist of whoever she fancied before leading them into a dark corner. And perhaps a kiss before the look-over, the proposition.

'You have to look less masculine,' Siobhan would say. 'Be a bit more subtle than standing there and sticking out your chest.' This was the kind of conversation we'd have walking home, just the two us, because number three had said no. In fact number three had usually said piss off.

Again, limbs flopped over the edge of the bed, I realized the whole escapade was beginning to drain me. Well, so I presumed. Because each time I thought this Siobhan would picture what the three of us would do together, who would be where and doing what.

'Imagine this,' she'd demonstrate. 'Her legs like that, your mouth here, and me sitting on top.'

And the rush would return, that tingle in the veins. What I guessed shooting heroin might feel like.

But then the come-down, the fear of losing Siobhan to someone else, man or woman.


Marissa worked in an antique shop on Wollaton Road, her dad's place. She was pale, red-haired and slight. Not that I was thinking about her body when I took in a photo of the grand-father clock I was hoping to sell. I just wanted a decent price for a damaged Victorian antique I'd found by the canal.

But the clock had nothing to do with it. Not once Siobhan sat Marissa down at the table in that narrow kitchen, stirring a milky tea while her father priced up my find. They were chatting about a thousand words per second when Siobhan reached out and stroked her hair. 'God,' she said. 'It's gorgeous.' She trailed her fingers, narrowed those very dark eyes.

'Natural shampoo,' Marissa said. 'Smell.'

Siobhan did. That close they could've kissed there and then. I was standing in the doorway with one eye on her dad peering into the back of my clock, and the other on the electric scene charging up the kitchen.

'Strawberry,' Siobhan confirmed.

Then Marissa's dad came from the lounge with his glasses perched on the end of his nose. 'The movement's fine,' he said. 'But the housing is irreparable.'

While I was helping him cart the clock into the back of his Volvo, Siobhan was inviting Marissa round for a drink later.

'Sure,' I heard her respond. 'Why not?'

Once I'd pocketed the fifty pounds and pulled the front door shut, I could smell the strawberry shampoo. As could Siobhan, standing at the window watching Marissa get into the car. She had the net curtain hooked back with a single finger. 'Isn't she a delicate wee thing.'

We got stoned in the afternoon because we were winding ourselves up about what might happen that evening.

'I tell you,' said Siobhan, leaning into the mirror and painting her eyelashes, 'she knew what I was thinking about.'

'I hope so.' I was lying on the bed with a hard-on I was trying not to touch. I thought about asking Siobhan if she loved me, but the word seemed wrong in the context of what I was picturing. So I told her not to get jealous.

'Me?' She looked at my reflection. 'You're more likely to get funny about it.'

Her dark hair fell about her shoulders, a frame for my favourite dress, the blue one printed with tiny white flowers.

'See.'

She was stunning. A seductress. Almost a witch. She twirled and lifted her hem to show that she had nothing on, that she'd shaved herself bare.

'How are you going to compete?'

And what more should I say than yes, another woman came to the house and drank wine in the narrow kitchen. That we got pissed and had a smoke and opened up the whisky. That Siobhan thought it'd be funny if I put on one of her dresses and paraded before them, fooling around until she volunteered Marissa to show me how it was done. And Marissa did, pulling off her top, intoxicating us with that strawberry shampoo, her little red bra.

Not long after that we were upstairs. Arranging limbs how Siobhan had planned. Legs here, mouth there. Tangled. Strung out on hormone.

But what does all that matter?

When I walked naked to the bathroom I thought I was some kind of Greek god. I had a barefoot piss with both my hands resting upon the cistern. Then I went back to the bedroom and they were kissing, entwined. The pale skin of Marissa burning on the dark flesh of Siobhan.

I was no longer that Greek god. I never had been.

I was a man who'd lie to old ladies to sell a pane of glass.

A man who'd fly across the Atlantic to court a married woman, while his future wife planned their wedding.

This.

From dawn I sat in a cafe on the north side of 23rd Street, waiting for Segur. With a plastic fork I pushed an omelette round a plate watching for him to leave for work so I could see his wife. I did have second thoughts on what I was doing. In fact I had third thoughts, but felt with the effort I'd made on the courier outfit I should at least see the plan through.

Such practicalities to absolve guilt.

It was just before seven o'clock when he swooshed through the revolving doors. Instead of turning left or right he walked to the edge of the sidewalk and *looked* left and right before, to my horror, jogging straight across to the very cafe where I was sitting.

I scrambled on my jacket to cover the courier shirt just as he opened the door. While he ordered coffee, I reached for, and dropped, the baseball cap.

'What the hell are the chances?' he bellowed as he turned and recognized me.

'No way!' I cried. 'Chris Segur!'

'You bet.'

I stood. We shook. I tried to mirror his surprised face at this seemingly remarkable happenstance.

'What the hell are you doing here?'

'I could ask the same.' I laughed, almost hysterical with nerves.

'Crappy as it is,' Segur began loudly, so the girl behind the counter overheard, 'it's the closest place to get a cup of Joe.'

I didn't care where he got his coffee. But what I did discern from his reaction was that Kay hadn't confessed to him about the field, the kiss.

'What brings you to the neighbourhood?' he asked, ripping open a pack of sugar. 'Sitting in my coffee shop at dawn.'

'I've been put up in Hell's Kitchen.'

'And you're walking twenty blocks for breakfast?'

I laughed, longer than his joke deserved. I laughed to buy time because I had no answer. None until my subconscious fired one out for me. 'Jet-lag,' I said, or rather a deep deceptive entity within me did. It was as though I'd just laid an ace on the table.

'You got to walk it off, huh?' And Segur folded his hand by finishing the lie for me. This was my chance to jump in, waffling about work, how I'd practically been put on the plane to New York by my boss, star man to run workshops between merging banks.

'He knows you're worth the air fare,' Segur complimented me. 'Well, hey,' he said, stirring his coffee before checking his watch. 'Why don't we swap numbers? I'm going to repay that favour by taking you to a Giants game.'

I said he didn't need to feel obliged, and that crashing on the way to the airport was hardly an act that needed reciprocating.

He shrugged his shoulders. 'You got her there on time.' I nearly asked him how she was, but let him go on. 'And I've got a box at Meadowlands. Besides, I want to hear you eat your words about rugby when you see some real tackles.'

We exchanged numbers, I muttered some comeback about rugby.

'Give me a call next Friday.' We shook again. At the door he turned to say, 'Have a good one.'

When I bent over to pick up the baseball cap I saw I'd left the fake Kay letter face up. What if he'd looked down and read the address? I'd like to know how my subconscious could have saved me from that one.

I WAS SPOOKED, TAKEN by surprise, the followed had turned upon the stalker. When Segur walked into that cafe I felt like a schoolboy caught stealing, the thief arrested with his hand in the till.

On the walk back to Hell's Kitchen, more than ready to change back into my suit and lose the courier garb, I resolved to stop the charade, the spectacle even, of a man chasing a married woman. We'd kissed, yes, and felt some undercurrent of emotion sweeping through us that day. But perhaps it was the crash adrenalin spiking a high that neither of us knew what to do with.

In an office tower on Sixth Avenue, on a desk with nothing but meeting agendas and diagrams of the bank's staff laid out like family trees, I was the diligent employee. Not knowing any of the New York consultancy particularly well, I could bury myself in work, once again allow myself to be carried through the day on sums and spreadsheets, the phone conversations of professional bullshit that were as far from emotion as twirling figures and calculator punching.

However, the workshops between vice presidents of the various departments were akin to warring generals deciding on terms of surrender. I had always believed that company mergers were more like the give and take of a relationship. What you bring to the other and what you lose of yourself, good and bad, ultimately decides identity, who you are in this two-into-one process. The acquiring company, the one with real command of how operations will now run, is the true power broker. Not that the acquired company doesn't have a say. The production lines don't whirr without the willing workers. But, whether the new company is a success or failure, identities change.

As they do in a couple when that *I* becomes *We*.

From facilitating a workshop where I suggested that men representing sectors as big as continents, men running operations in Asia, the Americas and the Middle East as if ruling their own fiefdoms, would now be managed by the new bank as if office juniors, I returned to my desk and there was Jenni, popping up on MSN Messenger: *Hey there worka-holic, don't forget the good fiancée.*

We rattled off a conversation, back and forth exchanges on the daily normalities usually shared in a mobile call at lunch, text messages or a chat in the evening over TV. She told me about her mother and her wonky hip, how the kittens had grown big enough to climb from their cardboard box and swing on the curtains. And what seemed banal, tedious compared to donning a disguise and trailing men home from work, was in fact a break from that state of hypertension. It was the steady heartbeat of routine, two people sharing a life.

We both signed off *I love you*, Jenni folding away her laptop in bed, while I logged off and turned down beers with colleagues who'd get me drunk and no doubt drag me to a strip club. I needed more connection with someone than slipping bills into stocking tops, and once out of the office rang Ruben, a friend who'd recently lost his job with Merrill Lynch.

'I'm a man of many hobbies,' he laughed when I asked how he was doing. 'I think it's called life, that thing that happens outside of work.'

I wondered if he fancied coming out for a drink.

'Sure, but fuck the city. Get yourself on the Q train, I'll meet you at Atlantic.'

I took him up on the offer, catching the Express from 34th Street out to Brooklyn, jammed with the commuters shuttling from Manhattan to the gentrified suburbs of Park Slope. I'd known Ruben from my first spell in New York, when times were good for those buying and selling mortgages. A hyperactive, fiercely intelligent and career-driven man, I wondered how he'd adapted to being jobless.

'Sammy boy,' he greeted me on the Atlantic Avenue plaza, a jazz soundtrack piping up from the brass band playing on the concourse. 'Now you're really in New York.' He wore scruffy Nikes, a pair of jeans and a leather jacket over the top of a Jimi Hendrix T-shirt.

'Who the hell are you?' I joked, not admitting I had to look twice to recognize him out of a suit.

'A man of leisure.' He laughed. 'And I know things are bad when they call in the Brits.'

I felt good in his presence, he was easy company.

'Miyuki's cooking teriyaki chicken, but we got time for a beer first.'

I followed him into a dim Irish bar called O'Connor's at the bottom of Fifth Avenue. A football game flickered soundlessly on a screen above the counter. Indie rock thudded about the narrow room while a tattooed barman wiped down the counter and folded away his tips.

'Two bottles of Brooklyn,' Ruben ordered, turning to me and saying, 'You gotta have the local brew.'

We took a booth seat, touched bottles and drank.

'Man,' he started. 'You gotta get out of this work thing. I tell you, best thing that ever happened to me was this crash.'

'You make it sound as if you're retiring.'

'For a month or two.' He shrugged. 'Who knows?'

'Miyuki wants a house husband?'

'Well I'm not getting a job in the city right now. You're more likely to see Elvis on Wall Street than a want ad.'

'You got the cash to sit back for a while?'

Ruben grinned, then leant over the table, closer. 'I did all right, okay.' But he only acknowledged his luck with a brief smile. 'And I know I'm not the only one. Look at Lehman. Kaput, fucked. Two thousand seven Fuld was CEO of the year. Last month he was up before some House committee. You know what he told them? That he earned sixty million in wages and, *and* two hundred and forty million selling stock.'

'Before it turned to toilet paper.'

'*A financial tsunami*, that's what he's calling it. And you gotta love that. That's as good as Clinton getting his dick sucked and denying sexual relations. Financial fucking tsunami. Come on, man, as if it was out of his control. A CEO of an investment bank saying that is like Zeus throwing down a lightning bolt and going, "What the fuck? Where did that come from?"'

'But I'm guessing you did pretty well from the fallout.'

He picked at the label on his bottle, and I asked if he was feeling guilty about it.

'Look, a week before we go under I get my bonus. I know we're sinking, I know others are getting fucked while I'm collecting.'

Ruben drank again. I told him he was telling me stuff I already knew. 'We're in a game,' I said. 'We know that. Winners and losers. Half the reason I got into the job was the competition, proving myself.'

'Bang,' said Ruben, sitting up straight. 'Adaptive market theory.'

I knew enough bits and pieces of economic theory to bluff most conversations, but this was a new strand of thought.

'Competition, you said, getting into the money game to prove yourself, to win. That's Darwin. That's adaptive market theory. People not numbers. Investor analysis is changing. The mathematicians, the physics professors, they've thrown in the towel. Numbers didn't predict any of this. Not the bubbles, the panics and the manias.'

'The crash.'

'Exactly. Because people don't do what they're supposed to.'

He had me now, my attention, and I asked him to explain.

'Natural selection. Competition and reproduction.'

'Survival of the richest.'

'Markets are like the ecosystem. Investors compete for profits, the natural resources. Different investors are different species. The hedge-fund manager and the market-maker go tooth and claw for the prey.'

There and then, it was easy to agree with the idea. 'A system measured by its ruthlessness,' I said. 'We evolve to stay alive.'

'Or sell a piece of shit mortgage.' Ruben shrugged his shoulders and held out his hands. What to do with it all.

'You're in a getaway car,' I said. 'A fast one.'

'Clean across the border, bro. Gone.' He finished the bottle, a gesture of disappearance. 'And you got your own bank job in the works?'

'Planning the getaway,' I said, overtly joking, but my insides suddenly coiling.

Ruben was about to say something when a text buzzed his phone. 'Miyuki.' The screen illuminated his face. 'It's chow time.'

We walked the tree-lined avenue beneath a dark blue sky, past Chinese, Thai, Indian and Mexican restaurants, even an English-owned fish and chip shop, and up the hill towards Prospect Park. Ruben, ambling, mellow as a stoned man compared to his once frenetic city personality, nodded hello to a woman carrying a chihuahua in her handbag. 'Five years ago this was a bad neighbourhood. Now we've got toy dogs in tartan jackets.'

'Is that what money's for?'

'Wait till you see what Miyuki's been spending my bonus on.'

I followed Ruben up to his brownstone apartment. At the top of the steps his wife, petite and pretty in that contained and precise Japanese way, opened the door. 'Good to see you, Sam.'

We hugged.

'And how's Jenni?'

'She's great,' I assured her. 'Looking forward to the wedding.' Jenni had flown out to New York several times on my last extended stay here. Apart from our upstate ski trips and tours of New York's Michelin-starred restaurants, she'd met and, as she usually does, charmed my colleagues and their partners.

Ruben slapped me on the back. 'Joining the married club.'

'You're a lucky man!' laughed Miyuki.

'That's what everyone keeps telling me.'

I slipped off my shoes and took a seat at the kitchen table. Miyuki returned to the hob and Ruben poured wine. We talked some more about weddings and I told them about Mark and Briony's extravagant bash, the horse and carriage, the marquee, how the happy couple got inside just before the skies darkened and split.

'So romantic,' gushed Miyuki, serving hunks of glazed chicken. 'I bet Jenni was so excited.'

I told them she was. I told them about the day as if it had been relayed to me by someone else. A version of me had been there, arm in arm with Jenni listening to the service, throwing confetti. But then another man arrived and hid with a woman in a field on a sunlit morning.

With an after-meal slouch Miyuki and Ruben sat together on a big armchair while we watched the McCain versus Obama presidential debate. I had one eye on the screen, the jerky, almost puppet-on-a-string twitches of McCain, the candour and confidence of Obama, generous to his opponent in the way a father might patiently educate his slow child, and the other eye on Miyuki curled over Ruben like a cat. Not jealous, just curious, studying how two people had grown into one.

'McCain,' Ruben snapped. 'Gets called brave for dropping bombs on villages.'

'And he was such a playboy,' added Miyuki. 'You know his wife had a car accident and got put in a wheelchair.'

'So he fucking leaves her.' Ruben shook his head. 'Leaves her for that psycho Cindy.'

'Imagine her as First Lady.' Miyuki laughed.

I made gestures of expected disbelief and carried on watching Obama dismantle McCain. I wasn't about to wade into a conversation about morally bankrupt men who leave wives behind.

When the debate closed and the two candidates shook, with the presumed triumph of boxers punching the air before the judges' decision, Ruben said he'd do the dishes and suggested Miyuki show me her sea horses.

'Sea horses?'

'About twenty,' she enthused, already heading from the lounge and beckoning me to follow. 'Always my dream to keep them, and now we have the extra space and Sam's bonus.'

The back bedroom had been transformed into a walk-in aquarium. Tanks filled with clumps of green weed and sea horses lined the walls.

'They only eat shrimp,' said Miyuki, sprinkling a handful on to the water. They eddied to the bottom, some falling on to the obligatory model castle where translucent sea horses bobbed over the ramparts.

'Don't you think they're beautiful?'

I crouched and put my face closer to the tank. A pale gold sea horse, propelled by its fluttering dorsal fin, swam towards the glass. I studied the dark roving eyes, each moving independent of the other, while it studied my own face, floating like a moon over that subaquatic kingdom of plastic castles and swimming horses.

'You know it's the male that has the babies?'

'The man?'

Miyuki clipped the roof back. 'They have a pouch in their stomach. After they dance with the female, and if they've danced funky enough, she puts her eggs into his pocket and he gives birth instead.'

Again, I bent down to the tank. 'I never knew that,' I confessed, watching a skinny pipefish zip past where the sea horses picked at the shrimp with their bony snouts.

'And you know they're not like McCain.' Miyuki chuckled. 'Sea horses are together for life. What's the word?'

'Monogamous.'

'They're monogamous. Same partner for ever.'

Miyuki bent to the tank, beaming, watching the sea horses twirl and flutter, gently bump one another and glide in the current, tails hooked together.

Coming back from Ruben and Miyuki's, standing on the open platform at 4/9th Street station watching the Brooklyn streetlights twinkle and wobble as if refracted through water, I pictured the sea horses bobbing around in the night sky. I could see them right there above the tracks, dancing, tails intertwined. And inside their translucent skin I watched the beat of their delicate organs.

Despite the chill wind cutting through my clothes, the home-cooked meal warmed my body like a log fire burning in the hearth. Not just the heat of the food, but the whole cliché of *the way to a man's heart is through his stomach* kind of thing. Soul food on a cold night. I wanted to hold Jenni, cuddle up with her in an armchair made for one.

I rode the train into Manhattan content, convinced, that I'd rid myself of the fixation, of *her*.

And when a succession of homeless men, toes poking from beaten sneakers, dragging body odour like a comet's tail of stench, trudged through the carriage and stopped to deliver their *Spare some change? A dollar, a dime, a penny* pitch, I gave them all the money I had on me, emptying my pockets. I also wondered which of them slept in a doorway because the woman they'd wronged had thrown them out of theirs.

Rising from 42nd Street station into the meretricious neon of Times Square, the tourist gawpers and bulbs of advertising, the ticker-tape news of folding banks, I was more resolved than ever to get over my hormone burst, my adolescent desire. I had a fine woman, a woman too good for me, waiting at home.

THE DAY AFTER I declared my good intentions, the day after Miyuki cooked teriyaki chicken and showed me her sea horses, I was sitting in a meeting when my phone buzzed in my pocket. Not wishing to incur the wrath of Ben Lucas, one of these red-faced managers who constantly appear to be on the verge of a heart attack, by being caught reading a text, I let the message sit in my jacket for over an hour. I guessed it was a goodnight from Jenni as early evening New York equals bedtime in London.

When Lucas wrapped up the seminar, a briefing which had turned into a troop-rallying speech from a man who liked to spur on his teams like a fist-pumping basketball coach, I walked into the corridor and checked my phone. The number was unrecognized. The message read, *Would you rescue my shoe if it fell in a river?*

I felt as if I was falling, my organs weightless in my body.

'Anyone home?' Lucas had been calling my name without my even registering him. He looked at the phone in my hand. 'I get it. Transatlantic love texts from your woman.'

I snapped it shut. 'Something like that.'

He laughed, spoke, said things I didn't listen to. 'Capeesh?'

'Loud and clear.'

He slapped me on the shoulder. 'Good having you here, Sam. But too much work and no play is bullshit. About time you joined us for a few drinks.'

'Friday.'

'Friday. A man could die of thirst between Wednesday and Friday. I know why you're not drinking, it's because you can't get a warm pint in this country.'

'You might be right,' I replied, gripping the phone in my pocket. 'But you know why American beer is served so cold?'

He turned to hear the answer as he jumped in the elevator.

'So you can tell it from piss.'

He laughed and called me a bastard before the doors shut. I walked back to my desk and read the message again. Then I checked the number, confirmed it was a US mobile. I was kidding myself with this detective work. It was her. Segur must have mentioned bumping into me, and Kay had scrolled his address book for my number.

'Shit,' I said aloud. The Guatemalan office cleaner briefly glanced up from her dusting, not that interested in hearing another man in finance swearing at his desk.

On the walk back to my apartment I twirled the phone between my fingers. I opened my door and threw it on the bed where it lay like someone waiting, a lover.

Then I went to the gym to burn off my doubts, strengthen my resolve.

When I came back from bench pressing and chin-ups, squats and sit-ups, thirty minutes on the heavy bag till my knuckles hurt, I was pumped with adrenalin, the rush of a workout. But on seeing the phone again I knew I'd failed.

Failed to douse the desire. I left the phone on the bed as I showered, washed and scrubbed. I got hard thinking about her, not Jenni. But this erection was comfort to my conscience. That was all it was, I thought, lust.

So I stroked myself and focused on Jenni. By coming with the image of her I'd kill the Kay hard-on. I thought of the time we climbed on to the roof of a starlit Greek ferry, the hidden cove in Devon where Jenni worked on me until we both collapsed and blissfully dozed while seagulls squawked and circled above.

But when I came it was Kay who flashed in my head, her legs wrapped round my back as I thrust inside her.

I took a towel off the rail, walked into the bedroom and picked up the phone.

*Yes*, I texted. *Yes I would.*

Finally, too tired to wait any longer for a reply, I fell on the bed and let go of my phone. I dreamed of clouds like smoke from burning plastic. Or a pyre of bodies. That was the leaden sky of my sleep, an expanse of roiling grey above a barren wood. No birds or green leaves, just a million naked branches. Like scoured bones. And between those pale trunks I could see a woman making her way through the dead forest, lost. When I followed her I had to fight my way through the rattling branches to keep up. She wore a yellow dress, ragged and torn. Was it Kay? Or Jenni? I couldn't see her face.

Then I was woken by the text, a short vibration on the bedside dresser. It was just before dawn. I was surrounded by office blocks and skyscrapers, not dead trees. I scrolled to the message.

*What if my shoe fell in the Hudson River?*

This time I didn't debate whether to text back. I typed, *Then I'd definitely need a kiss for returning it,* and hit send. In my half-awake state it seemed unreal to question my acts. I simply replied.

Within seconds she answered, *The Bethesda Fountain, Central Park. Noon. K.*

Before I had time to think about what she'd just done, what *we'd* just done, my phone buzzed again.

*Wakey wakey lazy bones.*

It was Jenni. A sweet good morning text to start my day.

First timers in New York often gush about the city giving them the sensation of being in a film. Seeing the Empire State Building flashed with sun, the yellow cabs and wraiths of steam that really do plume from the grates and manhole covers, they assume movie star status, believe, for a moment, in their own selves on a silver screen with a downtown backdrop.

But when your own life takes on a dramatic quality beyond the everyday, and perhaps this is the lure of many affairs, not that I counted what I was doing as one, the scene is superfluous and character is king, the chemistry between leading man and leading lady.

However, the New York stereotypes were certainly represented on set. From the overweight cop at a hot dog stand to the Fifth Avenue trophy wives dashing from limousines to designer stores. These extras were there when I crossed the road and walked into Central Park, past the T-shirt sellers and portrait artists, the clip-clopping carriages toting European tourists with digital cameras pointed at skylines and NYPD patrol cars.

And the horse-drawn carriages also carried my memories of that day in August, the joyous bride and groom swirled in confetti, talk of my own wedding.

On the ice rink, not yet cold enough to be open to the public, the blank whiteness waited to be coloured by skaters, by amateur couples fumbling around in hats and gloves, couples flown across continents to circle a frozen pond in a fairy-tale city.

As Jenni and I had done two winters ago, when she'd joined me on a short break to celebrate her latest promotion.

When I looked down on the rink I peered through time itself. I swear I could see us looping the ice, hand in hand. What if I'd looked up on that January day and considered the future? Could I have pictured myself sneaking off to rendezvous with another man's wife, lying my way out of interviews and seminars to risk the love of my fiancée for an illicit meeting? The way I felt about Jenni then I'd have laughed at the suggestion of my chasing someone else. But here I was, and there I was. A man in love on an ice rink. A man on his way to another woman.

Deeper into the park that guilt was replaced by worry. While I walked towards her, I scanned the paths and bushes for *him*. I was jittery, paranoid enough to wonder if I was being followed. What if Segur had found out that Kay had texted and this was a set-up? Perhaps he was hiding in the park, skulking in the undergrowth and watching me walk into his trap.

So nervous I was sweating in my jacket on a cold day.

I<small>T WAS THE WEEK</small> before our engagement party, before friends and family raised and clinked glasses to the declaration of our love, that I sat on the bed watching Jenni dress.

'Get over it,' she snapped, pulling clothes from the wardrobe.

'It's strange,' I replied. 'That's all.'

She was heading into Hammersmith to meet some of those friends, one of whom, Mike, happened to be her ex from university.

'*And* Clara,' she reiterated. 'The *three* of us are having a drink before she flies to Brazil.'

'You already told me.'

Watching her lift a bra strap over her shoulder, my imagination whirred with scenarios. From Mike and Jenni hugging their hellos and feeling a flame reignited, to them waving Clara through the departure gates and stealing away to a hotel for a one-for-old-times'-sake fuck.

Before I even commented that she seemed to be putting on more lipstick than usual I knew the words were war talk.

'What the fuck, Sam.'

But I still said them.

She spun round. I was sitting, head down. She stood over me in her boots. 'Just think about what you're saying. Think about me. And think about your fidelity, or lack of it.'

She swore she'd never been unfaithful.

'Not once. Not with you. Not with Mike. And not even with Philip fucking Cross from the sixth form.'

The 'fucking around period' that Jenni called my university years was not a state of being I wanted to return to. One-night stands and blurred memories, condoms, morning-after pills and fear of STDs. But after two years' work in the plastics factory, the all-nighters drinking and taking drugs merging into dawn shifts before I raced to college to study for my A levels, arriving on campus was as good as unpacking a suitcase in a holiday hotel.

I wanted, needed, to be with women, I knew that much about my messed-up self, but had no concept of a relationship.

'You know, I think I'd be happier about it if you'd just been shagging them and not craving some love at first sight, or first kiss, or whatever it was you thought you wanted after a few hours in the union bar.'

I thought that telling Jenni that my conquests were emotional, that all I wanted was to be needed by another for a night, would exclude me from the playboy tag.

'Oh it does,' she'd say, during one of the many arguments we had throughout our second year together, a period of resistance from both our hearts. 'But what does it mean? That I'm not enough for you?'

'No,' I'd protest. 'Not true.'

'Siobhan wasn't. And fucking hell, she brought other women into the relationship for you.'

I disagreed. I argued. I told Jenni she was the only woman I wanted, needed, loved.

ABOVE THE FOUNTAIN, PIGEONS roosted on the wings of a bronze angel. A few tourists wandered, took pictures, bought overpriced cans of Coke from the burger carts. When I saw her sitting on the wall by the lake edge, tearing up a pretzel and throwing it to the ducks, my stomach fluttered. I walked down the steps and across the terrace as if on a stage before a hushed audience. The spotlight of the low sun cast my shadow. Kay saw it and turned. 'Hey, you.'

A sharp thrill to hear her voice.

She checked her watch. 'You're three minutes fashionably late.'

She stood. She wore a mid-length suede jacket with black leggings and black boots. We nervously hugged and kissed hello, like two cousins meeting only at Christmas times. Then she stepped back, looked me up and down and said, 'You're here,' gesturing to the New York skyline with open hands.

I looked at the scene, towers steaming from air-conditioning units, sparks of helicopters and planes the only marks on a bright blue sky.

'So quiet for the middle of the city,' she said. 'Imagine the apartment blocks and offices are castle ramparts, and Central Park is the courtyard.'

I looked around, thought of standing in castle grounds.

'Do you know what I mean?'

I said I did. 'We're back in the fairy tale from the field.'

She smiled. 'Do you want to take a walk?'

I thought she might hold my hand, but she kept hers in her pockets. Perhaps someone she knows might see us?

Or perhaps she wanted to meet so she could say what fools we were, risking it all for a kiss?

We walked round the lake, alongside weeping willows that draped their branches in the water. Stacked neatly by the boathouse, rental skiffs had been turned over to mark the end of the season.

'Let's go in the Ramble,' she said, pointing to the overgrown maze of winding paths that ran behind the restaurant.

I said sure. I wanted to get lost in there. No, I wanted us to lose *ourselves* in there. Lose the regret I had in my gut for even showing up. Lose the third person who seemingly strolled by my side.

We passed comments on the leaves, copper tipped and bronze, clinging to branches or slowly twirling through the air. Squirrels, busily scampering about with acorns, stopped and cocked their ears when we walked by.

'They have no memory of where they hide their food,' I said.

'They must.'

'That's why they bury hundreds. Come winter it's just a lucky dip.'

'No memory of what's going to keep them alive?'

And as she pondered this I again studied her wide mouth and full lips. The sight, sound and smell of her was undoing things inside my body at a subatomic level.

When she looked across and saw I was rapt with her she quickly looked away, focusing on the mosaic of fallen leaves stuck to the path.

Wordlessly we followed the trail to the lake on the west side of the park. We went past a handful of strolling tourists and locals walking dogs before coming out on the water's edge, cordoned off from the public by a plastic mesh fence.

'I hate this,' said Kay, grabbing the top it and shaking it. 'Come on.' In one swift movement she swung her leg over. 'Before a cop sees us.'

I jumped after her. Memories of running from school as a child, adventures into the out of bounds. I followed her through the undergrowth, and once we were down by the lakeside the trees hid our trespass.

'I love this spot.'

It was almost a windless day. The Manhattan skyline mirrored on the glassy surface. On the other shore we could see joggers, a woman sitting reading a book, and an elderly couple ambling along with linked arms, each with a walking stick in their outside hand.

'We forgot the sandwiches, again,' said Kay, sitting cross-legged on a rock and facing the water, inviting me to do the same.

I sat beside her. For the first time since the airport goodbye in August we touched, brushing thighs. I felt hot, that same melting sensation deep in my chest. But unsure what Kay wanted from our meeting I resisted reaching over for her. Either from fear of rejection, or some remnant of guilt about Jenni. Though I have to be honest with myself and say it was most probably not the latter. There and then, in Kay's intoxicating presence, all sense of right and wrong had been suspended.

'Did you get my postcard?' she suddenly asked, picking small stones from the dirt and tossing them into the water.

'The Statue of Liberty.'

'The lady in the harbour. I was surprised how long it took me to choose the picture. Why not the Empire State building or the Brooklyn Bridge?'

'They're male things. Bridges and towers.'

'So I sent a woman instead of a phallus.' She smiled. 'Good.'

I picked a stone up, too. 'It was a shock, seeing it there on my desk.'

'Did I scare you?'

I tossed the stone into the water. 'I tried to throw it away.'

We watched the ripples spread across the lake, and I asked her why she posted it.

'To make that day real,' she answered. 'Worth something.'

'I'd have sent a picture of Buckingham Palace in return.'

'But no address.'

'Just Chris's business card.' By simply uttering his name I cheapened what we were doing, harmless as it was at that point, two people sitting by a lake.

'And you just happened to be in a cafe on 23rd Street when he came in for coffee?'

I felt like a stalker. 'People do strange things.'

When I bent to pick up another stone, she reached out and took my hand in hers. She inspected the back, the palms. 'You have a lot of scars for a finance man.' She ran her fingers along the creases. 'I like your hands.' Pressing her palm against mine, she saw my long fingers, slender, but most broken at some time or another.

I was only just listening. Her touch was electrifying, volts in my being.

'This is supposed to be your life line,' she said, tracing a fingernail over the deep crease in my palm. 'Yours gets stronger toward the edge of your hand.'

'I'm going to get better as I get older, like a good wine.'

'What about mine?' She turned over her hand. 'See how it's all splintered at the start, strong in the middle, then suddenly stops.'

'Come on,' I said. 'It's rubbish.' I hated seeing the halt of her crease, the end.

'I always worried about it when I was younger, running out like that.'

I turned her hand over. 'Why would you think that?'

She looked away to lower Manhattan, squinted at the golden storeys of glass. Then she pulled her coat tighter across her chest from the cold. 'I have a good life, so do you?'

'Depends how we're defining "good".'

'*Compared to what I had*, that's one way to define it.'

The history of her, a cause for why I was willing to risk it all with Jenni, was what I wanted. I needed to hear why my body had brought me here. 'You tell me yours, and I'll tell you mine,' I said, the jokey tone masking my fear of finding things out.

'You wouldn't believe me.'

'Make it a story then,' I suggested. 'Imagine you're talking about someone else.'

She thought about this. She studied my face while she considered what to tell me. 'No,' she said abruptly, shaking her head. 'Whatever happened in that field, under that umbrella, that was us. Me and you. No story. Everything I say to you is the truth.'

At that moment, on that particular day, we'd still done nothing wrong. Or had we? Though no physical betrayal of our lovers had occurred since the kiss at Heathrow, do the thoughts of another qualify as infidelity? Conscious or not. What if one wakes in the dead of night, as I had beside Jenni, from the pulsing dreams of a different bed, a different woman?

'I'm from a small town in California, just outside of San Diego. West coast girl. I grew up with mountain ranges, not skyscrapers. My mom tried really hard with me, but she was all alone and things were hard with no father around. She thought the only break for a woman working as a secretary at a car dealership was another man coming along.'

'Where was your dad?'

'Jail most the time. He lost his job at a sawmill, started drinking, thought it a good idea to drive drugs across the Canadian border.' Kay scratched at the rock with her pebble. 'See, I come from good stock.'

'Yeah, and I'm a real thoroughbred, too.'

And then I let her talk. I listened as if I were in her story. As if I were her. She told me how aged only sixteen she moved up to Seattle, swept north with the grunge scene, the wrong crowd.

'I got a job working a bar with fake ID and a tattoo.'

'Why did you leave home?'

Kay shook her head. 'The guy my mom was seeing. I knew something was going to happen.' She paused, left this part of the story and jumped ahead, told me how she met a guy in a band who talked her into quitting high school, promised her she could go on the statewide tour that never happened.

'And then came the drugs. Fun at first. No one takes acid because they hate it. And good weed, stuff from the hills. The Seattle sound was playing on radios all over the world and my only worry was getting high.'

'Something changes?'

'I was young, okay? Remember that when I tell you I got involved with a Mexican guy, a drug dealer. I thought it was all so darkly glamorous. And, not that I knew it at the time, I was getting back at my mom for inviting a man into our house who checked me out every time I walked into the living room.' She took a deep breath, looked to see if I was listening, understanding. 'The "something changes" was heroin. One minute it was all acid and weed, then best friends were stealing each other's TVs to buy deals.'

I'd never taken heroin, but seen enough of it, known kids from school who'd withered into old men over the course of a few years jacking up. Kay had smoked it at first, kidded herself that it wasn't an addiction. Then before long she was injecting.

She looked at me for confirmation that I understood, believed her. Perhaps she was looking for judgement, for the moment I'd back away.

'We've all messed up,' I said.

'But some messes can't be cleaned up, can they?'

She was probably right, but I wasn't going to agree.

'Have I turned you off yet?'

No, she hadn't. From the pang at the base of my spine when I saw her again, to a history others would've hidden. I was no saint, either. She'd turned me on to who she was, started colouring in the sketched woman. I told her this.

'Well, you're still sitting here.'

I was. The knowledge she'd lived out as much drama, if not more, as I had wasn't something that made me want to move.

'And I just tried to scare you away, tell you things I never share. With anyone.'

I asked her if Chris was that anyone.

'He knows enough, put it that way.' Her body seemed to jolt on his name. 'Anyway, maybe I've started explaining why we're hiding by a lake in Central Park. A married woman who seemingly wants for nothing, and a man about to marry his perfect fiancée.'

I looked away. I didn't want to think of Jenni and look at Kay simultaneously. And while I wanted to ask Kay about Segur, why she was with him and how much he knew of her past, I had no desire to bring him further into the conversation. I studied the lake bed. 'Are there any fish in here?'

'Nice change of subject.'

It wasn't. 'Perhaps there are things we should avoid.'

'For now,' she said. 'But not for too long. It's who we are, the people we live with.'

She angled her head to look me deep in the eyes. Her hand was palm down on the rock, and I reached out and took it in mine. We gripped, testing, as if babies trying out their grasp. But we were still awkward, fearful, afraid of what a kiss might do.

'We should walk some more,' she said, standing and brushing a dead leaf from her jacket.

I followed her up from the lake edge. We climbed back over the fence, returning to the winding path that cut between the trees and rocky knolls. I felt we'd left something behind by the water. A moment that had happened minutes ago was already years old.

'So you just got transferred to the New York office?'

'I was asked, and at first I declined.'

'What changed your mind?'

I let the answer hang for a while, a pause. 'The letter K.'

I was close to grabbing her right there, kissing her. Kissing her hard. I wanted her hair in my hands, her tongue in my mouth. But the timing seemed wrong. I sensed she was waiting, turning over the idea in her own mind. Right and wrong, logic versus desire.

We came out of the Ramble by the Swedish Cottage, a timber cabin oddity in the middle of Central Park that was home to a puppet theatre production of *Neverland*. Just past the cottage was the open-air Delacorte Theatre, famous for running Shakespeare plays through the summers. We stopped before the bronze of Romeo and Juliet, two elongated figures captured arm in arm, lips not quite touching.

I said, 'I suppose I can admire their dedication as lovers.'

'Death and sadness?' Kay waited for me to turn to her. 'I think we can do better than that.'

I nearly leant forward, pressed my lips to hers, but she took my arm and led us towards the Great Lawn. 'Let's get out of the shadow. It's cold.'

Then she took my hand. I felt like a boy. We walked into the low autumn sun, past a group of kids pinging baseballs into the cloudless blue, all of us focused on the arc of stitched leather hit skyward. I had a flashback of playing cricket in the park years ago, the simplicity of a struck ball falling back to earth.

Then Kay suddenly stopped, and we both stood very still.

In the middle of the Great Lawn, beneath that dome of city and space, we were like two figures in a Manhattan snowglobe. Kay turned. 'You didn't cross the Atlantic just to talk to me.'

I hadn't.

'So?'

So very slowly I moved towards her lips. She took a deep breath, so did I. And we kissed, very gently at first, as if testing the water before diving in, submerging our bodies wholly in the other.

THE ETERNAL HOMELESS FEELING I carry in my bones has nothing to do with a roof over my head, possessions. I know this because I have a home, things, objects that I bought in a shop. They all meant nothing in my rented bedsit, my rooms and flats. Nothing until I moved in with Jenni. For the first time ever, I felt a sense of place. That our bedroom looked on to the roof of a Chinese takeaway, and that mice scampered about the kitchen, meant nothing because we had each other.

So when did I once more feel that twitch in my toes? As if the floor beneath my feet, the carpet and polished tiles, could fall away with each step I took. A year later? Three years? A day in August on a wooded hillside?

Or in the middle of New York when I stood in a park?

Because we kissed.

Because we kissed and I believed again that if a home could be found anywhere it was in the heart space of another.

WE STOOD VERY STILL, embracing in the centre of that expanse of grass, set square in the middle of the city. If I'd been asked my name I couldn't have answered. Mute to who I was because I already wanted to be part of someone else. A woman who could reach into my soul and grab hold of it with both hands.

'Hug me tighter,' she said.

I pulled her pelvis hard against mine.

She bit my neck.

I traced her eyebrows with my thumbs. She hooked her hand behind my ear and pulled my hair, pulled me back to her mouth.

We were on view to the whole park, but screened by distance, I presume. Because if any of the joggers, strollers, or mothers with pushchairs noticed us I didn't notice them. I looped my arms round her waist, felt the small of her back, slipped my hand under her top and followed the knobbly contours of her spine. She broke away from our kiss, studied my face, trailed a finger over my cheekbones, my nose.

'You owe me your story,' she said.

'Which bit?'

'A truth,' she said. 'Something that hurts.'

*Something that hurts*, I thought, letting the words choose the memory.

'When my mum and dad were married, when my mum was pregnant with me, they were out of work and renting a run-down house in Nottingham. An Indian family lived next door, Sikhs. One morning their little boy came round with a tiny black kitten wrapped in a towel. He begged my dad to take it. His own father had said he'd kill it if it was still there when he got back home. Reluctantly, my dad took the kitten, worried they couldn't afford to feed it.'

'Are your mom and dad still together?'

'They split when I was three.'

'You lived with your mom.'

'And then my stepdad.'

Kay shook her head. 'I know something about them.'

'Till he kicked me out.'

'But your mom, you still get along?'

I used the words *passed away*.

'Oh, Sam. I'm sorry.'

And then I told her how long ago and nothing else, quickly carrying on, not wanting the story to turn into my mother's.

'Before we moved the cat lived with us, me, my mum and sister. But once she met my stepfather the cute kitten was long gone. Dinx was mean. Hissing, scratching and biting. She wouldn't come in his house. She caught birds and drank milk from a bowl outside the back door. Anyway, my dad would take us out every other weekend, parking out front, never knocking on the door. Just sitting till me and my sister got in the car. This one Saturday morning he saw Dinx on the path and got out. When he went to stroke her I warned him he'd be scratched, but he scooped her up like a baby. She was purring like a kitten, transformed in that single cuddle from my father.'

I'd told the story staring into space, through the scenery of Central Park all the way to an estate in the Midlands. When I checked to see if she'd been listening it was as if she was standing on that pavement with me.

'That's sweet,' she said. 'But what hurt?'

'After that she was the cutest cat ever. What hurt was she'd been angry all that time, when all she needed was a single moment of affection to change.'

'I want more,' she said. 'You. Tell me something else.'

I did. Between hugging and kissing I told the abridged story of what I thought amounted to who I was, the weekend dad, a stepfather counting down the days till he could kick me from his world.

'That's tough,' said Kay. 'Being thrown out, and then losing your mom like that.'

She was kissing my jawline, talking softly into my ear. We eased our faces apart, looked at each other. I focused on the rust-coloured flare in her iris, a tiny, iridescent flaw. Scars and blemishes. Physical and psychological, but she was richer and more beautiful for them.

'What's this?' I asked, tracing my fingertip over the line of her eyebrow, a healed score of lighter skin.

'Another time,' she said abruptly. Then she looked beyond me, beyond the Manhattan skyline. The moment she turned away I felt alone.

'Hey,' I said, gently putting my palm under her ear. 'Just here.'

When she raised her head she was crying. Tears magnified her eyes, drops streamed down her cheeks.

'I should go,' she said. 'I have to go.'

'Why?' I asked, feeling her body recede from my grip.

'We both should.' She wiped her eyes with the back of her hand, looked at me once more and turned.

'Kay,' I called, as she walked away, hearing a voice seemingly not mine. At least until I said her name a second time, when she did look again, briefly, walking backwards as I watched her get smaller, falling into distance. I had a terrifying thought that I'd never see her again. That I'd be nailed to this spot for ever. When she disappeared beyond the pine trees at the back of the museum I turned and walked in the opposite direction.

I went back past the Delacorte Theatre and the Swedish Cottage, taking the path alongside the edge of the lake we'd looked at from the rock. Long shadows stretched over the water, trees and rooftops. It was cold now, and the people we'd seen had gone, the dog walker and the woman reading the book. I overtook a man pushing a pretzel cart and followed the road round to Strawberry Fields, the John Lennon memorial. The black and white mosaic spelling *Imagine* was ringed by fresh flowers. Tourists took photos of each other. A Spanish couple asked me to take a picture of them in front of the tributes. But I apologized, backed away. I'd had enough of the park and headed for the exit on to 72nd Street, between the stalls selling Lennon memorabilia, photos of him and Yoko, the *I love NY* T-shirts and circular sunglasses.

From the gate I recognized the Dakota apartment building where he was killed. Shot dead by a man obsessed.

For two days I was a zombie. By this I mean that I walked and talked, functioned in my job, sat at my desk and performed sums, read business reports and digested statistics, yet I was numb. The living dead. Numb to the world, my own life.

The kiss, Kay walking across the park, her hands, played on in my mind. Too vivid to be called memory. Two days in the past, yes, but if reality is how we make sense of it all, how the brain transforms information and understanding into whatever a self is, then the very fibre of who I was now contained that day, her.

When she didn't reply to my third text I rang. Hearing her voicemail I hung up, with the thought that Segur could discover my message.

I wondered if she'd heard my story and changed her mind. Decided I wasn't worth the effort. I could think up a thousand different reasons why she walked away, but was still no closer to why she'd slipped from my grasp the way she had.

And I was daydreaming this when Lucas came up and asked for the agenda for his communications workshop, a plan, I suddenly realized, I'd been detailed to write up.

'No bullshitting, Sam. This is a big one.'

I was supposed to have an outline of how he was going to help the banks announce their merger to both media and employees. The timing of this was crucial, as stocks and shares could rise or fall on a press release. It was similar to a plan adulterous lovers might make for when and where to finally tell their partners.

'What the fuck, Sam?'

He wasn't happy. My slack work meant he had to wing a workshop the consultancy had been handsomely paid to carry out. I apologized, swore at myself.

'You can curse all fucking day but it won't change my meeting now.' With that he shook his head, looked at the clock and stormed off, no doubt mentally preparing the memo that would be sent to the London office.

When I caught the train out to Park Slope to join Ruben and Miyuki for an 'Election Party' I was hardly in the mood for socializing, getting excited about a presidential race I was ineligible to vote in anyway. Obama and McCain had ruled the news networks for days, and bubbling optimism among the New York democrats was palpable on the streets, in the bars and train carriages.

'That's not the attitude, bro,' said Ruben when I told him I was having trouble being enthusiastic. 'If you're President of the US, you're practically world leader. This affects you too.'

He handed me a bottle of beer. There were about twenty people in his apartment, drinking, glued to the results coming in on the TV and high-fiving when a state came in blue.

'I can't tell you how bad that sounds,' I replied to his 'world leader' tag.

'McCain in charge?'

'Presuming you're planet boss if you run the US.'

Ruben laughed. 'We've got to get it while we can, because this recession is going to bust whoever's balls end up in the White House.'

I sat on the sofa, chatted with his friends, young professionals, some out of jobs, some waiting to be told they were out of one. But none were gloomy about the prospect. A house full of Democrats on that particular night was about to be ecstatic, the cheers and whoops getting louder and louder as more blue states flashed on to the screen.

When the count put Barack Obama in the White House, firecrackers rippled in the streets only seconds after his face appeared on television sets across the nation accompanied by the words, *President Elect*.

The room exploded with streamers, popped corks ricocheting off the ceiling. The party quickly spilled into the streets, mostly the young Brooklynites bouncing with chants of 'O-ba-ma, O-ba-ma', while older residents watched from their stoops.

'*Yes we did*,' bellowed a flag-waving black woman.

'No more Bush,' called a guy wearing a jacket covered in Obama badges.

A crowd gathered at an intersection between two packed bars, manically cheering when a pair of hands hoisted a life-size cut-out of Obama above their heads. A crowd hero-worshipping a man who looked as if he were walking on air, and perhaps that night actually could have.

I saw Ruben and his friends dancing in the road. More fireworks crackled above the rooftops, amplifying the cacophony of car horns and cheers.

I stood in a doorway, oddly detached, as if it were all occurring on a news network and not the actual street I was watching from. When the joyous came past looking for high fives I had no choice but to reciprocate. Awkward and English. A fraud. A fraud in the celebrations, in my own life. Somewhere in my locked heart I was happy Obama had been elected, but perhaps too selfish, too wrapped up in my own drama to care about an entire country's.

I slipped away, walked to the subway. More flag-waving Obama supporters and honking carloads came noisily into the night as I descended into the station, a text buzzing my phone seconds before I lost the signal.

If I were a praying man I'd have prayed it was Kay.

*Wow! Must be amazing for you to be in the US tonight! You enjoying yourself at Ruben and Miyuki's? Call later. xox* Not Jenni.

So if indeed I were a praying man that would mean I believed in God and that God could see my stained soul.

THE DAY AFTER THE election I walked to work between a parade of Obama faces staring out from the newsstands, T-shirts and badges. The buzz on the sidewalk was a black man in the White House, as if the historic election had put a spring in the national step of my fellow commuters, Democrat or not. Even the staunch Republicans in the consultancy managed a sense of pride when the rest of the world was thanking the US for finally making the right decision. Others – well, mainly Lucas – warned that Obama was a 'Commie bastard' out to steal tax breaks and bonuses. 'Kiss the USA goodbye,' he bitterly predicted.

I was hiding from his bullshit at my desk, trying to catch up on a multitude of tasks I was getting behind on, when Segur rang. I let the phone rattle on the desk, paralysed by fear when I saw his name flash on the caller ID.

Then I answered.

'Hey, Sam. Catch you napping?' His voice was as sparky and snappy as usual.

'Working hard, working hard,' I fired back. 'To what do I owe the pleasure?'

'Well, fucked economy or not, we got this swanky awards dinner for financial securities tonight.' From his tone I presumed he knew nothing of Kay and me in the park.

'A black tie do?'

'Black tie. Champagne, you know the scene. Listen, a guy at my table bailed out on me this morning and I need someone not part of the company to take his seat. You in?'

'You need a man off the substitute bench.'

'The seat was for the husband of an area sales manager. Turns out he's off with some secretary, yada yada, we know the story. Anyway, free champagne, and save a lady from feeling uncomfortable sitting next to an empty name tag.'

I said yes.

I said yes because I guessed Kay would be there, too. Seated across the table. Whatever she wanted, or didn't want, from me, I needed to see her.

'The Ritz Carlton, Battery Park. Seven o'clock. Get yourself a dinner jacket, shine your shoes. You'll enjoy it.'

For the rest of the day I sat at my desk and made mistakes, divided by decimal points when I should have been calculating with hundreds. Not the pressure of work, but the pressure of *her*. Come five o'clock the sun beamed into the midtown office with all the fiery intensity of a dying star about to consume the world. I had the thought that if we all went up in flames at the same time it wouldn't be so bad.

Then that star dipped, set behind towers of steel. Downtown Manhattan looked like a silhouette cut from paper and pasted on to the sunset.

I thought of the phone call I'd promised Jenni after work.

'W'HY DOES IT FEEL like a million years since I've heard your voice?' I was sitting in Bryant Park behind the New York Public Library. Jenni had the phone to her ear as she cooked up a late Italian meal for one in our Maida Vale kitchen.

'Sorry, sweetheart.' And I meant it. 'I've been busy as hell. You know how it is over here.'

'You're missing the cats growing up.' She laughed. 'God, listen to me. Talking about them as if they were our kids.'

'Can't you starve them a bit?' I joked. 'Keep them the same size for when I get back.'

'Aaah, don't be cruel.'

'You know I don't mean it.'

'I've had a bugger of a day,' she said, triggering the two of us swapping complaints about work, colleagues and clients. 'And the more dippy CEOs I meet, the more convinced I am that women will run the world sooner rather than later.'

I told her I didn't doubt it, that men were only clever enough to know what fools they were next to women.

She laughed. 'Well, knowing that much is a start.'

But in the humour she heard a fade in my conversation, a distance.

'Are you missing me?' she suddenly asked, a waver to her voice, a doubt that struck me with sadness.

'What a question to ask,' I said sharply. 'I don't want to be here. I want to be sitting down in our flat, a glass of wine and one of your Italian specials.'

'I should hope so. New York has nothing on me.'

Above the park, a rash of starlings swirled.

'It hasn't,' I lied.

'Shit,' snapped Jenni. 'The pasta.' I heard the hiss of water on the hob. 'We're bubbling over here.'

'Don't burn yourself.'

'It's your fault,' she said. 'Mr Distraction.'

Just as she was turning the hob down, stirring the spaghetti and balancing her phone to her ear I said, 'You know I love you.'

'Who the hell burns pasta?' She hadn't heard me. 'What a mess. What were you saying, darling?'

'Nothing, just mumbling. Do you want me to call back?'

'After the inferno. Might be better. Are you going out with colleagues or anything?'

I didn't want to mention the black tie do with Segur. And Kay.

'Possibly.'

'You don't sound that keen.'

'Sitting in some sports bar drinking bad beer.'

'Well ring me in the morning. We can talk properly then.'

We said our goodbyes, the habitual 'Love you'. I snapped the phone shut and watched the flock of starlings set down in the bare branches above the park, screeching and jostling with one another before flowing back into the sky like a swirl of smoke.

From Bryant Park I walked up to Baldwin's Formals on 45th and Sixth, pushed open the door and announced to the young Asian tailor that I needed to hire a tuxedo.

'What kind of event, sir?' he asked, hands pressed together, tape measure dangling round his neck.

'An awards dinner,' I replied. 'Something simple.'

I was shown an array of jackets, from wedding tails to flamboyant white creations.

'Can I try on the two-button Ralph Lauren?'

'Nice lines. The lapel works with their laydown collar shirt, too.'

'You're the expert.'

He showed me to the fitting rooms, slipped the tape measure from his neck and set about calling out my numbers to the other sales assistant.

'Not too tight,' I requested.

'No problem,' he said, kneeling to measure my inside leg. 'Thirty-four.'

I felt like a cow at auction, my presence in the world defined by inches, what space my flesh occupied. I took the clothes into the fitting room and tried them on. Down to my underwear I turned to the mirror slowly, and saw my body. Taut from walking, press-ups and sit-ups, a diet from nerves that began the day I met Kay. I studied the scalpel mark on my right shoulder, an operation to keep me playing rugby when I should have retired, now a pink caterpillar of sewn-up skin.

'How are we doing, sir?' called the assistant from beyond the curtain. 'A good fit?'

I wondered what Kay would think of seeing me naked, if she ever would. Then I buttoned the shirt and pulled up the trousers, slipped on the tuxedo and stepped out before the assistant.

'Perfect.'

He tugged on the jacket sleeves, checked the cut at the sides. Again, I saw myself in the mirror, and barely recognized the man staring back.

THE YELLOW CAB DROPPED me outside the marble steps of the Ritz Carlton foyer. A top-hatted concierge opened the door, welcomed me with a 'Good evening, sir', and swept an open palm towards the entrance should I get lost between the taxi and the hotel.

'Evening.' I greeted the other dinner guests, men dressed as penguins, as I was myself, in black and white tuxedos, accompanied by trophy wives, mistresses parading as wives, and wives in their fifties trying to look thirty in dresses from shop windows on Fifth Avenue.

I followed jackets and high heels up the staircase to the reception area on the second floor. Bow-tied waiters balanced trays of champagne. I recognized names and faces from the Premier League of world banking, the uber-CEOs with more financial clout than entire countries. If money had a smell this was it. The off-season tans and glowing smiles. Height and size, a physical bulk in wealth. And even the small men swaggering like giants, because a figure in a bank account filled their frame, a voice, the raucous laugh from a row of zeros and a decimal point.

Scanning for Segur and Kay, I had the desire to run out of the room and be done with it, escape the tension and the lies.

But above the sound of a grand piano, jazz accompaniment to begin an evening of back-slapping and self-congratulations, Segur called out my name. 'Sam the man.'

I turned as he scooped two glasses of champagne off a tray and strode over. 'Look at you in a tux.' He passed me a drink.

'Good of you to invite me.'

'You're doing me the favour on such short notice. And hey, you clean up pretty good.'

Segur stepped back and admired the tuxedo. 'Could have shined your shoes, though,' he added, joking but condescending, perhaps getting points back because I had 'cleaned up' pretty well, was suddenly feeling smug that yes, I was ten years younger than him.

'Let's go find the boys.' He put that big hand on my shoulder and guided me towards the function room. 'You know we all feel the irony of this whole dinner.'

'A financial securities awards dinner.'

He leant closer. 'A celebration of the system that's fucking the economy up the ass.'

'And what a week,' I feigned, my interest in the world of money waning by the hour. 'If the market falls any faster we'll need parachutes.'

Segur laughed, then greeted other men standing with glasses of champagne, portly men beside slim women dripping with gold and precious stones. And when I stepped back from the hellos it suddenly appeared ridiculous. A magic show where I could see behind the curtain, the mirrors and the trapdoor. From the Wall Street players, the bankers and brokers, to the homeowners about to be kicked out of houses they deluded themselves into believing they could afford. Not that I too wasn't part of the mirage.

'This is Hal Gibson.'

I shook hands with a man who had teeth as white and shiny as a cartoon shark.

'Watch this one,' said Segur. 'Could walk away with CEO of the year.'

'Not if you've been slipping brown envelopes into jacket pockets.'

Segur smirked. 'Learned it all from you, Hal.'

We walked on, into the main reception room. I heard snippets of conversation about job cuts and bonuses, banks on the brink of going down, the captains, the first officers, the men in command rowing away with the treasure while the deckhands drowned.

And there she was, the siren in the bay. In a red, strapless dress. Her dark skin gleaming.

'Say hello to Kay,' said Segur, pointing her out as if I hadn't noticed her. 'But don't drive her anywhere, please.' He laughed, apologized for leaving me to 'talk some bull with a Dutchman'.

Kay was sitting beside the woman I was accompanying. With the skill of an Oscar-winning actress she said hello as if we hadn't even met since that day in August.

'Sam.' She stood. 'It's great you could make it.' We leant and air-kissed cheeks. And how strange it was to greet so coldly. To lean in like mannequins and barely touch. 'This is Margot.'

I greeted my 'date' with the same formality as I had Kay.

'I'm the jilted one, if you're wondering.' Margot was already tipsy. Bloodshot eyes and a smudge of mascara on her cheek. 'But if I've swapped my son of a bitch husband for an Englishman I'm in luck.' She laughed a smoker's cackle. And Kay smiled, caught my eye long enough to acknowledge what had happened between us in the park.

'You have a drink, Sam?'

My champagne glass was almost empty. Kay got the attention of a waiter, but he was carrying a tray of breadsticks.

I saw a full glass unattended on the table. 'Shall I grab this one?'

'I think that's Chris's,' said Margot.

Automatically I reached out and took the drink. I knocked back half the glass, staring at Kay. 'I'm sure he'll get another from the bar.'

Margot laughed. Kay looked away, did the thing with her hands on the tablecloth, each one gripping the other hard.

I SLIPPED OUT OF work early the next day, gave Lucas some story about a secret meeting with a phantom stakeholder from the acquired bank who had dirt on a couple of his own men, and headed for the Hudson River. I criss-crossed blocks down from the Port Authority bus station, past defunct lots and concrete underpasses, empty garage forecourts fenced off with rusting razor wire, shuttered doors flaking paint. Perhaps this district boomed when the economy did, I'm not sure. But I know now that if you look back at shiny Manhattan from there it looks like the border between two different countries. At least until you get to the water, where a landscaped riverside is home to rollerbladers and cyclists, the ubiquitous New York runner.

I took out the note Kay had slipped inside my jacket pocket when we'd danced, when Segur had passed her over to me as if she were a piece of real estate I could use for the evening.

Then I followed the Hudson River Park south, the view of the Jersey shoreline across the water on my right, apartment blocks of the West Village on my left. Just after the Chelsea Piers sports centre rotted piles jutted from the water like the stumps of a razed forest, or the tops of ancient trees that poke through sand on stretches of the Yorkshire coast.

When I thought of walking an English beach I pictured myself with Kay, not Jenni.

My stomach knotted, and for a second my knees felt as if they were made of jelly. I could collapse here and never stand again.

But instead I lengthened my stride, speeded up in the hope of outrunning my conscience, passing more joggers and dog walkers, two policemen on horseback, a tiny Asian woman in a leotard tap-dancing on a plank of wood she'd laid down on the concrete.

By the time I got to the Rockefeller Park I was thirsty and drank from a water fountain. I still had ten minutes before Kay was due to meet me there and popped into the public toilets to check my hair. Looking in the mirror I couldn't recall the last time I was concerned about my appearance with Jenni. The thought held my attention for about a second, the time it took for me to turn from the mirror and walk into the park, a green spit of land on the edge of the Financial District, two blocks over from Ground Zero.

I looked around, beyond the paths, a bandstand and the basketball courts, but couldn't see a phone. I opened the note again. *Rockefeller Park. The phone. 4 p.m.*

Maybe the phone had been removed since she last came here. I walked down to the plaza, dotted with bronze sculptures, a pair of feet, half a head and a clenched fist, a tortoise and a giant coin.

And a bronze phone sitting on a stone table. This was what she meant. I sat by the sculpture as if I expected it to ring, waiting for her to call and say she was running late. Because after fifteen minutes I was fidgety, checking my mobile to see if she'd texted. After thirty minutes I was worried she wasn't going to show, that I was waiting at the wrong place. I wanted to call her, but if she wanted to speak to me she could call me, too.

I was looking at the sculpture of a bronze bulldog growling at a bronze cat when she appeared. And appeared was the right word. As if a woman had walked from my mind.

She apologized, said my name. 'I was terrified you wouldn't wait.'

She was over half an hour late, but I was hardly going to complain. 'I think I'd have been here until a cop kicked me out for being a tramp.'

Again, I sensed a kiss hello wasn't right.

'I don't have long,' she said. 'Let's go by the water.'

We followed a path across the park to the Hudson River and sat on a bench facing Jersey City. Towers and office blocks marched into the bay towards the Statue of Liberty, very green beneath the overcast skies.

'You enjoy last night?'

'Not sure "enjoy" is the right word,' I answered, watching laden barges ferry stone upstream, screeching gulls diving in their wake. 'No. I didn't,' I added flatly, thinking about how Segur had put his arm round her. 'And you?'

'When he told me you were coming I was afraid.'

'Why did you walk off in Central Park?'

She looked at the passing boats, those swooping gulls. 'I couldn't keep hold of myself, my feelings.'

'I guessed you had second thoughts, changed your mind.'

A mother with a pushchair and wobbling toddler walked in front of the bench. Kay smiled at the little girl, and when the woman was out of earshot she said, 'I didn't want to make you feel guilty, mess up your world.'

'My pretend world.'

'Is it? You have a life waiting for you. Finish your time in New York, then go back to your fiancée and make some wedding plans.'

I shook my head. 'Remember what I said on the hill, about being an actor in your own life? Suddenly I don't feel that. All the jolly pretence has gone.'

She reached over and firmly took my hand. How abruptly my life in England seemed so wrong. A diary-filled future of work and marriage. Days watching computer screens then commuting home to a woman who didn't know who I was. I looked at Kay's fingers round mine and lifted her hand to my lips, kissed her skin.

I could've asked her why she was seeing me, why she was doing this. Instead I told her that I wanted every single part of her body. '*You*. All of it.' Then I leant over and kissed her cheek, her neck, inhaled her.

'Sam,' she said. '*Sam*.'

And when she repeated my name, uttered it so gently into my ear, I wondered if I'd ever known how much another person could confirm my very presence in the world.

'Kiss me,' I asked, begged.

She pushed her tongue into my mouth, curled it round my teeth. She pressed the full force of who she was against me. And I pressed back hard, the blood racing in my veins, that rush as if a sea were kept beneath my skin.

'*Mommy*,' shouted the little girl. The mother and child had come back. 'What are they doing?'

She stood and stared, blond hair and big blue eyes. We both laughed nervously. It was a good question.

'Come on, sweetie,' called the smiling mother. 'Let's go feed the squirrels.'

Once she'd gone past we stood.

'We attract interruptions,' said Kay.

'We are the interruption.'

We headed towards the moorings, a small harbour. I wanted to hold her hand as we walked, but when I reached for it she said, 'Not here. We're not that far from Wall Street.'

I didn't want to ask about Segur, but I did. 'Is he still at work?'

Kay bit her bottom lip. 'He's in Boston today, but the guys he works with might be around.'

'Is that why you didn't text? You're afraid of being found out?'

She tapped the railing as she walked, impatient, frustrated. 'Aren't you?'

I asked her what he'd do if he knew.

She shook her head. 'I don't want to think about it right now.' She beckoned me on, and as I followed I clenched my fists in my pockets, tensed before a future I finally acknowledged was coming.

When we got to the yachts we stopped and stood, awkwardly apart, surrounded by darting office workers starting their journey home. Kay turned and looked out to the river. Lights on the New Jersey shore shone in the gloom. A speck of setting sun burned orange between leaden cloud, the reflection leaking on to the river's grey surface like a fiery slick.

She said, 'It's the sunset being carried out to sea.'

I watched the river slide past, plastic bottles and bobbing driftwood. 'Can you get away?' I asked. 'For a night. One night.'

Kay turned, looked beyond my shoulder, perhaps scanned the plaza for a familiar face. Then she reached for the lapel of my jacket, turning it over and over.

'We owe ourselves that much,' I said.

That evening I changed the wallpaper image on my phone. A photo of Jenni, proudly standing on top of Arthur's Seat in Edinburgh. Her father had paid for the weekend trip last year. 'A celebration,' he said, 'of marrying my daughter off to a man who can hold a cricket bat.'

Joking aside, I knew he was happy, that he approved of my proposal with a plastic ring fallen from a Christmas cracker.

And when I think back to that Easter weekend in Scotland, the silk sheets of the five star hotel, the wild salmon and malt whisky, I mourn for us both. Jenni, intelligent and funny, beautiful. A woman to spend a life with, to have children with, to live for.

But the sadness for myself, the man who took a hilltop photo of the woman he loved, is as if I am mourning the death of someone I knew, a good-natured and well-meaning friend. Dead and buried. Laid to rest in a suit and tie.

Catching the subway to pick up a rental car from 86th Street, the very day I should have been catching a flight to go skiing with Jenni in Italy, I wondered if there was time for that body to be resurrected.

Could I return from a weekend with Kay in the Catskills and pull him from the earth, dust down his suit and present him again before his fiancée?

KAY WAITED ON THE steps of the Natural History Museum between two giant shrubs cut into the shapes of *Tyrannosaurus rex*. And on time. She wore a black beret and a slim-fitting tan suede jacket. I thought I'd driven on to the set of a 1950s film, a chauffeur calling to pick up Lauren Bacall or Greta Garbo. She came skipping down to the car and opened the door.

'You look fantastic,' I said, leaning across to take her bag.

'I feel it,' she answered, giving me a quick kiss before the getaway. She was so excited she stomped her feet. I'd have done the same if I weren't driving.

'North,' I said, pulling out. 'And this time I know the way.' I'd meticulously gone through the road atlas, making sure I knew every inch of highway until we got to the cabin I'd booked in the heart of the Catskills, a small town called Phoenicia, a short drive from Woodstock.

'And no swerving for geese.'

'Straight through.' I chopped the road in front of the car with my hand, thoughts of that day in the Cotswolds playing as I made my way to the Henry Hudson Parkway, driving parallel to the water until crossing the George Washington Bridge.

'Don't you love bridges?' asked Kay, looking out of the window. 'I always feel lighter, somehow.'

The rippled water sparkled. Sun shone through patches of cloud, flared on green hills in the distance.

I felt lighter, too. As though if I wound down the window I'd be blown from the car like a feather.

Kay looked from the river to the sky. I had to watch the traffic coming off the bridge, but managed a glance across to see her smiling, relaxed, more than at any moment since we'd met. I reached for her wrist, lifted it to my lips and kissed her.

'Where the hell am I?' I asked.

'Right here,' she answered. 'In my world. The sign says you're entering New Jersey, but it's a lie.'

Coming off the bridge I could barely concentrate on the directions, honked at by taxis and trucks for erratically changing lanes. I accelerated aggressively, darted through the snarl of cars.

'Look at you,' said Kay. 'Driving like a New Yorker already.'

'You impressed?'

She told me she would kiss me if I got us there safely. Enough incentive to focus on the road, navigating the sprawl of parkways before finding the I-87 to arrow us all the way into the mountains.

Kay switched on the stereo, skipping past ads and the empty harangue of DJs afraid of silence. When the opening piano section from 'Court and Spark' tinkled into the car I reached over and turned up the volume. We listened to Joni Mitchell sing about love coming to her door, a man dancing up a river.

'That's such a beautiful line,' said Kay.

My body thrummed with the music. We waited for the next song, Van Morrison singing about rain and water.

After Van finished crooning, Kay searched for the next station to miss the inevitable ads, letting out a little whoop when she heard the scrambled guitar and thumping bass of Nirvana.

'Gotta pay homage to my guys from Seattle,' she said, turning the volume first up, then down, guessing it didn't catch me in the same way Van Morrison and Joni Mitchell had.

'I just don't know the song,' I answered. 'That's all.'

Kay turned the volume up again, sat back, thought for a second before sitting forward and turning it down again. 'You know, I'm glad you don't love the song. I'd be freaked out if it all worked.'

She was right, and the trip would perhaps uncover what was real and what we'd projected about each other. Talk of the first food stop gave away some more of her life.

'Anywhere but McDonald's,' she insisted as we shot past a rest area presided over by the giant golden arches, the red and white clown in his oversized shoes.

I laughed. 'That would be a turn-off.' The fibreglass giant smiled his stupid smile. 'If you couldn't go past a McDonald's without needing a thick shake.'

'You're not kidding.' She sat up a little, put her hand on my thigh. 'Can we do the ugly truth thing again? I got a good Happy Meal story.'

The weight of her palm was wonderfully heavy on my leg. I said I wanted to know everything, and she started telling me how things had got bad for her in Seattle. Picked up by the police a couple of times, possession charges, shoplifting.

'Miss a few court dates and soon enough it's an arrest warrant.'

I looked away from the road, at Kay. I wanted to see her face telling this story, this biography. But she was turned to the rushing scenery passing by the window, trees and billboards, perhaps picturing the Californian landscape she saw from the freight train she jumped to cross state lines and avoid the warrants.

'And I was starving, crazy hungry. All we had to eat in the boxcars were pumpkins. Hacking them up with keys.' She shook her head. 'I was so screwed up. All I was doing was hustling for a fix. Simple as that. Get money, get high. Whatever it took.'

I shuddered on the word whatever. I thought of my brief but fierce battle with cocaine, the hollowed-out nights and petty theft. And a friend I'd played rugby with, a hulk of a kid who went from upending fly halfs to injecting, and then turning over off-licences. He was finally caught when a policeman pulled over to buy a pack of cigarettes as he had a rounders bat cocked above the cashier's head.

What saved Kay was getting arrested with a dealer. A background check and the warrant in Oregon.

'They extradited me. Two days in a downtown jail before three days on the road in a van.'

She'd taken her hand off my leg now, so I reached mine out and put it on hers, a reassurance.

'That was what changed a lot of things, not the rehab, but that van trip. I was shackled, hands and feet. Can you believe it? And I was the only woman. Me and four guys chained to the seats. Of course we couldn't get out at the gas stations, so when the driver stopped one of the guards picked up some food.'

'Happy Meals.'

'Burger, fries and Coke. Morning, noon and night. Three days of Happy Meals, shaking for a fix. Hell. Pure hell. I asked the guard if he could at least get Diet Coke and he laughed. That was it. There and then I vowed I'd get clean.'

'Well, I'm guessing you did, because you're here right now.'

Cat's eyes zipped down the windshield. A straight road hemmed by trees.

'I had no choice. Because I'd jumped rehab before the judge banged that hammer and gave me a month in jail.'

She told me about crawling up the walls of a prison cell, that a barred room was a better way to quit smack than being in a group session with some namby-pamby counsellor.

I reached out for her hand. I told her I thought more of her, not less.

'Why?'

I was looking back and forth between the road and Kay. 'I know something about hitting rock bottom,' I said. 'I had my own drug problems, once. After my mother, a bad break-up, I couldn't leave the house without doing a line.'

'You see yourself inside out,' she said. 'You know you. The best and worst. The extremes.'

I nodded, agreed. 'Only then can you know someone else.' And I added this with some confidence. Because I knew the core of myself. Or at least believed I did, sitting behind the wheel of a car fired like a missile at the future.

THE NIGHT WOMBLE WALKED into the Grove with an empty sports bag I was single and broke, once again hanging around with the local gangsters I'd gone to university to avoid. Siobhan and Marissa were an item, and I'd returned to selling double glazing after the foreman at the plumbing supplies warehouse caught me napping in a bathtub.

It was also the night before I moved from Nottingham back to London, when I realized I was falling down a hole I soon wouldn't be able to climb out of.

Within minutes of finishing my beer I was helping Womble strip lead from a factory roof. A few years older than me, Womble worked on the bins. When he wasn't stealing. He knew I needed money for a free-wheeling coke habit, walked into the bar looking for a willing partner in crime, and saw me sitting in a corner.

Like a pair of shadows above the terraced homes of sleeping families, we scrabbled across gables and eaves, trod and hoped for a beam beneath our feet. When the moon crested the clouds, the lead gleamed in our hands.

'Bastard's gettin' heavy now,' said Womble, dragging the bag across the rooftop like a corpse he had to get rid of before morning.

He shared a flat with his brother, Maz. Before Maz was raided he bought a Reliant Robin because drug dealers don't drive plastic pigs, and he guessed that a fibreglass three-wheeler wasn't the kind of car that aroused much interest in the police.

The evening Womble saw squad cars outside the flat, a carnival of blue lights and sirens, he screeched a U-turn and stamped on the accelerator. A bottle of vodka later, a round-about was a tricky island to navigate.

But maybe it was the only shore for a marooned man, a man driving with no destination.

The Pig finished its tumble on the other side of the barrier. Splashed with blood, Womble lay slumped over the steering wheel. Cars passed, headlights flashed on the shattered wind-screen. He crouched behind the dashboard until the road was clear, then put his shoulder to the Pig and pushed.

No wreck. No crash. No one looking for the driver. In one growling effort, he shunted the Pig down the hill until it smashed through the undergrowth. Knackered and drunk, Womble crawled inside and folded back the passenger seat.

The next morning he woke to a blue sky beyond the treetops, the constant hum of traffic. 'Not that different from the sea,' he tried to tell me, insisting it was better than turning up for work or going home with the police after him.

Looking around the clearing, a cover of branches and bushes, he found a drain that ran through a short tunnel into a paddock of cows. This would be the front door. The train tracks into town were across the road, and it was just a stroll to the Grove when he felt like a game of pool or had some junk to sell.

At night he walked into the industrial estate and pulled tarpaulin off skips. He transformed his refuge into a princely den of leather sofas and glass-topped coffee tables, wiring a TV to the car battery, nailing his dartboard to a tree trunk.

I sat with him on the broken sofa and listened to the whirl of traffic beyond the trees. On that island I had no thoughts of my own life, how a degree had done nothing but put me into debt. That my mother was gone. Once I was down there with Jeff, taking mouthfuls of poteen from a Lucozade bottle. As we watched jets streak across the sky, Womble scratched *The eye of the storm* on the bonnet.

Until he turned up outside the Grove towing a brass bedstead on wheels, those who heard that Womble lived on a traffic island said it was rubbish. And then the same doubters slowed driving the roundabout on their way home, trying to see over the crash barrier, past the covering of leaves, circling as Womble sat watching TV and doing word-searches from tattered quiz books, grilling burgers on the bonnet of a Cortina, fixing bikes and selling kettles.

Though I was hardly doing much better. Two months' rent due on a dump of a house, a daily tour of abuse selling windows to people who already had them. And a dumb paralysis of grief because my mother had left without a goodbye.

So when Womble had asked if I wanted to earn some 'easy money', I'd downed my beer and walked out, no one looking at us, no one wanting to know what two men were doing with an empty sports bag just before last orders.

We worked our way up and down the eaves, breaking slates, prising up nails and peeling off strips of shining lead. Now all we had to do was haul the bag to the corner of the building where we first climbed up. I remember looking down, thinking the fall would kill me. I imagined the shape I'd take as a dead man. The passers-by and drunks walking home, stopping to see my final pose in life.

'Straight across the gables,' instructed Womble. 'Bastard's too heavy to drag across the slates.'

I didn't have a better idea. I wish I had. Fragments of slate broke beneath our feet and skittered off the roof into the car park. They made a tinkling sound like breaking glass when they hit the ground.

Then, very slowly, my handle began tearing from the bag. Then *tore* from the bag. The weight yanked Womble round to face me, nearly pulling his arm off because he wouldn't let go. He just had time to say 'Fuck' before the slates opened up and swallowed him whole.

Lights came on in the car park. Womble had gone, vanished from the night. I crawled over the hole and looked down, past the broken slates and dangling plaster, the cartoon outline of his fall through the ceiling.

He was on his back and smiling, circled by a crowd of shift workers who stood at the sort of respectable distance usually reserved for holy men or deities.

'HE WASN'T DEAD, WAS he?' asked Kay, about Womble.
'He was fine,' I answered, no memory of the stretch of highway I'd just driven while telling the story. 'Until the police came.'

'Were you arrested?'

'I was running across those rooftops like Spiderman.'

'You got away?'

'Jumped down on to someone's shed. The whole thing collapsed. I leapt over their back fence and didn't stop running till I got to my place.'

'What happened to Womble?'

'Locked up. Not for long. They thought it was better for him than living in that wreck on the traffic island.'

'You still know him?'

'Well, *of* him. He's all right, sort of. He's got a council flat, last I heard.'

'Good for him. And you.' Kay laughed, playfully pushed my knee. 'The city boy stealing lead from a roof.'

'A quality crime.'

'Aren't churches good for that kind of thing?'

I shook my head. 'That was it. Seeing Womble fall through that roof, the thought of me ending up like that.'

'I think Jenni comes into the story soon.'

I looked across at Kay. 'You're pretty sharp.' She gave me a sad smile.

And I drove on, flying past more exits for fast food, speeding towards those green mountains. But reversing through memories. I told Kay about packing my bags and catching the train to London the morning after the Womble escapade, ringing the universities and practically begging for a place on a Master's.

'I'm guessing you got on one.'

'Business,' I answered, gripping the steering wheel tighter. 'I walked into that first lecture and sat down next to her.'

'Jenni.'

'I should talk about something else.' I hoped Kay would agree, because I had a strange sensation in my arms, like pins and needles.

'You okay?' she asked.

I shrugged my shoulders, rolled my neck.

'I can drive if you want?'

'I'm fine,' I lied, my skin prickling.

'JENNI,' SHE WHISPERED, HOLDING out a hand to be shaken. 'Sam,' I whispered back, the lecturer darting an angry look at two students daring to not pay attention in the first class of a London Business School MBA. Between taking notes on 'Ethics and Corporate Social Responsibility', I flicked glances at her slim fingers round her pen, the neat handwriting. When the class finished I asked if she wanted a coffee, and we sat in the campus bar and did the usual intros of why we were taking the course.

'Putting off the real world,' she joked. Her small and perfect lips. 'And you?'

'Keeping me from a life of crime.' Thinking that sitting in halls overlooking manicured lawns was better than stealing lead off a factory roof.

'After that lecture,' she said, 'I think the best businesses are the most ruthless. The ones with criminal bosses.' She laughed at the thought of what she was about to say. 'I can learn from you, then.'

She let me borrow her notes when I missed a class, which I often did, working part-time shifts with a temp agency to pay my rent. My friends from university had mostly left London, flown off to teach in Japan, taken jobs in France and Italy. In a class of nearly seventy students I thanked my lucky stars that I'd sat next to her. Between mind-numbing placements in various offices, each stint too brief to make any real friends, she was one of the few people in a city of seven million that I could actually talk to. Nottingham was just over an hour away on the train, but that was suddenly a past life I wanted to distance myself from.

After a month of eating picnics in Regent's Park, feeding crusts to the pigeons and walking off lunch along the Grand Union Canal, I asked her on a date.

'To Hampton Court,' she pondered, pausing in the middle of a sandwich. 'I was supposed to be heading back to Marlow on Saturday.'

I suggested we could go earlier if she wanted. 'But I won't be able to buy you a meal if we do.'

'See,' she said, that sharp, knowing smile. 'The MBA is already working. Cutting costs on a lady.'

But I did buy her dinner, sitting in the bay window of a pub overlooking the Thames. When the waiter lit the candle and the soft flame glowed on her pale skin, I thought she was stunning. And although she was obviously beautiful, the belle of the class with her striking, Germanic looks, and that high and bright laugh, I hadn't found her attractive until that moment.

Or is this another lie to myself? Perhaps I always wanted her, from when I first saw her in the sunlit lecture hall, but knew she was a woman who'd demand a better man.

After a day walking the grounds of a palace home for kings and queens, a lavish room for each of Henry VIII's six wives, I was enchanted. Not just with the fallow deer running free in the park, the peacocks and the architecture, but now with Jenni.

And brave enough to tell her, to kiss her.

I remember going back to my flat that night, the sum of my life in a rented room, the taste of her in my mouth. This is something, I thought. Someone.

Within months we had a place together, shared a bed.

'My bad boy,' she'd say, lying naked, running her hands through my hair. 'You know I could blackmail you with all those confessions.'

We had all the abandon of new lovers, the vigour and heat, youth. And then after sex, after the shudder and cry, came the murmured calm, talking. Steadily I'd told her stories, selling the rental car and reporting it as stolen, burgling a snooker club. Womble and the factory roof.

'And now look at you. Star student on an MBA, and in bed with a girl who's never even stolen a penny chew.'

At the beginning of our relationship, pulling her into my world, my heart, I used these tales as bait. I realized she got a buzz from my history. But after a year together, finishing third in that class of seventy students, I stopped talking about where I'd been and what I'd done, and planned my career with all the measured guile of the young business exec I was training to be.

What I got from her was something better than myself. What she got from me was the feeling that she was someone I'd changed for. A woman with enough presence in the world to alter mine.

'You need to give me more about your family,' she'd say, probing beyond the anecdotes. 'You must be angry, sad. Something. Your mother. How do you feel about her? That doesn't just go away.'

But that was done, wasn't it? Or so I thought, and hoped, once I found Jenni and believed she was the one, the only.

AFTER I TURNED OFF the highway we followed a glittering lake, driving beneath blue sky and trees, the autumn leaves brushed a million different hues of red. I didn't say anything because I knew I was being ridiculous, but when a silver Lexus took the same exit I almost believed we were being trailed, checking in the rear view mirror until it took a side road just before Phoenicia. We went through the small town with Kay reading out the directions.

'Should be up a way on the left.'

We took a bridge over a shallow, fast-flowing river. Two hundred yards on was an ensemble of timber cottages set below a stand of pine trees. I took one more paranoid look to see we hadn't been followed, worried that Segur himself had shadowed us there, then took the turn into the lodgings.

'Here's home for the night,' said Kay, peering through the windshield.

I drove along the gravel drive and pulled up by the reception. Then apologized to Kay.

'For what?'

I looked at the painted brown planks holding the cottages together. 'It looked grander in the photos.'

'Hey,' she said, reaching and touching my chin. 'Come here.' I leant across and kissed her. 'I don't care where we are, really. All I know is that we're about to close a door on a room that's ours.'

I checked us in by writing Mr and Mrs Smith in the guest book. The receptionist read the names and looked over her reading glasses through the window. Kay was taking her bag off the back seat.

'Just give me a call if you need anything.'

I thanked her.

'But not after nine,' she added. 'It's just you and the critters then. Well, and your wife.'

I faked a smile, then walked out to the cabin, my steps crunching on the gravel drive.

Kay was waiting by our cottage, leaning against the front door. 'Take a good look at those hills,' she said. 'Because we're not coming back out until it's dark.'

I didn't turn round. 'I've seen hills before.'

When I put the key in the lock my hands trembled. Kay was kissing my neck as I opened the door.

'Home sweet home,' I joked, taking in the rustic furniture, a huge brass bedstead.

Kay walked over to the bed, the floorboards creaking. She smoothed down the quilt with her palm and said, 'Shut the door and come here.'

I closed and locked the door. I walked over to the bed where we stood and faced each other.

'You hear that?' she asked. 'The river, the wind in the leaves.'

I could hear all these sounds, layered over the bass of my thudding heart. I pulled her hands to my lips and kissed her fingers. 'You're cold,' I said, looking for the fire.

I flicked on the gas and sparked a flame from the snapping electric. The orange bars quickly glowed, illuminating the room, us.

She said, 'If I'd remembered my umbrella, none of this would be happening. Not you in this room. Not me doing this.' She reached out and started unbuttoning my shirt.

As she undressed me I felt as if I was being dismantled. The world beyond the door of that wooden cabin lay heaped on the floor.

Only when I was naked did I lean forward and kiss the nape of her neck, breathe her in. Together we pulled at her clothes, tugged off her boots. I cupped her breasts and took her dark nipples between my lips, gently, until they were hard in my mouth. After unbuckling her belt I pulled down her jeans. She stepped out of them and grabbed my hand, pulling it between her legs. How wet and slippery against my fingers. I bent and kissed her stomach, her hips. The insides of her thighs. I was thrilled to have her standing before me. Thrilled to be stripped, nothing between us but skin. I told her to lie down and knelt on the rug, pushing her legs apart, pressing my tongue against her, both of us trembling.

'Inside me,' she sat up. 'I want you inside me.'

I stood and she pulled me to the bed, on top of her. Then she reached down, gripped me hard in her hand and guided me into her heat. And without words, thought or guilt, I became one with her.

I SWEAR I COULD hear the Earth turning. I was wired to every sense. The sound of the river, the scent of Kay, her breath steady on my skin where she lay curled against my chest.

'If I could have any power right now it would be to stop time.' I ran my hands through her hair, kissed her head. 'Just run this minute on a constant loop.'

In that bed, beneath a heavy duvet, a wooden roof and a stand of pines, beside a rushing river surrounded by mountains tinged with rust-coloured trees, we'd made a bunker. The two of us naked and warm, wrapped around each other.

We lay like that till the dusk turned to dark. Through a window that framed the peaks, a tangerine sky deepened to violet, then black, punctured by points of starlight.

'Are you sleeping?' I asked.

She kissed my chest, pulled tighter against me.

We showered together. We took a long time washing down each other's bodies, studying skin and scars. Over her right shoulder blade was a scarlet patch. 'I had a tattoo removed.'

'Of what?' I asked, smoothing soap across her back.

'Can I tell you another time?'

I rinsed away the suds and wondered what kind of design she might have chosen, why she didn't want to talk about it.

Before she told me anything about her life, the journey that made her who she was, how she arrived at herself, I'd guessed certain histories from the blue veins running along the inside of her forearms, the soft skin scarred.

We stepped from the shower and I wrapped her in a towel.

'You going to brush my hair?'

She sat on a chair by the heater. I drew the brush through her long black hair, gliding through the strands, playing it out over my palms and running it between my fingers. Every few strokes I leant forward and kissed her on the temple, her eyebrow.

And I never knew I could be so haunted by a scent, the aroma of another. Not perfume, but the feral inhalation of a woman who burned in the core of my chest. A spark that had become a flame, crackling, catching my bones the way a brushfire might sweep through a tinderbox wood.

'I could get used to this,' she said, leaning her head back and closing her eyes, smiling, her whole body glowing.

We LEFT WORDS ALONE until we dressed. Silent with our bodies because there was no treachery when we were skin on skin, pressed tight against one another so no thought could get between us. But then came the words, the guilt. After desire, conscience. To try to escape the sin that had broken into the cabin, the sin that sat on the cheap and faded furniture, the patchwork quilt, and then the sinner who watched from the cracked mirror as I combed my hair and buttoned my shirt, we drove out to Woodstock.

Kay took the wheel this time. She drove fast, confident on the dark bends winding the tree-lined roads.

'Do you think there are bears in the woods?' I asked, looking into the forest shadows.

The headlights illuminated the nearly naked branches. Moths like torn bits of paper flared in the beams. I had a flashback of my dream, the woman in the barren wood. I looked across at Kay, focused on driving. What was a dream and what wasn't seemed a tricky thought right then, in a car on a dark road in a country where I wasn't born.

We parked on the main road, outside a boutique clothing store selling designer dresses and hats.

'It's not the sixties any more,' I said, looking at the jewellers next door.

'This is a cute town now. You won't find Janis Joplin raising hell with a bottle of whiskey.'

We had some minor disagreement choosing a place to eat as we both wanted to defer to the other for the decision.

'Heads the Thai place,' I proposed, readying the quarter on the tip of my thumb. 'Tails the Italian.'

I flipped. The coin came down in South East Asia. And because we had no idea how to act, what to be, we sat and ate like two people on a first date, spending most of the meal looking at each other, reaching hands nervously across the table. The fairy bulbs strung from the ceiling did nothing to put what we were doing into the stark light of reality.

During a walk along the quiet streets, strolling hand in hand, I wondered if this sight would be a worse one for Jenni to come across than the two of us naked in bed. An ocean away, I was still terrified we'd turn a corner and find her standing there, and suggested to Kay we should head off.

'You okay?' she asked, knowing I wasn't.

I drove back to the cabin, Kay against my shoulder, both of us watching the ghostly branches in the headlights. White as dead coral. I wanted to talk about something, but the words wouldn't come. I wanted different visions from the one of Jenni sitting there on the back seat. Only when we arrived back in Phoenicia did I find my voice again.

'Not a soul,' I remarked on the empty road.

It was very dark off the main highway, and the array of unlit cabins appeared deserted.

'Are we the only ones here?' asked Kay, sitting up.

I looked at the glitter of stars above the silver hills. 'Or the last ones left.' I switched off the lights.

We kissed, our lips and the faint wind hissing in the pine the only sounds.

Not that we were alone.

When I opened the door and took a moment to stretch, I heard a twig snap under the weight of a heavy step.

'Hello?' I wobbled.

'Is there someone there?' asked Kay.

Another twig cracked, followed by a huffed exhalation of air. 'Who is it?' I shouted.

Then a black mass shot past the front bumper.

'Shit.' I jumped back to the shelter of the car. 'What the hell was that?'

'Look,' screamed Kay. 'A bear!'

As surprised by us as we were by him, the bear scrambled up a trunk, the sharp claws noisily digging into the bark.

'He's in the tree,' said Kay.

'Right above our cabin.' My adrenalin was pumping.

'My God!' Kay laughed. '*You* frightened *him*.'

I was standing behind the open door. When I flicked on the headlights his eyes burned red, claws fastened in the trunk, watching, working out if we were a threat or not. And he decided we weren't because he looked at the two of us hiding behind the car and climbed down.

'Get back in,' I called to Kay.

We shut the doors and watched him slope down the trunk, his oily pelt gleaming in the bright beams.

'How beautiful,' said Kay as he dropped to the ground, took one look into the headlights, and ambled away into the darkness.

I parked as close to the cabin as I could, and we scampered inside laughing with fear that he'd steal us away into the night before I got the door open.

'Quick,' panted Kay. 'Close the door.'

We were playing the encounter up, but both of us were excited by the bear, fooling around like sugared-up children.

I slammed the bolt across. 'That was close.' I was breathless. 'I wasn't really scared,' I said untruthfully.

Before I had a chance to slow my beating heart Kay pulled me across the room, pushed me on to the bed, and hungrily kissed me.

The bear had saved us. Saved us from thoughts about others. Fear had reduced us to flesh and blood, body.

Kay sat astride me, slowly unbuckling my belt, popping the buttons on my jeans and pulling them down to my ankles. Then she crawled back up the bed and took me into her mouth, looking me in the eye, slowly pushing me down her throat. She took me to the brink of coming on her tongue before kissing me again, the taste of myself on her lips. When I put my hands between her legs she stood up and stepped out of her skirt, lost her clothes. Then finally, balancing with her palms on my ribs, she sat back on her heels and slowly lowered herself on to me, very carefully, feeling every moment of the glide. I held her hips and worked a rhythm with her. Each time she came she collapsed over my chest, kissed me, and reached back and put a finger inside herself, alongside me, before sliding it into my mouth. And then into her mouth. So when we kissed the taste was neither her nor me but us.

I woke staring at the cabin ceiling.

My dream about the woman in the wood.

This time I was running after her. And she was running from what I thought was a bear, slashing his way through the dead branches. But it was a man chasing her, or a half-man, half-bear. Or a man eaten by a bear and become bear himself. I was snagged by the branches, my flesh hooked by thorns. When I woke, before the woman was caught, I checked to see that Kay really was in my bed, not lost in a dead wood.

'You awake?' I kissed her neck. Sleepily she turned over.

'I am now.' She kissed me back. 'You were having some crazy dreams.'

'I know.' I didn't want to tell her about the woman. 'That bear got in my sleep.'

'I'll protect you.' Kay planted kisses over my cheeks, draped her hair over my closed eyes.

But the dream was still playing. Even when I walked barefoot across the wooden floor and into the bathroom. Splashing water over my face I tried to wash the vision from my thoughts.

'Shall we go for a walk before breakfast?' I called into the bedroom.

'Sure,' answered Kay. 'Hike along the river.'

Clouds dappled the wooded hills with shadow, and the bronze peaks flared and faded with the passing skies. We followed a fast stream, shallow rapids where the river was torn into spray on submerged rocks.

On a small wooden bridge above calmer waters, we paused to look at our reflections below.

'Like two ghosts washed into the sea,' said Kay, leaning back from the rail, our mirrored selves. 'That would be the way to go. Evaporate and fall as rain.'

'Come back to earth in a thunderstorm.'

She dropped a leaf into the water and watched it float under the bridge. Then she linked her arm around mine and we walked on, not talking much, already thinking about the drive back, the questions without answers.

I<small>T WAS ON THAT</small> highway south to New York, a pause between conversation with Kay, a pause between reaching across and feeling the warmth of her thigh on my palm, heat pulsed from her thudding heart so I could feel it in mine, when I was suddenly a child again with my sister in Betty's living room, our neighbour. We were kneeling at the window looking at the angry boil of clouds that towered over the estate.

'How do you know the distance to a storm?' Betty asked, tipping a mug to her mouth.

I knew the answer and told her. And my mum, just back from work to pick us up and take us home. 'Count the seconds between the flash and the bang.'

Which was what I did when sheet lightning lit the black sky.

'May as well have another cup of tea, Jan,' said Betty, almost interrupting my careful counting down to the rumbling thunder.

'Four,' I shouted. 'That means it's four miles away.'

'I'd better get the kids' dinner on,' my mum replied to Betty's offer.

'Can we have pilchard pie?' my sister begged. My mum had made us believe her cheap meals were treats worthy of a restaurant, and I joined in the pleading.

'Go on then,' she said. 'Get your boots on.'

We raced to the porch and pulled on our wellies. My sister got to the umbrella first, and we wrestled as to who was going to hold it.

'Neither of you are,' said my mum. 'You're not tall enough to hold it over my hair.' She was always getting it cut, having it blow-dried and styled. Ten years old, I already knew why. 'Two kids or not,' I heard her telling Betty, 'I've no plans on being a single mum for ever.'

She took the umbrella from my hand. Rain crashed against the frosted porch glass.

'I'm going to run,' I bragged, opening the door and feeling the fat drops pierce my T-shirt before sprinting across the road to our house, my sister chasing behind.

The back door was locked. We turned and shouted at my mum to hurry up.

If the door had been open I wouldn't have turned and seen her splashing through the puddles, kicking up the rain.

Neither would I've seen the simultaneous strike of light and sound, the thunderclapped vein of white that connected earth and sky, cracking the glass in our kitchen window, jumping from a metal garage door to the umbrella my mother clutched.

Like the blaze of the sun that burns on your vision when you turn from its fiery core, for a few seconds it robbed me of my ability to focus.

Then she stood, as if resurrected, and ran to the house with smoking hands.

DRIVING BACK INTO MANHATTAN I felt like a shuttle pilot re-entering the atmosphere, the front end of the Mustang glowing with friction. I'd watched the Catskills shrink in the rear view mirror, and then the neat suburbs cluster across the bonnet. And now the rising towers.

We'd been chatting like children at the start of a friendship, when that remarkable finding of each other feels like a gift, the shared knowledge unwrapped. She'd talked about her brother, his childhood illness, how she loved to play nurse, spooning him juice and pretending it was medicine. And her mother, sitting on the deck and painting sunsets. One of her earliest memories was mixing up reds and oranges for the flame-lit skies. Although she spoke with a serious focus, zooming in on tiny moments from decades past, toys and dolls, a dressing-up box filled with the clothes her father left behind, she made fun of herself too, laughed easily at the thought of the little girl playing with imaginary friends. 'I had whole tea parties with dozens of guests. I set everyone places all over the house.' She shook her head and laughed. 'What a crazy kid. My poor mom.'

But a city climbed up the windscreen, loomed and judged. I nearly said I'd like to meet her mother, but held the thought, the careless words.

Then she said, 'We have to talk about them.'

I'd rather have pumped up the music, U-turned, and spun out at the beginning of a real getaway. But I held south on 87, kept the New York skyline a target.

'How did you meet him?' I fired the question abruptly, because I wanted to know, but didn't. I'd have been happy to never hear his name again, have us both lobotomized of past lovers.

No, no, that isn't true. To wish that would be to wish the very death of another.

'Don't let my imagination fill in the gaps,' I said. 'Tell me.'

She hesitated, tapped her fingernails on the dashboard, then talked. After jail and rehab meetings, she had to get out of Seattle, away from the same old friends doing the same old things. I knew something about that. In an effort to at least try to escape my old self I'd had to escape my home town.

'I needed a fresh start. Something. I had a few hundred dollars saved from waitressing, thoughts of finishing the performing arts course I bailed out on. So I took everything I had and flew to New York.'

'Did you know anyone?'

She shook her head. 'That was a reason to come here. I had to build myself up brick by brick. Away from family, the counselling. It had to be me. I had one month's rent for a room in Green Point, one month to get a job. I shared a tiny apartment with two Polish girls who spoke about a word of English between them. I walked around a few diners, gave my number to the managers, but nothing in those first days but tired feet. Then one of the Polish girls got sick and said I could have her kitchen job till she was better. Doing dishes, cleaning the ovens. I convinced the owner to let me waitress when the Polish girl came back to work.'

The Jersey skyline was growing on the horizon.

'I was making enough from tips, just, to cover my rent. Daytime I was getting myself back in shape, jogging, sneaking into dance classes without paying.'

'It must have been hard, though.'

'I didn't mind working seven nights a week, because it kept me busy. But waking up in the morning, seeing myself in the mirror, knowing I had the day to fight off before I could hide in taking orders and arguing with the chef, that was the test.'

Apart from exercise and reading books, when she could focus, she walked.

'A lot. Hours. I'd walk the Williamsburg Bridge into the city, just drift along with the crowd.'

She started writing letters, apologies to her mum and brother. She'd stolen from them all at some point. Lied.

'I put my brother's record collection in a bag and took it to the store. Got fifty bucks.'

I looked over to her, wiping a gleaming cheek. 'Hey,' I said, reaching across, one hand on the wheel and the other on her arm.

'It's okay,' she said. 'I know they forgave me for the shit I did. Those letters were epics. My mom would write me back with her own apologies, wishing she'd been a better mother. Saying she had no idea what was happening with my stepdad.'

Then I said that I'd listen if she wanted to tell me about it. How sorry I was to hear that someone had hurt her. How angry it made me. And that I'd guessed certain histories from the pauses in our conversations, things I hoped I'd misunderstood.

'It happened all right,' she said. 'I nearly killed him. And my mom. I set fire to the porch one night and ran.'

It was hard to find the right words to console, to empathize. I told her I'd spent a childhood imagining the murder of my stepfather, and a good part of my life hating my mother too.

'Well, once my mom found out, she took a carving knife and put it to his throat and told him never to come back. She asked me to move home again, but I was still a construction, unfinished.'

Then she said she wanted to move the story on, to New York. 'I was feeling better about myself for sure, and looking better. I swear I ate nothing for two years but Baby Ruth bars and chips. A couple of months' exercise, dance, pirogi, borscht and potatoes, and I have my body back.'

I doubted it could have ever gone away. But she said she was a skank getting off that plane at JFK, rail thin and pale. Though come springtime her tips were up, and she was turning down dates from customers.

'And not all drunken jerks, some decent guys. But I'd worked so hard to get me back I wasn't ready to share with someone else. Though I couldn't be a waitress for ever.'

She was ready for a change when a man came into the restaurant who owned a few clubs in the city.

'I was sceptical, sure. But his wife was part of the sales pitch.'

I was afraid of where the story was going, another dark turn.

'He writes down his number, and then his wife drops a fifty dollar tip on the bill. I left it a few days, but when I paid my rent for that month, saw I had peanuts to live on, I called him up.'

Then she paused for a moment, took her time, looked at the houses flashing past the window, as if only just noticing the outside world.

'It leaves a mark on you. Sex that young. With a man your own mother has brought into your home. A man who replaced my dad.'

I was hoping the car would break down before we crossed the Hudson. Before I had to watch her open and close the door, step out alone.

I took her hand and kissed her wrist, up and up, to the soft curve of her bicep.

Hearing about Kay on her own, the rise from a tragedy in her life to here, the two of us in a car aimed at a teeming city, I wanted to be part of someone else more than I ever had. I told her so.

'Tell me you mean it,' she said.

I told her she turned a lonely past into something shared. Because she too knew what it was to be empty of love and adrift, not only of family and company, but a very self. It was as if she was there the night I slept in the park. The day I sat under the tarpaulin with my mother's abandoned furniture.

She touched her palm under my jaw and kissed my cheek.

I asked her to carry on, whatever she wanted to tell me, I wanted to know. But the present jolted. Signs for roads we didn't want to follow. When we'd driven out of Manhattan I'd felt as light as a feather coming over the bridge. This time I felt heavy enough to buckle the steel girders. I needed the rest from her, all of it, but the sight of the skyscrapers had broken the rhythm of her story.

'Shit,' she swore. 'I should turn my phone on.'

Driving into Phoenicia we'd made vows not to even look at them till we got back. As Kay delved in her bag, I slipped mine from my pocket and brought it to life. Both our phones buzzed and bleeped with messages waiting.

'I don't have to ask who called you,' said Kay.

I put the phone to my ear and listened to the answer messages, jolted at a voice. 'Probably the same man who rang you.'

'What?' She was shocked, scared. 'Why's he calling you?'

'You tell me.'

'What does he want?'

'The first one is Jenni.'

*Hey there missing person. You're either somewhere with no reception, lost your phone, or switched it off because you're working too hard. Give me a ring when you can. Love you.*

The sound of her voice in my ear seemed to put her right there in the car. My stomach tightened. I still had Segur to listen to.

*Sam man. What's up? Tried you a few times and nothing. You back in the Cotswolds with my wife, because she's out of range or something, too. I'm busting your balls. Just calling to remind you of the Giants game tomorrow. Call me when you get this.*

'What's he want?' she asked again, anxious.

'It's okay,' I reassured her. 'He's reminding me about the football tomorrow.'

'That's going to be weird.'

I nodded, turned on to the parkway. 'I could think of weirder things.'

'What do you mean?'

Hearing his voice, knowing she was going back to him, I trembled with a jealous rage, gripped the steering wheel till my knuckles whitened.

'What do you mean?' repeated Kay. 'Weirder things?'

'Nothing,' I said. Two blocks till I dropped her outside 86th Street station.

'Don't end the trip like this,' she pleaded.

'How do we end it, then?'

'It?' she asked. 'Or the trip?'

The light changed to green. I pulled across 87th down to 86th Street.

'Everything,' I said. 'And everybody. The whole fucking mess of *It*.'

I wanted to talk more, say something that would make both of us feel better, but within seconds of stopping a traffic cop came banging on the roof. 'Move along, move along.'

'You better go.'

The traffic cop turned to the window. 'I said *move along*.'

Kay snatched her bag off the back seat. I grabbed her wrist, hard. 'I want you,' I said. 'You do know that?'

She stopped, clasped my chin, then kissed me goodbye. In the rear view mirror I watched her go down the steps into the subway.

WHILE ON THE PHONE to Jenni I could smell Kay on my hands. 'What happened to your mobile?' she asked. 'I couldn't get a ringtone all yesterday.'

I was back at my apartment, my open suitcase, clothes strewn around the room.

'I thought you might have lost it.'

I apologized, called her sweetheart. 'I went out with some of the guys from work and didn't even see the battery was dead till this morning.'

'A big night out with the boys?'

It was a lie she believed, but wasn't impressed with. 'Not what you think,' I said. 'Few too many drinks, usual bullshit guy talk.'

'Another strip club?'

'No.'

'What time did you get in?'

'Around two, maybe later. I only got up an hour ago.'

And how easily the words fell from my mouth. Not a rehearsed lie, shamefully, but a natural one.

'I want a Saturday with you, Sam. Take a walk on the Heath.'

'You can still do that,' I said, my heart sinking.

'Wandering around Parliament Hill pretending I have a dog. Sounds like fun.'

'Only another week.'

'The bed's so empty without you.'

When she said this I had my hand to my mouth, inhaling Kay. I looked at the bed I hadn't slept in and told her mine was empty, too.

'Well I'm glad you feel the same. You know, I couldn't stop touching myself last night, thinking about you.'

'Hey.' I cut her off. 'You know what I'll end up doing if you keep that up. I'll be lacklustre all day.'

'Sorry,' she snapped, annoyed. 'Once upon a time we'd make each other come just by talking on the phone.'

'I know. That's what I'm afraid of. I need a workout to get rid of this hangover.'

'I'm being rejected for a set of barbells.'

'Let's talk later, when you're in bed.'

'That sounds like a better idea.'

I told her I couldn't think about her till then. 'I'll lose my verve.'

'Well, have a run and sweat out the booze. Pour a bucket of cold water on yourself. Isn't that supposed to do the trick?'

It would've taken more than cold water to bring me to my senses. More than a workout shifting steel and pounding the digital mile. Not that the calories burned helped me sleep that evening.

Because it was that night, after the call. When I lay awake twenty storeys in the sky above New York, hovered with the half-dream, half-thought that I owned a gun. A sleek black pistol I pulled from the dresser. A cold barrel that I lifted to my temple and pressed against my skin and then, with the most precious and terrifying movement, as if the bidden acolyte in the final, complete act of supplication, pulled the trigger.

A dream so real I was surprised to find myself alive in the morning.

I MET SEGUR OUTSIDE Madison Square Garden. He wore a Giants cap, a navy blue bomber jacket and jeans. Interchangeable with the other red and blue fans making their way to Penn Station. A man in a crowd, as was I. The difference being that the two of us were joined by a woman.

'At least you didn't wear red.'

We shook hands.

'I was worried you were going to turn up looking like a 49ers fan and make me sit next to you in the nosebleeds.'

'Nosebleeds?'

'Bad news about the box. I promised it to some Canadian clients in town. We got seats in the upper tier, where the air's so thin you get nosebleeds.'

I laughed. Not the first time that day I'd have to manufacture a reaction.

'Right, we got a train to catch.'

We went under the Gardens into Penn Station. Segur walked and talked. Economy, Obama, Sarah Palin. 'Was an act of fucking suicide picking her, I tell you.'

Segur paid for my ticket. When I offered the money he said, 'Get outta here.'

On the train, carriages jammed with fans wearing blue,

numbered shirts over the top of ski jackets and hooded tops, thickset men and a sprinkling of keen girlfriends, Segur and I talked football. He was curious how I got interested in the sport.

'Remember when the Bears won the Super Bowl? William "the Refrigerator" Perry splashing over for that touchdown?'

'Nineteen eighty-six.'

'American football had quite a following in the UK. Teams popped up everywhere. I was already playing rugby, and more sport running with a ball and tackling was perfect.'

'You like the rough stuff, huh?'

When I said I did, I knew where the conversation was heading, the conversation I'd told myself as a budding rugby star that I'd never have. The war stories. The game reports of ex-players that can only be embellished by time and telling. And I was just as guilty. Segur and I swapped tales of match-saving scores, bone-crunching tackles and last-minute acts of heroism. Part fiction, part fact, events from years ago that had fallen into private legend.

'Wanted to go on defence,' replied Segur when I asked what position he'd played. 'But I had a natural arm, and I was good at leading people, so I played quarterback.'

Captain of the ship, the team. I could see him in charge. Not because he was a man others would naturally follow, more that he seemed a man who wouldn't take instructions from another.

'Got to college on a scholarship, but a dog of a linebacker fucked up my knee.'

Beyond the huff and puff of our conversation, the macho give and take of sports talk, I sensed a prying, a test

189

of who I was. What else was I beyond the man who'd given his wife a lift to the airport?

'Don't get me wrong,' he said, 'rugby is a hell of a game, but you're not going to convince me it's better than football. And when I say football I don't mean some faggoty kids kicking a soccer ball, I mean *football*.'

'Rugby. Football. Arguing which is better is like arguing about a favourite colour.'

'Two shades of blue, at that.'

'They're both evolution of a caveman hunting party.'

Segur laughed. 'Spearing that sabre-toothed tiger.'

'Men in shorts fighting over a scrap of leather. That's rugby.'

'And football.' Segur was excited by the primal metaphor. 'Shit, we should go over and see the guys in the lot, usually have a tailgate party, few beers. We might get a game of touch going afterwards, get to see you make some moves.'

Meadowlands stadium sat like a concrete bowl on a tarmac table, streams of coaches disgorging fans into the parking lot. It was a bright blue sky with a biting wind, fans bundled up from the cold wearing sunglasses. We walked from the shuttle bus, Segur and I, buddies for the day at a football game.

'You want a hot dog?' he asked as we passed the smoking barbecue carts. 'A burger?'

We had a quarter pounder each, both of us squirting in extra mustard. 'Fuck,' said Segur, chewing a mouthful of beef. 'I've been hanging in my executive box too long. This is better than any fucking canapé.'

We ate and walked. A gang of drunken men played touch football with a roast chicken carcass.

'Told you about fighting over dead animals.'

The quarterback threw deep and the carcass disintegrated in the wide receiver's hands, shining his jacket with grease and chicken skin. Segur shouted, 'Plaxico would have put that in a sandwich then run in the touchdown.'

The guys laughed at Segur's joke. A watching security guard high-fived him. 'You got that right.'

Segur turned to me. 'Plaxico's the star receiver. Lot of talent, but the guy's an asshole.'

Once patted down by the ticket inspectors – 'None of this shit before 9/11,' Segur had added – we rode the escalators to the upper tiers. He took the step ahead of me, and looked down from a height as we talked. He loomed above, asked questions about what I'd been up to in New York, work, Jenni. 'And I bet you're missing her,' he said, smiling. 'She's quite a catch.'

'She certainly is,' I replied, wondering for a moment if he'd looked at me that bit harder when he mentioned her.

'So is Kay,' he said in return, just as the escalator turned back on itself and dropped us at the top.

'We're having a beer?' I said, quickly changing the subject.

'Make that singular a plural,' he answered, pointing to a drinks stand. 'Two Millers,' he called out. The barman pulled the bottles from the ice and snapped the tops off. 'The Giants,' toasted Segur.

'To all sports with odd-shaped balls,' I added.

We weaved through the crowds, more fans in ski jackets and hats, dads carrying beers with sons clutching sodas.

'Five minutes to kick-off,' said Segur, checking his watch. Just as we exited the tunnel into the stadium a thunderous boom cracked the clear skies and two F-16s roared overhead. Men whooped and cheered, beat the air with their fists.

'Gonna be some game,' Segur shouted over the sonic booms.

Four rows from the top of the stadium, the lip of the concrete bowl, were two empty seats on a full row.

'Take a breath,' said Segur. 'Atmosphere gets pretty thin this high.'

By the time we'd shuffled to the seats it was time to stand for the Stars and Stripes. The entire crowd rose in silence, put their hands on their hearts and listened. No one cheered or whistled. No one sang along. No one said a word until the singer had sung and the fireworks fountained a gateway of sparks for the Giants to come running through.

'Yea*aaah*,' screamed the man in the baseball cap beside me. 'Go the fucking Giants.' Miller slopped on my sleeve when he raised his bottle. Segur apologized on his behalf.

'Don't worry about it,' I said, brushing the beer off my jacket.

'This is where the real fans sit. Hope they don't scare you.'

I laughed. 'We invented the hooligan.'

'Can get pretty wild up here. Winning and losing. Some men just can't handle it.'

We sat and watched the kick-off, one team running into another, head on tackles and crunching blocks. The whack of body on body could be heard even at the height I was with Segur, already on his feet when the kick returner nearly burst into open field.

'Fuck,' he bellowed before sitting again. 'That was a touchdown if he'd broken that tackle.'

'He's fast.'

'Lightning.' Segur took a swig of beer. 'The fucker's gone if you give him a yard.'

I drank my Miller before Segur finished his, and offered to get us another.

'Pace yourself, buddy. Remember a football game can last three hours.'

'Are you telling me you can't keep up?' I was bullshitting already, hiding myself in machismo.

'Don't worry about me. You want to get us some more brewskis then go ahead.'

I had to slide past him to get to the aisle. I had to feel his hands on my shoulders when he steadied himself as I nudged my way through. In that moment I felt what Kay had, *his hands on her*, and shuddered.

'Double up,' he called down the row. 'Buy us two each and save yourself a trip later.'

As I went down the steps the Giants went deep, the spiralling football hanging above the pitch before Plaxico leapt and snatched it from the air, landing then pirouetting, sprinting from the cornerback into the end zone. The fans jumped and whooped and high-fived the score.

Maybe it was the distance of our seats from the action, or maybe it was the half a dozen beers, but anything else of that game is just a faint recollection of tiny red and blue men on a green rectangle, like toy soldiers arranged on a table top.

It was what happened in the parking lot that I remember.

'First home game of the season and we got the W,' Segur boasted after the final whistle. 'Asshole or not, when Plaxico fires on all cylinders we got ourselves a player.'

We filed down the steps, shuffled away with the other happy Giants supporters. This time I stood on the step above him, riding the escalator down from the upper tiers, both of us halfway to being fully drunk.

'Could be a Super Bowl year?' I offered, not feeling as if I were actually talking to him but rather making up words to fill the time. As the game had drawn on I'd downed more beers in the hope of numbing the oddness of sitting next to him, close enough to be touching, body heat through our clothes.

Most of the fans flooding from the game were in a hurry to leave, but Segur was intent on finding a touch game to join. 'Show you I still got an arm,' he bragged, practising by throwing an invisible ball to invisible receivers when we got down to the entrance plaza. A grown man imagining himself saving a match, for a moment lost in his fantasy until he got hold of a real piece of leather, picking off a pass between two kids tossing a souvenir football back and forth.

'He takes the interception and *he is gone*,' he commentated on his own move, sidestepping fans. 'Here you go, Sam.' He arrowed a pass into my chest. I took it with both hands and tossed it to the kid whose ball it was.

'What the fuck, Sam,' he shouted over the crowd. 'You fumbled. Shit. Gave away possession.'

He was joking, I think, but the beer had definitely spiked his aggression.

'It's all about the pig skin, man.' He was swaying, scanning the tarmac. 'There.' He pointed to some college kids playing five a side in the car park. 'There's our game.'

Segur walked right in, said he had a Limey with him who needed to see a real sport.

'It's just touch, though,' said a skinny blond guy in a hooded top. 'But blocks are cool.'

I played on one team and Segur the other. Marking me.

'Come on, Sammy boy,' he baited me, readying to block. I squared up, face to face. I could see the paleness of his blue eyes, broken veins in his nose.

'Hut, hut, *hut*,' called the quarterback. I stepped to go round Segur rather than through him, but he came off the line fiercely, two hands in my chest, a heavier man pumping me backwards. I swayed, deflected the brunt of his weight and went past. I dipped inside and the blond kid fired the ball into my chest as the black guy playing linebacker tagged me on the shoulder.

'My Limey just burned you, man,' called the blond quarterback to Segur. 'First down,' he bellowed, making the sign of the line judge.

'Fucking lucky,' cursed Segur.

How quickly he'd turned ugly. How quickly the jovial drunk had got angry with a man who'd simply taken a pass in a game of parking lot touch.

What would he do if he knew I'd slept with his wife?

'Let's go, then.' Segur hurried the quarterback.

'See what you got this time,' answered the blond kid.

Again Segur lined up opposite me, but this play dropping into a zone instead of man to man. On the snap I made a run past his outstretched arm, round the back and cutting into midfield. The quarterback was chased by a defensive tackle and threw out a looping pass that wobbled rather than spiralled. But I stopped and took the catch, turned to run and took two steps before Segur buried me with a full tackle. The ball cannoned from my hands. I crumpled face first on to the tarmac, my arms pinned by Segur's. I came down on my left shoulder, my bad one, and scuffed my cheek. I heard the college kids saying, 'What the fuck?' and 'Come on, man.'

'*Now that's a fucking hit*,' Segur gloated, on my back, his weight pressing my cheek to the ground, his beer breath in my face.

I flipped. I wanted him off. I levered myself up and elbowed him away, threw my arm back far and hard enough to catch him in the ribs.

'Motherfucker,' he spat.

And then he snapped. Or maybe he already had. He cracked me on the temple, got a shot in before I turned and came over the top with a left. I caught him on the ear, pulled back to swing again before both of us were garotted away by the other players.

'Cool it, guys.'

A skinny redhead had me by the collar, and the black linebacker had Segur's jacket bunched in his fists.

'You're supposed to be buddies, right?'

'That was a cheap shot,' I said, wrestling the kid from my collar and standing. 'I wasn't expecting a tackle.'

Segur stood, too. 'Way out of line,' he said, raising his hands in apology. 'I deserved the elbow.' He rubbed his ear where I'd caught him with my punch. 'And probably that, too.'

'Shake on it,' said the black guy, barely out of his teens and telling two grown men to shake hands.

'Shit, Sam, I just get carried away playing football.'

'Me too,' I replied, stepping forward to shake his outstretched hand. 'It was a good hit, I'll say that much.'

'A cheap shot, hitting a guy when he's not looking.'

I think we shook again before walking across the parking lot to the taxis. Segur looked dishevelled, almost like a tramp, in his torn jeans and dirty jacket. When he bent to pick up someone's discarded can of Coors he really was a forlorn bum, not a millionaire who'd popped bottles of champagne at the Ritz Carlton. Then, and possibly only then, did I feel sorry for him. Because once we got in the taxi, and he finished that beer and looked for a while at the swamps and factories of New Jersey flying past the window, he suddenly turned and slurred, 'Kay's hot, right?'

I pretended not to hear him. 'What?'

His eyes were bloodshot. Instead of a forty-something athlete he suddenly looked old, a man past his prime. 'She's some woman, Kay. I tell you I lucked out.'

'I'm taken. Eyes for Jenni only.'

'You're not blind, though. She's a great-looking woman.'

'She is.'

Segur looked back out of the window, at a passing coach full of fans. 'And hell, there's no one like her. Shit. You could fill Meadowlands with women and there wouldn't be one as good as her.'

'That's quite a compliment,' I acknowledged, wondering how long the journey back to Manhattan would take.

'You know how I met her?'

I didn't. She'd nearly told me in the car back from the Catskills, but New York had got in the way.

'Well keep it to yourself,' he said, grinning. 'She was tearing up the stage at a downtown strip club. Twirling a pole and slipping dollar bills into a thong.'

I felt nauseous, feverish.

'And I got attached, I really did. I fell in love and thought that no other man should be seeing her naked except me. And bang. I offered her my life, more money than she'd ever

197

need.' Segur paused, then leant a little closer across the back seat. 'And a man, a real fucking man, who'd take care of her no matter what, who'd never let her go.'

I fantasized about pushing him from the speeding taxi, opening the door and shoving him on to the highway, then waving the driver on, all the way into Manhattan, her apartment.

SEGUR THOUGHT HE OWNED her. That Kay belonged to him. He owned her as much as she did the toy horse her father had given her as a child. 'I'd hold it to the window when we drove to my grandma's,' she told me on the way back from the Catskills. 'Gallop him up and down the hills, pretend I was riding him across the fields.'

Walking back from work that Monday after the Sunday football, hungover, grey clouds dulling what should be gleaming steel, because, like the sea, New York mirrors the sky, my mood was as downcast as the city. I'd been tying up loose ends in the office, wedding plans for an arranged marriage between two banks, companies as idiosyncratic as people counselled into an awkward pairing by our consultancy. Advised on a partnership by me, the adulterer.

I rang her a dozen times.

No answer.

I sat in the window of a plastic Irish bar on 23rd Street across from their apartment building, watching the revolving door to see if she might step from the spinning glass. Yellow taxis flashed across my vigil, buses, bikes and freaks. Men living out of shopping trolleys. In the bar-room neon shamrocks glowed a putrid green, Gaelic football flashed on multiple TV screens. I drank Jameson, looking either at the amount of whiskey left in the tumbler or through the window at the top-hatted concierge in his white gloves, smiling at the residents. Twirling the door for seemingly everyone in the building but Kay. Or him.

And by the time I was on my fifth or sixth double it was probably a good thing that I didn't see either of them. Full of whiskey and half crazed. At Segur. At myself. At Kay for making me feel this way. Even at Jenni. Why couldn't she stop me from what I was doing?

I hazily recall walking into the kitchen looking for the lavatory. Lifting a bin lid and starting to unbuckle my belt. Then a barman, firmly on my elbow and pointing me out the door, hailing down a cab before I stumbled across that road and hammered at the windows of the Caroline, screamed her name, and made a big enough fool of myself for her to forget I was ever in her arms.

That was the thought I opened my eyes to in the wreckage of a hangover dawn. Woken by ragged pigeons flapping about my balcony.

I WAS AT MY desk with a whiskey-pounded headache, feeling the graze on my cheek from Segur's tackle, thinking about how he'd met Kay, when she rang.

'I didn't think you'd call,' I answered, dashing from the office into the corridor and bursting out of the fire exit on to the roof, no one to overhear me but the Midtown skyline, the mast of the Empire State Building spearing a rain cloud.

'Weirdo,' she called me, confused at how I'd answered the phone. 'I said I'd ring.'

It was Jenni, not Kay. Even though I'd seen her flash up on the screen, I'd somehow read Kay's name.

'You did, you did.' I hurriedly repaired the conversation with talk of being stressed, overworked.

'Well I'll start running you a bath now, put a couple of Chardonnays in the fridge for when you get home.'

I was due back in just over twenty-four hours. Due back in my flat with the woman I'd asked to marry me.

'Three weeks has gone by so slowly,' Jenni complained. 'It seems like an eternity since I last saw you. But I guess it's not that long, is it?'

'Not even three weeks, actually.'

'Long enough.'

Long enough for what, I wondered.

She laughed. 'As long as you don't bring back some American woman.'

'Don't be daft. They don't get my jokes.'

'Who does, except me? Oh, did you get a chance to meet up with Chris's wife after the football game?'

If I took the question on its exact syntax it wasn't a lie to say, 'No, I didn't. I had a drink with Chris and came back here.'

It was a truth. I didn't meet her after the game.

I met her after the call, later that night. She rang when I was walking down Sixth Avenue, when I was about to walk all the way to her apartment building on 23rd Street. When I was resolved to stride in, stone-cold sober, and knock on their door and tell Segur everything.

Would I have really taken matters into my own hands if she hadn't?

'Catch the train to Brooklyn,' Kay told me. 'I'll meet you outside Giovanni's, the restaurant where I used to work.'

There was no dilemma. I rode across Manhattan Bridge, scared, shaking as much as that rattling stretch of cabled steel. When I looked back over the East River the lights of the financial district seemed as cheap as an imitation Christmas tree.


By the time I got to Giovanni's it was already full of diners. I looked through the windows and tried to picture Kay waitressing.

I was late, directed ten blocks in the wrong direction by an elderly Polish man. When Kay came out of the restaurant and saw me there on the sidewalk it was as if I'd been raised from the dead.

'Sam,' she snapped. 'Don't do that again.' She hugged the breath from my lungs.

It wasn't until we were sitting at a table and she took her jacket off that I realized what had caused the reaction, the panic at my delay.

'I thought you weren't coming.'

'What's this?' I saw blotches of red skin at the top of her arms.

'It's nothing.'

'Did he hit you?' I asked. 'Does he know about us?'

She shook her head.

'Speak to me, Kay.'

'After the football game. He came back drunk, angry. I thought the Giants had lost and he was pissed at that, but it was something else.'

I mentioned the football in the lot, the scuffle.

'More than you two,' she said. 'Things he sensed between us.'

'The Catskills?'

'He didn't believe I was seeing my friend in Warwick.'

Segur had tried to shake the truth from her, and the bruising on her arm was there because of me. I apologized for everything, for coming into her life and ruining it.

'Don't you dare,' she glowered, insisting I was making her life worth while, not destroying it. 'Too long,' she said. 'Too many years with a man I thought was someone else. Who thought I was someone else.'

I asked her if she knew me.

'Enough to take a chance. To be here.'

When the waiter came to the table carrying a bottle of red wine, I tried to turn my attention to the taste, sipping from the glass to confirm it was to my satisfaction. I could've been drinking vinegar and wouldn't have known.

And looking back on that moment, it's as if I was already at the point in the future when Jenni would hear of this, when she'd say, 'No woman in the world wanted you as much as she did right then. Not me.'

'Come with me, Sam.' That's what Kay had said. 'Come with me.' She was leaning across the tablecloth, over the plates of free food the owner had presented us with after kissing her on both cheeks and asking why she hadn't returned to see him sooner, a meal we'd barely touched.

For the first and only time New York had stopped, and would only start again with my answer.

'You really want that?' I'd asked. 'To leave? Go, just like that?'

Her eyes welled, and she wiped her cheek with a napkin. 'Do it, Sam. Come with me.'

I reached over and took her hand. She laid her wrist limply on the table, as if waiting for me to either kiss it or cut it open.


On the wet streets outside the restaurant, I'd flagged down a car to take us back to the city. There was rain on the windscreen, Manhattan neon warped by the streaked drops that veined on the glass. Amber and gold, beads of red.

Kay in the nook of my shoulder.

It was then that I grasped, or at least thought I did, a difference between understanding someone and knowing them. And perhaps that was the reason I gave up everything that night. For something less tangible, maybe, but more *felt*. I'm not a churchgoer, a believer in a benevolent man with a beard of stardust hovering around the planet. Yet I wondered if faith, loving something that you can only imagine is there but trust will never abandon you, is the same as being in love with another person.

I swapped the real for something imagined, the understood for what I believed was the known.

Later that night I looked from the dark of my apartment to the snarl of traffic that roared across the intersection. I was afraid to turn the light on and see myself reflected in the window pane. Afraid this love was as fleeting as a bird hovering above the vows of a wedding.

I WAS PACKED AND ready to leave New York. My own shoddy work or not, two banks would merge using a plan of action pitched by our consultancy. A success. I'd crocodile-smiled through a farewell drink with Lucas before heading back to my apartment and throwing my world into a bag. Suddenly the boardroom chess of men and women in suits, distractions from the business of living, seemed a trivial pastime now I was out of the game.

After I handed the keys to the super and tipped him ten dollars, he wished me a safe trip back to England. I thanked him and wondered how long it would take me to get there.

Outside Penn Station SWAT teams brandished machine guns, stood with dogs on leads. None of the lantern-jawed officers smiled at the odd tourist naïve enough to travel on the day before Thanksgiving. On a day al-Qaeda had reportedly plotted to blow up a subway train.

I waited by men in black flak jackets and visored helmets. I searched the faces of Americans heading home for turkey dinner and pumpkin pie, their gathered families. And I knew I wanted nothing but us. I wanted who I was when she held me, kissed me. I wanted the voice I heard when I talked to her, the body I belonged to when I was inside her.

'That your bag, sir?' asked a policeman, a sub-machine gun slung over his shoulder.

'Yes, sorry.' I'd wandered away looking for Kay in the crowd, terrified I'd miss her.

'Liable to get taken away and destroyed if you leave it unattended.'

I apologized again, stood beside my bag, next to the SWAT team and the dogs. I waited there in case Segur showed before she did. In case he wondered where she was going with a suitcase in the middle of the afternoon. My mind raced with thoughts of him catching her leaving, hitting her, beating her until she told him where I was. I'd seen him angry at the Giants game, seen him snap in a game of touch football. What was he capable of doing when pushed aside by his wife for another man? I didn't care what he'd do to me, I truly didn't. I was almost waiting for it. I was tapping my feet thinking what I'd do to him if anything had happened to her. Murderous thoughts of blood. I saw his doppelgänger three or four times, men hurrying for trains, checking their watches. All Segur for one horrifying second. The paranoia of terrorism in the station mixing with my worry for the woman I was running away with.

So when she came jogging through the crowds, crying with the force of what we were doing, I hugged her off her feet, kissed her and erased the concourse, the police and the guns, the station announcer and the bustling passengers.

'I thought you wouldn't be here,' she cried. 'I ran. I couldn't stand it, the tension.'

The SWAT team stared like stone-faced judges. Before I offered to carry Kay's bag I realized she didn't have one.

'No luggage?'

207

'He isn't working today. He's at home watching football on TV. I said I was heading out to the grocery store.'

I held her hand that bit harder, and then checked from which platform to catch a train to Newark airport. In case she changed her mind and returned home with a bag of shopping.

# III

D ID WE REALLY THINK we could board a plane, rise into the clouds then land in a new life? There and then, perhaps we did.

My own father had. On the train to the airport I wondered about the day he got in a car and drove from the woman he'd pledged to have and to hold, till death them did part. The woman who bore his first son, who was about to give him a baby girl. But he drove from one house to another, and stayed there. For good. The fling that became a divorce, another marriage. The man who became the weekend dad, picking us up every other Saturday and taking us to the park, playing football and feeding ducks, to petting zoos and Sherwood Forest, before dropping us at the end of the driveway as my mother watched from the living room window.

I truly believe that our father loved us. But from a distance, in a hidden space in his heart. We were always the symbols of his guilt, the son and daughter who reminded him of the woman he'd abandoned. When my half-brothers were born, twins who seemed no more my blood than any other boys, my father removed himself from our life as if he'd tendered his resignation from one parenthood to begin another.

To save his future he cut the cord to his past. Once we moved in with Les he saw us less and less, till the weeks became months, finally a once a year gathering at Christmas.

And he was still alive, wasn't he? He'd survived the break-up A happy man now, a wife and family. If he could do it, then I surely could too. Neither I nor Kay had kids, and I wasn't even married.

These were the thoughts I had as we rode that train to Newark airport. The cold comfort. The two of us stood in a vestibule, too nervous to sit, too afraid, perhaps, to even talk. We kissed and held each other, kept private any misgivings we had about running. I simply took the tightness of her hug as her conviction, and hoped this passion could replace what we were about to lose.

ALTHOUGH THE IDEA OF my father's elopement had made mine less difficult, even getting a last-minute flight the day before Thanksgiving wasn't easy.

We were hoping for west coast sunshine, but had to take a plane to New Orleans. A hurricane-ruined city wasn't a tourist hotspot for the holidays, yet busy enough to mean we could only book separate seats. I'd leant over the passenger next to Kay, kissed her as if we weren't going to see each other for days, then sat three rows back. I studied her dark hair, imagined running it through my fingers. I was thinking about Kay between looking at my watch and working out how long I had before calling Jenni, before she turned up at Heathrow and waited for a man who'd got on board a different plane.

I sat beside a woman in a business suit reading the in-flight magazine, glossy photos of exotic beaches and foreign climes. Once we'd taken off and Manhattan had shrunk to a model souvenir, I ordered a rum and Coke from the flight attendant and asked her to send a drink to 'the woman in 22F'.

The attendant played along, and when Kay took the glass off the tray she twisted in her seat, sat up and silently toasted our getaway. And it was a getaway. Temporarily separated by three rows at 35,000 feet, once the plane touched down in New Orleans we would be together.

I was terrified. The captain might as well have announced the engines had failed and we were going down in flames.

My hand shook, rattling the ice in the glass as I knocked back the rum. I stared at the TV on the headrest. The choice of movies seemed ridiculous when I had a drama playing out in my own skin. But when I switched off the screen I saw myself reflected, the leading man, scared and guilty. So I closed my eyes, wondered if Kay was having second thoughts. Wondered if Jenni had chosen the outfit she planned to wear for my Heathrow welcome.

When my head felt heavy and I rocked forward, I couldn't tell if I was fainting or sleeping. I fought the sensation only once, jerking upright and looking from the cabin window to the cloudscape.

How long I slept I wasn't sure. In my dream I was sitting on a high stool in some Wild West saloon, drinking whiskey from the bottle. A bona fide cowboy. And the girl pouring my drinks was beautiful and dressed up in all that frilled finery of those times. All lace gloves and stocking tops. Kay. It was Kay. Flirting with me and laughing and kissing and pushing away the other men sloping over the bar and crassly trying to pick her up.

And in this dream a man walked into the saloon wearing a beaten-up top hat and two long-barrelled pistols stuck in his waistband. He was dusty and dirty and spat on the wooden floor. When he looked at Kay he grinned and I could see his foul yellow teeth. I drew my gun and shot the man through the heart as if there were no more substance to him than a paper target.

Then, as dreams will have it, in the next scene I was suddenly riding a horse. Kay was across the saddle and I wanted to kiss her, but she was looking past me and back to where we were coming from. I asked her what was wrong and she just shook her head before a long shadow advanced from the sunset. I could see that the shadow wore a top hat and when that same cowboy I'd killed in the saloon was level with us I knew it was Death himself, tall in the saddle and laughing.

I woke and unbuckled my seatbelt, apologized for asking the woman next to me to move, then walked down the aisle and leant over to Kay and kissed her. To know for sure that she was real, that I was.

WE TOOK A TAXI from the airport to the French Quarter, holding each other tight on the back seat, feeling as small as children in the night. It was too dark to see the shattered houses Katrina had left beyond the highway, but in the shadow and flicker of a foreign city on a car window I saw the flash of a country lane fading into dusk, stone walls and a farm. It was the last break we took together, North Wales, the three of us, my mother and my sister. We had a holiday cottage choked in ivy, damp rooms with musty blankets, a short drive from a golden beach whipped with surf where my mother, alone, would sit and read on a deckchair.

'All this,' said the Moroccan driver, waving his hands over the rooftops. 'Water. And this part of the bridge, broken. Like a road into sky.'

He dropped us outside the Hotel St Marie, a few blocks from the tacky neon of Bourbon Street. Ironwork balconies, unnervingly like my flat in Maida Vale, looked on to the cobblestones. I paid the driver, took Kay's arm and walked into the foyer. A bouquet of fresh flowers sat on a glass table beneath a crystal chandelier.

'I don't care that it'll be expensive,' I said. 'In fact the more the better.' An abandonment of all values seemed appropriate, and I wanted a flagrant hotel bill to match the

216

excessive act of eloping. Though what room could have cost that?

But Kay stepped ahead of me to the counter. 'Neither of us is paying.' She waved a credit card, a joint account with Segur. She was so intent on spending his money that I didn't protest.

We kissed in the elevator. When the doors slid back I picked her up and carried her along the corridor to our room. Like newly-weds. She opened the door still in my arms, and I kicked it shut with my heel and fell with her on to the bed.

'Lock us in,' she said, unbuttoning my shirt.

I did. Then I pulled off her boots, desperate to enter our world of touch and skin, trailed fingers, that strange elation of lovemaking where the body of another can lift you from your own mortal flesh and put you at some height above a bed of twisted sheets and tangled limbs, with no way of knowing where one self starts and the other ends.

'W E HAVE TO TELL them,' said Kay, naked on her back beside me, both of us staring at the ceiling. Street sounds of taxis and people heading out to drink filtered through the wooden shutters, erasing our refuge. 'You're supposed to be getting off a plane in a few hours.'

I turned, laid my hand on the ridge of her pelvis. 'And you were due home with groceries.'

'Let's get it over with, make the calls.'

I wasn't feeling brave, and suggested we text.

'Text the end of six years?'

'Shit.'

Kay sat up. 'They have a minibar in here?' She found the fridge, pulled out a can of Coke and two shot-size bottles of Captain Morgan.

'Dutch courage?' I asked.

'Something like that.'

We drank, no toast this time. If we'd raised our glasses we'd have been no better than killers toasting a murder.

'I can't do it in front of you,' she said.

'I'll go on the balcony.'

I turned and walked out through the wooden shutters. Beyond the tiled roofs of Toulouse Street downtown New Orleans glowed. I was wrapped in a towel, in a city trying to resurrect itself from a devastating storm, and about to call my fiancée to tell her I was running away with another woman.

I scrolled to her name and pressed call.

On the second ring I hit cancel and looked at the skies above the Central Business District, the clouds illuminated by an electric glow. I could see bats flitting around TV antennae silhouetted like Chinese pictograms. It was humid, but cool. I had a couple of minutes before I'd get cold, and once again flipped open my phone. This time I scrolled to compose and typed: *Work has gone haywire, so, so sorry, but I have to be here another week at least . . . will call later, might have to switch off phone that busy. x*

I was a coward. And a liar.

But Kay wasn't.

'He went fucking crazy.' She was on the chair, head down and crying, sniffing. 'He didn't understand at first. He could hear me, but it was as if he didn't get the combination of words, that I was leaving him.'

She wiped her nose on her hand, said she was sorry. 'He just kept repeating, "No, no, no." And then before he hung up he said, "Who do you think I am?"'

I pictured his smashed phone fracturing into a thousand pieces. I imagined I was him. What rage would I be capable of if I were the one wronged?

'We knew it wasn't going to be easy,' I said, wondering if Kay was saying sorry to me, or to Segur.

'What did she say?' asked Kay, raising her face, looking up at me with tear-streaked cheeks and bloodshot eyes. 'You did tell her?'

'Kind of.' Now I felt guilty twice. Adultery and breaking the pact with Kay.

'Kind of?'

'I said I wasn't coming back.'

'Ever?'

'Well, not on that plane.'

'Don't do this, Sam.' She cried again. 'Don't make me feel alone.' She dropped forward to the floor like a puppet suddenly cut from its strings.

I had the sensation of my organs melting. I knelt before Kay, cupped her jaw and told her to look at me. 'I am yours,' I said. 'I am you. Trust me. I'm here. I've come this far because of you. I'm in this room because you are, no other reason. You.'

I kissed her wet face. I kissed her eyelids, her cheek and nose. She kissed me back and we rolled over and kissed again until sex was a drug, soma from our selves, the lives of others.

IT WAS JUST AFTER midnight, officially Thanksgiving, and we were walking towards Bourbon Street for a drink.

After the meltdown in the room we needed to get out, pretend, no matter how difficult the charade was to believe in, that we were a normal couple for an evening. We walked between the bars hand in hand, together. No threat, we thought, but our own fear and conscience.

We had chicken burgers in a restaurant waiting to close, the two of us and a room full of empty chairs, before heading back out to Bourbon Street.

'Where is everyone?' I asked, looking at bartenders leaning in doorways offering two for one on cocktails and shooters.

'Day before Thanksgiving, biggest family day of the year.'

I thought of my mother, the strange idea that she was for ever frozen in time. Then I put my arm round Kay and brought us closer.

We walked some more, had two beers in a Mexican place watching an old couple slowly waltz to music twice as fast as their steps. While peeling the label from her bottle Kay asked if we'd ever become like them, two dancers with no cares if we kept the beat.

'Why not?' I tipped back the end of my drink, veered from the dark thought that a future together was a fool's

221

paradise. I fought off the plain facts of where we'd live, a new job. 'Butch and Sundance ran to South America,' I said, pointing at a portrait above the bar of Mexican revolutionary Pancho Villa, posing in twin bandoliers.

'They got shot in Bolivia,' Kay reminded me, adding she'd be happy to get stuck on the Gulf somewhere, find a beach and rub suntan oil into my back.

I hooked my arm round her waist, grabbed her hard. She said I had so much to discover about her, whole novels under her skin.

There and then, I nearly confessed that Segur had revealed how they met. But I stayed with the thought of stories inside us waiting to be told, and kept this idea running till we finished our beers and walked back to the hotel, past a strip bar.

I watched Kay stare through the doors, glimpses of legs wrapped around steel poles. She turned to me, and before she repeated something I already knew, I told her.

'He talked about it after the football game, the fight.'

She shook her head. 'It was such a secret. He was always scared his Wall Street buddies would find out he'd married a stripper. And then he goes and tells you.'

We walked on. I said it meant nothing to me and that I'd advertise it to anyone and everyone without a care.

'It was after that guy in the restaurant dropped his card and that fifty as the tip,' Kay said. 'And more than the money, it was a way of affirming myself again. I know that sounds fucked up, taking your clothes off in a roomful of strangers builds confidence, but on a night off I went into Manhattan and sat down in one of his clubs. High class places. The women strutted on stage and owned it. Every man in the room was pinned by them, by their bodies. I wanted that primal command over another, over a man.'

We'd turned on to Toulouse Street, and could see our hotel on the corner.

'Fuck it,' she said, stopping. 'Lets exorcise that demon.'

I didn't know what she meant.

'I want a drink in that strip club, then I never want to go in one again.'

We took a table at the back of the club. A circular stage, joined by an illuminated catwalk to a pair of velvet curtains where the women emerged, was the island at which everyone looked. Men on their own, college kids and couples. Boyfriends daring their girlfriends to walk up and slip dollar bills into G-strings and garters.

Kay was quiet to begin with, watching the first two women dance and barely looking back at me. I watched them get naked, too, shedding what clothes they were wearing, skirts and jackets, an Army uniform, finally reduced to honed bodies obsessively taut and tanned.

'What do you think?' asked Kay after a tall black girl picked up her silver bikini and vanished behind the curtains.

'You're the only woman in the room.'

She shook her head, smiled. 'Fake tits ruin a great body every time.' Walking into the club she'd taken on the air of a different person. Defensive, tougher. A strutting femininity, yet vulnerable, younger. While sipping at her rum and Coke she told me how the girls she stripped with all came from some messed-up background. 'And nine times out of ten it was something to do with a man.'

I thought about her own flight from home. The stepfather.

'Or just plain egomania.'

If Kay was ready to tell me what had happened, a story of abuse, I was ready to find out. Odd as it would be while women danced around us in nothing but high heels. But she carried on talking about stripping, perhaps to avoid the history. 'And nowhere is it more right now than being completely naked.' She took a breath with this statement, waved the waiter over and ordered us two more drinks.

'Then you put your clothes back on and walk outside, see your wrinkles in the mirror. The effort of being you. But at the same time wonder how these shiny young women working as secretaries get up every day and do the same shit.'

'And then you met him.'

Kay swirled the ice in her drink. 'And a while later an Englishman holds out his umbrella.' She smiled, took out the lime and sucked up the juice.

'You stripped,' I said, grabbing at her chair and hauling her closer, 'while I slept in a park and stole things.'

I leant in and kissed her. She put her hand behind my ear and softly bit my lip. We only pulled back from each other when the next dancer stepped down off the stage and walked the tables, a peroxide blonde with short spiked hair, her body pierced and painted with tattoos. Kay asked if I'd guessed her own design yet.

'The one lasered off?'

'The only one.'

I didn't want to guess and get it badly wrong, so I joked. 'An anchor, or your regiment in the marines.'

'You know, I love your fooling around as much as everything else. Nothing is taken too seriously. I like that.'

'So it was the anchor?'

She waved me off with her hand, sat back with her rum and Coke.

'You have to tell me now.'

'Work it out.'

'I need a hint.'

She thought for a second. 'It's the only bird that can fly backwards.'

I stalled, asked her why she had it lasered off.

'I didn't.' She drank again then shook her head. 'He paid for it to be removed. Chris. He insisted I lose that part of my past.' She swirled the ice cubes to get the last drop of rum. 'As if your memory is kept in the ink of a tattoo, just erased when the picture is.'

AGAINST THE BLACK SKIES and slate grey water of the Mississippi, above the moss-clad trees that stumbled through the swampland like a ragtag army of grey and bearded men, the flames of oil refineries burned in the gloom.

'Could it look any more like the end of the world?' Kay looked from the road to the fires on the horizon. She was driving the rental car we'd picked up in New Orleans, heading west into a storm, an alien landscape that helped keep us disconnected from what we were actually doing.

I glanced from the elevated highway to the waterlogged forest, thought of alligators and snakes. 'Keep your eyes on the road,' I warned. 'We'll get eaten if you crash here.'

'You're the guy who totals signposts.'

I saw tumbledown shacks on rafts of barrels, chimney smoke drawn from sagging roofs.

'Shall we live in one of these hillbilly homes?'

Kay shuddered. 'Can you imagine?'

'How far would you follow me into the swamp?'

She shook her head. 'We'd be dead by sundown. Locals or the gators.'

Deeper into the black and towering clouds, past the refinery, a floating city of pipes and flames. Kay drove fast, accelerated into the rain when it came hard and spattering against the windscreen.

'At least I bought a coat.'

We'd woken up and gone shopping in New Orleans, Kay buying a suitcase and a whole new wardrobe as she'd travelled with nothing but her self and the clothes she was wearing, the clothes she had on when she walked out the door. Before leaving the hotel she'd unzipped the suitcase and thrown the old ones in the bin.

It wasn't until we had the hire car, again paid for on Segur's credit card, that we talked about the night before, the strip club, the lasered tattoo.

'I should've given you a harder clue,' said Kay.

'But I only got it in the dream.'

That morning I told her she had another life in my sleep. Another form. That I'd again been in the forest of dead trees, walking, and this time there was no running woman. I'd broken through the branches, clambered over fallen trunks, until I heard the applause of pebbles turned in breaking waves. I could see a woman curled up on a beach, the way a child might be found in a fairy tale, hatched from a stone. Gulls lifted on the breeze like scraps of paper. Giant sequoia towered along the shoreline, and the wind through the higher boughs was oceanic, as if some ghost of sea tangled there with the clouds.

'It was you,' I'd told Kay in bed, the two of us lying side by side, her stare fixed on mine as though she could see the dream in my eyes.

'You sat up. The wind blew your hair from your face. You said that if I looked along the coastline I might see San Francisco, your old house.'

But all I could see was a salt-sprayed wilderness, a shore of rock and rain where bears, ignoring our presence on the beach, had climbed down from trees and hooked fish in the foaming surf.

'And the man was you?' she'd asked. '*You* were standing there watching *you*?'

Beyond the haze and spray of broken waves, a figure had appeared. A man, walking, emerging from the distance.

'I think it was me,' I'd guessed. 'But I wasn't sure if it was actually the beach sliding towards the man.'

He, me, the man, stepped over driftwood, past scoured and polished trunks. He walked up the beach towards Kay. She heard his footsteps crunching on the stones, and so did the bears in the surf, turning back to the dark of the woods.

'You saved me from bears,' she'd said, kissing me on the cheek, the forehead.

'Only for you to turn into a hummingbird when I tried to hug you.'

She'd gasped when I told her this, jumped up on the bed before turning her shoulder blade to show me the scar. 'It was a hummingbird,' she'd nearly shouted. 'And you dreamed I was a hummingbird?'

I'd said I really had.

'Did I fly away?'

'You fluttered around my head. I could see dazzling emerald green. You were a tiny thrumming jewel, hovering over the flowers which had bloomed between the pebbles.'

'See, I was just showing my wings off to you.'

I'd leant forward and pulled her back down to the bed, kissed her neck and shoulders.

I don't think I lied, retelling the dream how I had.

I'd just refrained from mentioning the end, how one of the bears that watched her from the trees had sharpened his claws on the bark before coming out of the shadows and across the beach.

About an hour past Baton Rouge we had a turkey dinner, 'With all the fixin's,' sparked the waitress, in a roadside restaurant chain called the Cracker Barrel.

'This is the high life,' Kay had joked, looking around at elderly couples too frail to be cooking up their own Thanksgiving meal, spooning on extra cranberry sauce, sneaking bread buns into bags then asking for more to box up and take home.

I ate mouthfuls of stuffing and gravy, tried to avoid the sudden ordinariness of where we were. In a mock southern diner with men dribbling pie down their plaid shirts.

'You're thinking about Jenni, aren't you?'

'Hard not to.'

Kay chased the rest of her turkey around the plate without catching it, as did I, before saying, 'We'd better get moving if we want to hit Corpus Christi before it gets dark.'

We'd decided on this as our destination for no other reason than that we liked the name and knew it was on the Gulf of Mexico. We got the bill and thanked the bus boy, an old black man who walked with a crooked polio limp and collected our plates, shuffling back to the kitchen with the knives and forks clattering on the china with each troublesome step.

'You want to drive?' asked Kay. 'Keep your mind from other things.'

I took the keys and walked to the car. The rain clouds had cleared, and bright sun beat on the parking lot. I could have cried. But instead I opened the door and clicked in the seatbelt, then fired up the engine.

'DON'T GET QUIET ON me, Sam.' We were well beyond the Mississippi delta, driving past towns that looked alike, a strip mall kit of gas stations, fast food restaurants and car dealerships lined with discounted SUVs. 'We've been through harder things than this before.'

When I switched lanes, pulling from between two thundering rigs, I said, 'It's not us left in the wreckage.'

Kay didn't respond for a minute, and I thought it was because there was no answer, no magic words to let us off lightly for abandoning our lovers.

'Well I don't know if you do, but don't feel guilty for Chris.'

Part of me did, and perhaps she knew that so told me something to erase that impostor of a feeling.

'Have you ever hit Jenni?'

'God, no.' I nearly swerved into another lane.

'Well, whatever I've thought of him in the past, he's not man enough to hold back on an occasional slap.'

If she wanted to upend my mood she had. The thought of Segur hurting her stirred up my emotions. I revved the engine, touched a hundred before she said, 'Better you're angry than sad.'

I slowed back to eighty, took a breath, and arrowed the car past Houston, south.

*

The afternoon sky was so blue, the morning rain seemed a feat of our imagination. Ribbons of cirrus burned away as soon as we noticed them. The odd jetliner, high and remote on the stellar edge, was hard to associate with the ancient landscape of dead creosote and rattlesnakes.

'We're in nut country now,' Kay had remarked as we left the Houston suburbs. 'And you know who said that?'

'You. Right then.'

'Way before me, the day he was shot.'

'JFK?'

'He whispered it to Jackie when they drove out of the airport.'

It was nearly noon, and very bright on the highway, chrome fenders and windshields dazzling.

'Nut country,' I repeated, looking at the stark landscape.

'It's so flat.' Kay had taken off her shoes and rested her bare feet on the dashboard. 'I love those mirages that look like lakes.'

The horizon wobbled, tremored with sun and distance. Silos and barns the only features. Passing the small towns, Wharton, Edna and El Campo, where county sheriffs sat with speed guns, where old men sat on porches and watched us drive by, Kay fell asleep, a smile on her face like a toddler. And I watched her chest rise and fall as much as I watched the empty highway, all that horizon, the empty sky filled by her.

She woke when I pulled into a rest stop outside Victoria. Although a break from the wheel was due, I pulled over because I needed her with me, talking. She stretched and sighed.

'How long was I asleep for?'

'A hundred miles.'

'I slept a hundred miles of my life away.'

'Not away.' I leant over and kissed her, as if rousing a woman from a spelled dream.

We walked across to the rest rooms. I splashed my face with water from the drinking fountain. Then I hurried from the building with a sudden fear of abandonment. A child's fear, that someone I loved could open and close a door and never return.

In the car park two teenagers were throwing rocks at a snake backed against a junction box. I warned them that if they left it alone I'd leave them alone. The boys eyed me warily and dropped the rocks.

'You told them,' said Kay, linking her arm round mine. 'No one's throwing things at me with you around.'

Taking the ramp on to the highway she said she had the memory that she might have once hitched from that very same spot.

'But I've never been further south than Austin,' she added. 'Maybe I inherited the memory of my dad. His life as a professional bum after Vietnam.'

'Do you know about his life before he met your mum?'

'The best, and only real conversation I ever had with him. He told me in a prison visiting room. Through my teens I got it in weekly instalments.'

'Vietnam?'

'Never. Just what happened after. How he made sense of the world through whisky. Days of drifting round the country on a Greyhound bus.'

I asked if he knew what had happened to her.

'Kind of. I think my mom liked to use it against him, say it was his fault and not hers.'

I drove on. Kay sat back in her seat to talk. 'Funny, but I felt like I should have been in a war, too. Those were the people I was hanging out with, vets, Vietnam and Iraq. About every bum I asked a light from had served somewhere. Some begged with their regiment scratched on the sidewalk, an empty sleeve flapping where an arm should be. The lost vets were the tumbleweed rolling down a deserted street.'

She told me about days and weeks erased from her life. Flashes of towns and faces still came to her in extraordinary moments. 'As if the thought had been put there by someone else.'

I reached across, stroked the inside of her forearm.

'He came back from war and took a job on a farm. Then quit a week later. All that space, nowhere for his mind to run and hide. He got a room above a roadhouse in Wyoming. Trucks rolled in and out all night, but the juddering rigs were a welcome distraction from his dreams. When he ran out of money the owner gave him credit for doing odd jobs like fixing up chairs and tables after bar fights, sweeping broken glass from the urinals and generally maintaining a run-down establishment.'

I stopped abruptly for a red light, nearly skidding, so taken by her father's story, which in turn had become her story, that I wasn't concentrating on driving.

'He shined the surface of the bar where he sat each night with his elbow. He only left his stool to piss, or follow women on to the dance floor. Later they'd slam into each other on his bed of broken springs then wake and both wonder how they'd got there.'

I saw tears in her eyes. 'You okay?'

'See,' she said. 'I'm my mom.'

'What do you mean?'

'He met her in that roadhouse. He watched her sit on the edge of his dresser and shoot heroin into her foot. He called her a dumb bitch then finished off a bottle of whisky. The third day in a row he vomited blood the owner put a hundred dollars in his hand and asked him to leave. He said he was sorry, but if he poured him another drink the police would charge him with murder.'

'And your mum?'

'Long gone. It was years before my dad found me, his daughter.'

Kay told me how her father walked, hitched, fell asleep in ditches and shook uncontrollably on the back seats of buses while his body rattled with drink and death. He hiked for weeks across the Midwest and watched storm clouds gather above the Great Plains. He walked through electric rain in Idaho and stood in the corn like some ragged scarecrow waiting for judgement. But nothing.

'And then the rain stopped, the fields turned gold, and he followed the setting sun all the way to California.' She said this with theatrical irony, throwing out her hands.

'And found you,' I stated. 'He came and found you.'

'He did,' she said. 'And then he just vanished again.' She looked to the fields beyond the roadside, acres of sky. Then she unbuckled her seatbelt and laid her head across my lap.

We were still an hour from Corpus Christi when it got dark, the deep blue rising up from the eastern horizon like a sheet of litmus paper drawing ink. Then for miles nothing but the road rushing beneath the wheels, kamikaze moths in the headlights. And no stars, thick cloud moving to blot out the universe. Maybe no light anywhere in space and time but the cone of the car beams. And the dashboard glow casting us in green, our ghostly faces. Then from the blackness came trucks howling and rattling, the rigs illuminated with neon so you could see the painted women on the doors. Women like the cartoon belles on Second World War bombers, reclining on a fuselage above smoke and ruin.

'The gods have pointed their fingers and cursed us,' said Kay, trying to find something to see in the dark night. 'We're forever bound to drive south Texas and never arrive anywhere.'

I hoped not. My blurry eyes knew nothing but car lights. Finally we saw a burn of white on the horizon.

'It's bigger than I thought,' said Kay, looking at the dazzle of downtown, the towers and office blocks lit like warnings for passing ships. Then the closer we got, the more we realized something was wrong with the skyline.

'Was that fire?' I asked. 'A burst of fire from the top of that building.'

Orange flares. Giant match heads igniting in the dark.

Kay leant forward in her seat. 'It's a city of oil pipes,' she said, studying the wraiths of flame.

The metropolis, hissing, torched and burning, was another refinery. Steel and fire lighting up the evening for miles, as if it were an automated hell built for show.

Half an hour later we pulled into a quiet Corpus Christi, both of us tired and car stale from the day's drive. It somehow seemed a let-down that we'd escaped New Orleans, dodged the diesel-chugging rigs and kept sane on the pancake flats and dead highways of south Texas to disembark without some kind of welcome. Driving about looking for a motel we had our first tiff.

'Just take this one,' said Kay, looking at a Best Western in the business district.

'But we're by the sea,' I countered. 'We can't stay in a downtown hotel when we can wake to a sea view.'

'Does it matter?' She was tired. 'We can go to the beach in the morning.'

I was adamant that we should open the curtains on to ocean, not office blocks. 'Let's at least try the sea front.'

Kay sighed hard, looked at the entrance to the Best Western. 'A bed's a bed.'

'A sea view would be nice.'

'Getting out of this car would be better,' she replied curtly.

I drove on in silence, then she apologized. And so did I. 'There's not many days in life like this.'

'We'll have better ones if we're lucky.' She leant across and kissed me. 'And the driver rules.'

'That sounds like a good idea. When I'm at the wheel.'

She playfully slapped my arm, not unlike the way Jenni would have, then perked up and wound down the window. 'There's definitely an ocean out there.'

I could smell sea, hear the squawk of gulls. The next junction I took a right on to the bay front, deserted and dark but for the sign of a Super 8 motel, yellow and bright.

'We've got our bed,' said Kay.

A FTER WE MADE LOVE in a motel bed, after Kay crossed her legs tight round the small of my back, she'd said, 'Don't you dare let go of me.'

I didn't dare. I lay for a while inside her, listening to her heartbeat, tasting the salt on her neck. Beyond the windows palm leaves rattled in the breeze, waves hissed as they broke on the shore. And when I woke still wrapped in her arms, the first light of dawn gilding the cheap curtains, I pulled the duvet over our heads and pushed my head into her cleavage and slept, lost myself for a precious while more.

The next time I opened my eyes I'd shifted to the edge of the bed. The first thing I saw was my phone. Jenni. I still hadn't switched it on. When I reached on to the dresser and powered it up the message waiting buzzed four times. Instead of opening the inbox I turned it off.

I felt that my being alive was only an illusion. Part of an even more elaborate illusion that would vanish in a puff of smoke if I switched on the phone.

I got out of bed and drew back the curtains. Yachts in the marina, a huge road bridge and a navy destroyer moored further along the bay.

'That's better than a sea view,' said Kay.

I was naked.

'Come here.'

We rolled around, mock wrestled each other. I let Kay grab my wrists and sit across my chest. I tried to shunt her off, but she put her knees over my shoulders. 'Hey.' She laughed, tickled my sides until I screamed. 'Stop, stop.'

She did stop and instead we kissed, slowed our breathing, tasted each other from the night before. I was hard against her stomach when there was a heavy knock at the door.

'Hello?' I jolted on to my elbows. No answer. 'Hello?' I called again. I could see the shadow of feet under the gap. 'Who is it?'

Kay pulled the covers over her bare breasts. On the next knock I got up and wrapped a towel round my waist and loudly asked again, 'Who is it?'

'Housekeeping,' came the reply, a heavy Latino accent.

'Come back later,' called Kay from the bed, sitting up and pulling on a T-shirt.

I watched a shadow move across the curtains, then walked back to the bed, the mess of sheets. 'That spooked me a bit.'

'Me, too.'

Then I walked back to the door and opened it a little, watched the cleaning lady push her cart along the landing to the next room.

'I think I need a run,' I said. 'Thirty minutes of Zen time, you know what I mean?'

'Do your thing,' she said. 'Just save some energy for me.'

We had the end room on the top floor. Kay was stretching and watching the news. Iceland was bankrupt, more financial doom and gloom that seemed utterly removed from our lives. I kissed her and promised I wouldn't be long, then shut the door and took the stairs into the lobby before jogging across the grass median between the palm trees.

Saying 'Zen time' to Kay now seemed ridiculous. That I could erase my thoughts and be purely a thing of body was impossible considering the situation. I'd come outside because I thought the power of feeling so alive had threatened to pull me to pieces. Guilt and joy competing extremes.

I ran harder to race the thoughts, shuttled up and down the rows of steps along the concrete wharf until I came to a pagoda-shaped watchtower built into the marina. I stretched and looked out to sea. I saw a dolphin's tail splashing as it dived. I watched the glassy water, waiting for it to surface, but decided I'd imagined it by wishful thinking. Or was simply looking for distractions from the fact I had messages on my phone from Jenni.

PARANOIA HAD GOT THE better of me, that's what I believed. That my imagination had put his face in a car on a Texas sea front. My guilt. How could Segur follow us from train to plane to rental car and finally a Super 8 motel?

But I decided to jog back, anyway.

Then that jog became more of a run, a lengthened stride.

When I saw a car parked askew in the motel forecourt I knew something was wrong. I hurried into the lobby and jabbed at the elevator button. It was stopped on the top floor, where our room was.

The Segur credit card, I abruptly realized. 'Fuck.'

'Everything okay, sir?' asked the receptionist. 'The elevator is a little slow, I'm afraid.'

I ran up six flights of stairs. I ran because the receptionist told me that a driver was here to 'pick up Mrs Segur'. I sprinted up the concrete staircase, my feet slapping loudly with each panicked step, no thoughts but Kay, and what I'd do to Segur if anything had happened to her.

The door was ajar. Before I turned into the room I heard the cracking sound of splintering wood.

Segur was kicking his way into the bathroom. Stamping his way through the panelling to where Kay had locked herself. Before he saw me he had her by the hair, yanking her out like a rag doll, *his* rag doll. So intent on taking her back he didn't see me until I'd hit him, a running punch on the point of his cheekbone, the firecracker snap of bone on bone. He hit the wall and dropped. I got hold of Kay, pulled her from where he lay slumped against the dresser.

'You motherfucker,' he called me, halfway to getting back up, pushing himself off the wall. 'And you said my tackle was a cheap shot.'

'Fuck off, Segur,' I shouted. 'Get the fuck out of this room.'

'That's it, Chris,' screamed Kay. 'We're done. Over.'

Segur stood. A blood vessel had burst in his cheek, already a purple swell. 'But worse than a blindside punch has to be fucking a man's wife.'

'It was coming,' spat Kay. 'And you know it.'

Low and measured, as if without malice, Segur replied, 'You stupid bitch.'

I flipped. I went at him, throwing all my weight into a right cross. Perhaps I'd have dropped him again, but Kay screamed, 'No, Sam,' and yanked the sleeve of my T-shirt, stopping the punch short. Segur hit me hard and heavy. I might have gone down had Kay not been holding my arm. Blood filled my mouth, gritty bits of tooth. I spat the red mess in his face when he pulled back to strike again, flecking his hair and shirt collar.

'Son of a bitch,' he snapped, wiping his face.

When he came at me again Kay beat me to it. She had the lamp stand by the neck, stood on the foot of the bed and swung as if she were chopping wood.

The first strike glanced off Segur's shoulder, the second came down the side of his head, the corner of the base splitting his scalp. He raised his forearm and took the brunt of the third blow on his elbow. Seeing his midriff exposed I swung hard and low, direct on his diaphragm. Air rushed from his lungs and he groaned, crumpled, knocked the TV to the floor as he crashed to the ground.

Kay was still on the bed, the lamp stand raised, crying, 'You can't pay for a wife. Some fucking warranty that lasts a lifetime.'

Segur levered himself on to his elbows. Both of us stood over him, all three of us breathing hard, mammals baring tooth and claw, streaked and scored with blood.

'Damaged fucking goods.' Segur smirked. 'No money back when what you're buying is faulty.'

If he hadn't looked so down and out, hair dyed red by the welt on his skull, I'd have kicked his jaw clean off to stop him from talking. But I didn't.

'You thought you had a bargain, didn't you?' He smiled. 'But you should know that we're the ones who set the prices.'

'You have no idea,' I answered. 'None at all.'

'No sale, Sam.'

'What?'

Then he reached into his inside pocket. 'No customer, no sale.' And pulled out a gun.

I froze.

Kay struck his wrist as he fired. I swear I saw the bullet leave the muzzle. I definitely felt it graze the heel of my hand where I held my palm up as if I might halt the lead. Right then I could see the world more clearly than I'd ever done. The pistol flash. The smear of blood down Segur's cheek. A peel of flesh loosed from the base of my thumb like a strip of fabric. And the sounds: not the shot, but the bullet ricocheting off the ceiling and piercing the mattress top, the dropped gun thudding on the carpet, bouncing up. Segur and I threw our hands to grab it as if catching back a wriggling fish on the boards of a skiff. I grabbed it first. Not that Segur could have done anything if he'd beaten me to it, because Kay was finishing off her wood chopping, bringing that lamp stand down like the final axe strike on a stubborn log.

She struck him square on the top of the head. He sat up straight for a moment, as a child might ponder his toys scattered before his outstretched legs, and then slumped against the dresser.

'Is he dead?' screamed Kay. 'I didn't want to kill him.'

'He shot me.' I held up my left hand, the gouged flesh pulsing blood. In my right hand I had the gun.

And this is what the maid saw when she stood at the open door and screamed. And ran, ran from a man standing over another with a gun in his hand. A woman standing over the two of them with the posture of someone who'd just chopped down a tree.

'Chris?' said Kay, stepping down off the bed, grabbing his shoulder and shaking him. 'You stupid fuck.' She punched Segur in the chest. 'You're not dead, Chris. Snap out of it.'

And he did, rousing from the concussion, blinking at the woman who was legally his wife, the woman who'd nearly killed him.

'Let's go,' I said.

Kay stood very close to his face. I was more afraid of her kissing him than of Segur hurting her. And for a moment I think she thought about it. That close for so many years, a natural action of two mouths within touching distance.

Instead she looked hard into his pale blue eyes and said, 'I'm going now.'

And we did, Segur swearing something as we ran from the room and along the concrete veranda and down the staircase into the car park. I jumped into the car and started the engine, swung from the space and took one last look at the balcony where our room was, where Segur stood with his hands on the rail like a preacher in a pulpit.

I screeched off the forecourt as the concierge ran from the reception waving the unpaid bill. Along the sea front I had us up to nearly seventy before Kay told me to slow down. 'The cops will stop us before he does.'

And if they did? What would they make of a man and woman covered in blood? The gun on the seat between my legs, my ripped palm pulsing red over the steering wheel and on to the floor.

'Your hand,' said Kay. 'Look at it.'

I didn't want to. I didn't care at that point. I wanted us on a different planet from Segur, let alone in a different country.

'You'll bleed to death.' Kay took her skirt between her teeth and tore a strip from the hem. 'Here.'

I drove with my right hand and held up my left as she poured water from a drinks bottle over the raw wound before binding it with the improvised cotton dressing.

I nearly ran a red light because I was watching her tie the bandage. A woman and two children walked in front of the bonnet. The boy looked back and stared. Not until I pulled away and looked down did I see the splash of blood. Like a spilt glass of claret. 'I should change my shirt.'

Kay was staring out of the window shaking her head. 'This is all fucked up. I'm so sorry.'

I told her not to apologize for him. 'We can do this,' I said, reaching across and touching her hand. 'Can you get a clean shirt from my bag?' She did, and like the tea makers at a wake she was glad of the task, slipping my old shirt over my head while I briefly steered with my knees, too afraid to stop for even a second in case Segur had got down the stairs in time to see what direction we'd taken. Not that it wasn't obvious, south Texas and a few hours from the border, a highway that forked both ways to Mexico.

'You should change, too,' I said, seeing my blood on her sleeves, her jeans.

'Shit,' she said, looking down. 'All I grabbed was that fancy new outfit.'

She yanked down her jeans, ripped off her bloody T-shirt, bunched it in her hand and threw it out of the window.

Then she pulled on her white dress.

ONCE OUT OF CORPUS Christi I opened up the car. Too much. I thought we were on an empty road, nothing but sun glimmer and two runaways.

'Damn it.' Kay saw the beacon in the mirror. 'A cop.'

Before I answered my own thought about speeding off, Kay did it for me. 'Don't do it. Just be calm, play it out.'

I pulled over. Kay checked the seats for blood, made sure my shirt was zipped up in the bag.

'Okay?' I asked.

'Shit,' she said. 'The gun.'

It was in the door well.

'Under the seat,' she said. I slipped it beneath me as the red and blue lights flashed in the mirrors.

'Be polite, call him sir.'

I watched the cruiser draw up to my bumper. The officer wore sunglasses and a wide-brimmed hat and stepped from his car with his hand firmly on the butt of his gun. I put the window down when he signalled me to do so.

'You know why I pulled you over?'

'Sorry, sir,' I apologized, noting the gleam of his golden badge. 'Was I speeding?'

He smirked, put his other hand on his hip. 'I had to look twice. You know how fast you were going?'

'I didn't realize.'

'Ninety-seven.'

'I had no idea,' I said, simply relieved that I'd been pulled over for a traffic offence.

'Can I see your licence?'

Relieved until he saw my bandaged hand opening my wallet.

'How did you hurt your hand there?'

'Oh, this.' I looked at the cloth. A raspberry stain of blood seeped through the material. 'I caught my hand on the rail adjusting the seat. Just pinched the skin a little.'

'That so.' The policeman had crouched down now and looked across to Kay. 'You folks a long way from home?'

'I'm English.'

'I live in New York.'

'Y'all visiting family?'

'A driving holiday,' I answered. 'No landscape like this in England.' My accent was becoming more pronounced, posher. 'I think I was speeding because I couldn't keep my eyes from this stunning country. We just don't get highways as long and straight as this on our little island.'

He liked that, the gum-chewing policeman. 'I bet you don't.' He took my licence. 'Can I see your passport, too?'

'Sure.' I handed him the burgundy book.

'Let's just check this out.'

He ambled back to the patrol car. We both watched him in the rear view mirror, thumbing through the pages, talking on the radio.

'If something has already been reported,' said Kay, 'Chris making up some bullshit story, then all we have to do is tell the truth, simple.'

'We're not running from a crime, though. We're running from him.'

The officer walked back to my window, his hand on his gun.

'Okay?' I smiled.

'Well the speeding's not okay. Twenty-five or more over the limit and I can arrest you.'

My stomach fluttered.

'But I'm being nice as you're not from round here.'

'Thank you,' I said, trying not to look too relaxed.

'These highways ain't no race track. If you want to take a look around you're best doing that at a slower speed.'

I agreed, ingratiating to the point where I was making myself cringe.

'Y'all drive careful now.' He handed back my documents, then stood and turned to watch another car approaching, slowing. 'I bet he wasn't driving as leisurely as that a mile back.'

All three of us saw the same face. Blood-caked hair, a swollen, ballooned eye staring down all three of us. And when the car had passed the image hung before me like a Halloween mask.

The policeman paused for a moment, considered what had just driven by. 'Unless that man was born this morning, that ain't no birthmark.' He jogged back to the patrol car, his gun and cuffs jiggling, then jumped in and pulled on to the highway, lights flashing. Within seconds I was wheel-spinning a U-turn and driving back towards Corpus Christi.

'You saw him too?' asked Kay.

'I could hardly miss him.'

'What are you doing, Sam?'

'Fuck this,' I said, flooring the accelerator. At the next junction I swung a right.

'These little roads go nowhere.'

'I'm not playing his game.'

I raced down a dirt track. Fields bounced in the windshield. The way the dust cloud trailed the churning wheels it looked as if the car were on fire.

Kay, knuckles white, held the door handle to stop her head from hitting the roof. 'Easy, Sam.'

I had the accelerator pressed so hard that I could feel the pedal bend beneath my foot. I swung us over crossroads, cut corners behind signposts to farmsteads and ranches.

But no one had followed, and there was no need to thrash the engine so I slowed, driving back roads between irrigation ditches and lonely farmhouses, barns filled with bales of golden hay.

'I'll get back on the highway once we've gone past that speedtrap.'

'Then what?' asked Kay. 'Back to Corpus?' There was a wobble to her voice.

'Or drive until Chris pulls us over?'

Kay twisted to see we weren't being followed. 'We should throw that gun out of the window,' she said. 'Get rid of the damn thing. Pass it here.'

Part of me wanted to keep it. I felt safer having it under the seat, at hand, should I again cross paths with a man intent on ending my life. But I reached down and grabbed the barrel when she asked. Kay took it from me and said, 'What the fuck?' then put down the window and tossed it with a splash into an irrigation ditch.

'And we should leave this car somewhere, too.'

I agreed. 'Not here.'

'Just park up in the city.'

'And then what?'

Kay was shaking her head, looking across that hammered landscape, flattened of everything but the sun and the sky. 'Get a bus to Brownsville instead of driving to Laredo, walk into Mexico from there.' She wiped her eyes. 'Or double bluff him and carry on to Laredo.'

I told her not to cry. 'Hey, we should be happy that we're alive.'

'If you'd never met me, you wouldn't be in the middle of nowhere, a fucked-up engagement, your hand split open, being chased by a man who wants to kill you.'

She was right about it all. But I told her it meant nothing because she was there, right next to me. The word happy was hardly appropriate, so I said, 'I'd forgotten what being alive was actually like.'

'Till you got shot?'

'If you hadn't hit his arm that bullet was going into my chest.'

We sat holding each other for some time. Kay cried into my chest softly. I gritted my teeth to clench my own tears. Through the windscreen I watched specks of birds wheel on that great sky, black birds like flakes of ash riding the heat of the fire that bore them. I watched the mirrors, too. Holding Kay tighter each time a car approached, thinking of how quickly I could pull away if Segur appeared. We stayed like that longer than we should have. If he'd doubled back it was an obvious side road to take, but we were both drained from the morning, the jilted husband with a gun at our door. A part of me wanted him to drive up right now, put a single bullet through both our hearts so that there would be nothing to break us in two, nothing for him to take, or for me to lose.

Kay or Jenni.

A part of me had blocked Jenni from my thoughts. Only when I paused did I recall that I had a life, a fiancée, a good job, cats and a house. It all seemed so removed from where we sat clutching one another, even the sun looked small in the vast blue. I scanned the misshapen horizon for cars, for him. In the bleached distance a red tractor laboured across a colourless field. A red tractor like a toy I'd once had and lost. A toy given to me by my mother for being good when my sister was born.

I pulled my phone from my pocket, put my thumb to the power button but didn't press it.

When Kay lifted herself from my chest to kiss me, when she grabbed the back of my head so hard it hurt, I dropped the phone back in my pocket.

'We should get rid of the car,' she said. 'Get a ticket out of here.'

I criss-crossed those dusty farm roads back towards Corpus Christi. When we saw the downtown towers I turned back on to the highway.

'If we can't get a bus tonight, that means we have to stay here,' said Kay, nervously checking the mirrors.

'It's not a big enough town for that.'

She knew what I meant. It wouldn't take much to track us down to one of the motels.

'What are the options?'

I pulled over to the side of the road. Trucks buffeted and rocked the car as they whooshed past. A trailer filled with cattle, and then four piston-thumping Harley-Davidsons thrummed by before I said, 'Fuck it,' and swung back on to the highway.

Neither of us wanted to sit out the night waiting for a door to be kicked in.

TWO BLOCKS FROM THE bus station I parked the car at the back of a shopping mall and waited while Kay went into the pharmacy. I argued that I should be going with her but she pointed out that the blood had seeped through the cloth and stained my shoes.

When I thought about Jenni again it seemed I was imagining a life I'd never lived. That world was so disconnected from the visceral circumstance of sitting in a hire car with a gouged palm. And I was too distracted by the fear that Kay was out of my sight to focus on anything beyond a mesh fence in a car lot, only lifting the bandage from my hand to see the streak mark of a bullet meant to kill. I wanted to call Jenni, say something. But even my phone seemed an alien piece of technology, unnecessary when I could lean across and kiss the woman I needed.

Jenni would soon be wounded, too. I dared to think that much.

Then Kay came back and tenderly unwrapped the stained piece of hem, already sticking on the exposed flesh, before blotting the caked blood away with an antiseptic wipe. She smiled, for the first time since that morning. 'Now it's my turn to play nurse, return the favour.'

'How long ago does that seem?'

'Last week. Or about ten years ago.' She kissed my cheek. 'Tomorrow.'

She picked bits of thread from the wound, then bound my hand. A mother tending her son, nurse and soldier. She tore off a strip of tape and fixed the bandage. I inspected her work, the neat dressing.

'All good?'

'I'll live.'

'Maybe,' she said sarcastically. 'If riding a Greyhound bus doesn't kill you.'

I locked the car, took the half-full holdall, lighter by the clothes we'd left in the motel room, and walked the two blocks to the station. I carried the bag in my good hand and rested my damaged one over Kay's shoulder.

Inside the terminus a rackety standing fan swung across the waiting room. The caged blades whirred in the corner of the hall beneath a mounted TV playing an episode of *The Simpsons*. Kay looked up at the departures board and saw that we had an hour to wait. I turned and studied the other passengers sitting in plastic bucket seats or flopped over cases on the floor. Families beside homeless and drug addicts. Clinically obese with walking frames. A woman wheeling her own breathing apparatus. This America riding the buses, the poor and the damned, without healthcare or a car. All watched over by a skinny security guard who stood nearly seven feet tall and swooped on a young black man taking sips from a bottle of malt liquor pulled from his jacket.

'Outside. How many times I have to tell you.'

The guard had him by his collar and picked him from the floor as if he were laundry.

I studied the indifference of the waiting passengers, those who'd just come in to watch the TV and feel the waft of the fan. The security guard came back through the door and stood tall at the entrance, scanning the hall for another body to throw out.

'We should wait somewhere else,' I suggested. 'A station is an obvious spot.'

'I guess so. But I doubt he's ever been on a Greyhound. The thought of a bus wouldn't even cross his mind.'

We were the only souls venturing the sidewalk, and so conspicuous that a black and white patrol car slowed and the officer took a good look at our faces before driving on.

'What would Chris say to that highway cop?' I asked. 'Make up some bullshit story to get us picked up?'

Kay bit her lip, looked worried. 'He likes to do things himself.'

'Two, three hours and we're gone.' I pulled her closer, kissed that scarred eyebrow, her cheek.

We went into an old-fashioned diner presided over by a pot-bellied man with tattooed forearms and a dirty apron who couldn't fathom what I was saying when I asked for water.

'What kinda speaking is that?'

I told him I was from England.

'Welcome to Texas.' He shook my hand. 'Helluva way from home.'

I eventually communicated my order, slid next to Kay. Around the diner men slouched and napped in chairs with local papers and books on military history. One man dozed with a dog-eared *True Tales of the American West* splayed across his lap.

Then over coffee at a Formica table, on a cracked leather booth seat, Kay quietly cried and nothing I could say or do consoled her until she suddenly grabbed a napkin, wiped her nose, and said, 'What the fuck am I crying for?'

I was still shaking from the fight, the highway cop and Segur. But when she said this I calmed, saw my hand was steady on the cup.

She reached up and grabbed my chin, smiled and joked, 'We're immortal, didn't you know that?'

There and then, in that tatty diner, a bag of luggage between us, two tickets to Laredo in my wallet, Kay in my arms, I nearly believed we were.

WE WALKED BACK TO the terminal, thankful to see the bus to Laredo idling in the bay. I looked about for Segur. So did Kay. Then we stepped aboard, joined Mexican and American passengers, a young serviceman in his desert fatigues, and a string-thin woman in her fifties who had no luggage but a plastic bag which she'd occasionally vomit into.

'Shit,' said Kay, standing up and giving the woman her bottle of water. When she sat back down next to me she said, 'There's a life I could've lived.'

The Greyhound pulled from the station. Ten minutes out of town we overtook two white deportation buses. Mothers with babies. Men sleeping with caps pulled over their faces. I looked carefully as we went past, as if for some reason I might recognize someone, feeling the odd sensation that I might see another version of me on another bus.

To the south thudded a Border Patrol helicopter. A mosquito outline harrying God knows who across the shimmering sand.

Kay leant against my jacket, wadded between the tinted window and the seat. I was afraid when she slept, left alone with my thoughts. When she woke with a jolt she told me about her dream. 'Well, it was something that actually happened in San Francisco, this Cuban guy I knew, a dealer.'

She rubbed her eyes, looked at the other passengers. 'I was right there when a guy walked up and shot him in the side of the head. On the street. His skull came away in pieces.'

I asked what she did.

'I ran the other way.'

'Was that the dream?'

Kay looked from the bus window to the scruffy outskirts of Laredo, gas stations and wrecking yards, hangar-sized warehouses. 'But it was Chris.'

I put my hand behind her neck, rubbed her shoulders. 'Just a dream. It was bound to be a bad one after this morning.'

'I know, I know,' she said. 'And this,' she added, meaning the two of us with nothing but each other, 'this is more than that.' She kissed me, held the back of my head with both hands. 'The closest I've come to this sensation, this buzz, was kicking heroin. Suddenly you can smell flowers and grass. See colours and taste your food. Feel again.'

I looked down the aisle out of the bus windscreen. I could see office buildings, hotels and a casino. And across the Rio Grande the biggest flag I've ever laid eyes on, the red, white and green totem of Mexico, strung from a pole taller than any building on the horizon.

THE SUN HAD NEARLY set by the time we arrived in Laredo. Yet the blue sky held the light, a royal blue. Even the most mundane of buildings seemed to glow. A run-down bowling alley and a liquor store. The Sahara Inn, where we got off, deciding it was smarter to alight before the bus station.

'He either turned down to Brownsville,' I guessed, 'or gambled we were coming here. A fifty-fifty chance.'

'Would he really have driven here?' wondered Kay. 'And wait for us?'

I didn't reply. But thought I knew enough about him to decide that he was the kind of man who would.

I would have.

In the air-conditioned reception a polite Mexican concierge drew us a map to the border bridge, and then came to the door and pointed out the road we should take at the junction.

'Gracias, señor,' said Kay. 'Gracias.'

We walked round the hotel swimming pool, a palm tree oasis in the middle of the car park, before heading down the street and turning left at the bodega as instructed.

'We hardly need directions with that giant flag billowing.'

As we caught a glimpse of the rippling banner, a drunken tramp came staggering across the road, arms stretched out from a dirty overcoat, swinging stiffly like an Egyptian mummy sprung from a tomb. I stepped in front of Kay and he stopped just short of her. Filthy-bearded, chest naked beneath the overcoat, the man held out his hands. He looked as though biblical revelations should howl from his mouth, verses from the Old Testament of pestilence and infanticide, adultery.

'Vamanos,' he shouted, casting his hand as if brushing us down the street. 'Vamanos, vamanos.'

He stumbled from the sidewalk. Cars and trucks honked. I told him to stay off the road and the man slowly backed away, still holding out his hands, repeating, 'Vamanos, vamanos, vamanos.'

We hurried, glancing around, nervous of every car that slowed or even stopped for a red light.

'Why's it so busy?' I asked Kay as we approached the city centre, crowds of Mexicans flooding from a huge mall on the approach to the border crossing.

'Day after Thanksgiving, biggest shopping day of the year.'

Families, fathers carrying bags, children carrying boxed toys, the women walking and talking with one another, trudged to the turnstile entrance of the International Bridge, a concrete and steel span that sailed high over the Rio Grande below.

'This is it,' said Kay, looking around, probably wondering if Segur had made it to Laredo or not.

We were in the line for tickets to cross. 'This isn't the customs, is it?'

'This is the toll. Mexican immigration is the other side.'

I studied the policeman and the two Homeland Security officials flanking him who stood by the turnstile talking among themselves and barely noticing who was passing from one country to another.

'I didn't think it would be as easy as this.'

'Knock on wood.'

I kissed her cheek, shuffled forward with the returning Mexican shoppers and bought two tickets to walk the bridge.

'Don't be nervous,' whispered Kay as we went past the armed officials at the gate.

'I am,' I answered, pushing through the clunking turnstile. 'But more of making all this worth it for you.'

And for me.

Kay gripped my good hand. We shuffled with the crowds, hemmed in by the eight-foot mesh railing designed to stop anyone, illegal immigrants, betrothed men accompanying wives running from husbands, changing their minds and diving into the river. Cars on the road were gridlocked, radios pumping, children fighting in back seats. I saw no other white people until the Mexican customs gate.

'No,' said Kay, pulling me back. '*No.*'

He was standing beside a Mexican official wearing a uniform with tassels on the shoulder.

Segur.

We could see his bandaged head beneath the cowboy hat. And he could see us, stopping, shunting the foot traffic behind us.

'Fuck.'

'He's slipped them some money.'

'We have to go back,' I said. 'Can we?'

Kay had already decided we could, tugging at my sleeve, pulling us both against the returning shoppers and knocking into bags as we barged along.

I turned and saw Segur wading through the crowds as a man might charge up a flooded river.

'He's coming.'

Confused faces parted as we hurried against the flow. At the turnstile Kay said to the gate official, 'We forgot his inhaler,' and without a question we were waved through, running once we were on the concourse and past the ticket desk.

Perhaps Segur didn't have his excuse ready, because when I looked back again he was arguing with the cop, pointing past the turnstile.

'Bastard,' screamed Kay, taking us down to a parking lot beneath the bridge.

'This isn't good,' I warned her, noting the lack of people around. 'We should have stayed up there.'

'Fuck that,' cursed Kay. 'Fuck *him*.'

She pulled me from the lot to the park that ran along the river front. A white Border Patrol jeep was parked facing Mexico. On the opposite bank boys swung from tree branches and splashed down into the swift waters below, to be carried by the current before swimming back to the bank. The braver ones taunted the Border Patrol by swimming out to the middle and waving.

'Keep walking,' said Kay, looking to see if he was still coming.

'He's on the stairs.' I could see his hat descending to the lot we'd just cut across.

'Crazy fuck.'

'We should stay around the Border agents,' I suggested. 'He won't try anything here.'

Kay shook her head. 'You saw him back there. He's gone.'

Maybe she was right. I couldn't convince her otherwise. I was hardly going to let her go while I waited for Segur and reasoned with him, talked calm into a man who'd already fired a gun at my chest.

263

We hurried on, past Mexican families having picnics, past another Border Patrol watching the river. From the park we passed into a neighbourhood where stray dogs wandered the streets and broken fences cordoned each yard from the other. Yards where women hung washing and men sat drinking cans of beer while enjoying the spectacular sunset.

'Buenas tardes,' I nodded, trying to look less like a fleeing couple than we were. When no cars came we ran, when we saw people we walked.

Kay was breathless. 'We must have made some distance on him.'

We both looked back down the block.

'I can't see him,' said Kay. 'Can you?'

'I don't think so.' Maybe he was at the end of the street. I couldn't see clearly in the haze of dusk.

'Up here.' Kay pointed. 'We'll get back to the main road and jump in a taxi.'

We followed the road across a rail track. Into another neighbourhood that was as ramshackle as the last one.

'Is this road going anywhere?' I asked.

'Shit.'

We stopped by a row of houses, built against spiked iron railings that had been bent and twisted to be climbed. Before one of the neater homes sat a man in a fold-out chair reading a copy of *Newsweek*. He saw us and stared.

'Hey there,' said Kay, glancing back to see if Segur was about before turning to the man. 'We were hoping that we could walk along the river.'

The man shut his magazine and stood. 'I only just moved here myself. But I know this fence cordons off a kind of buffer zone. Not that it stops the Mexicans.'

'They come across here?'

'Pass through my yard like coyotes every night.' He gestured to the back of his house. 'And I've only been here a week.'

I looked to the fence, saw a section where a railing had been torn out. Then I looked back to the corner and saw Segur walking towards us. Calmly. A figment of nightmare come true. When Kay saw him, too, she thanked the man and without speaking we made the same decision.

'Hey,' he shouted as we ran through his yard. 'That's trespassing.'

We could see tall grass beyond the iron railings. We slipped between the bars like children skipping school. Kay snagged her top. We followed a worn dirt path littered with burrito wrappers and soda cans, plastic bottles.

When we came upon two men dripping wet and drying themselves off with a rag of material they scattered like rabbits.

'They must have just got here.'

Then she pulled me along, smashing through the dry and brittle reed stems towards the river.

She was the woman in the wood from my dream, running.

THE BULB GLOWED FAINTLY, protected by a steel grille. A cockroach worked its way across the concrete, pausing in the strips of light that beamed through the wire. I was curled on the bloodstained floor of a prison cell.

Again, I heard a key in the lock, and stood up, presuming another questioning. The metal door swung a brighter light into the room. Silhouetted, the comandante stepped past the young guard who that morning had slipped me a cigarette through the bars.

'I have no reason to keep you here.'

I stared at him, blinking.

'Do you have a reason to stay?'

'This room?' I gestured at the stone walls, the slop pail. 'Or Mexico?'

The comandante tipped his hat to study me. He'd been doing this for three days, again and again asking me about 'the woman'.

'I recommend you go home,' he said. 'And not through the US. They hang men in Texas.'

He shouted back to the corridor. Another guard walked in with my clothes, washed and folded, held out before him as if he were my footman.

'The blood didn't come out in the laundry.'

He watched as I set the clothes on the wooden bunk, and then stripped off the soiled and rank cotton shirt and prison issue trousers I'd been wearing since the second morning.

'Come,' he said once I'd changed back into my own outfit. I felt as much of a stranger in it as I did in the prison garb. 'You must sign for your money and credit cards, your watch and phone.'

I followed him through the corridor. In other cells I saw the Mexican men who'd been calling out to me since I was brought into the station, handcuffed on the banks of the Rio Grande.

DAY AND NIGHT, IN the dark of that cell, I'd seen nothing else. Kay had been running ahead of me towards the river, slashing at the reedy grass with her hands. She fell at speed, sprawled and crumpled in the dirt. I dragged her up and pushed her on, desperate, every thudding second expecting the bullet in my back.

When we got to the bank I shouted, 'Swim.' She threw off her shoes and dived. I looked down at my laces, then looked back along the path.

'Jump, Sam.'

I did. Shoes on. Because he came thrashing through the grass, pistol in hand.

It was the way he calmly took aim that was so terrifying. Like a man at a shooting range.

THE COMANDANTE WALKED AHEAD. A guard held my elbow, firm and guiding, as if I might fall if he let go. 'I apologize for your lack of exercise,' said the comandante over his shoulder. 'Now you can see why you were kept separate from the others.'

In an open cell where men were caged like exhibits at a zoo, one man with spider web tattoos wrapped round his upper body mimed slitting my throat by drawing a finger across his own.

'And he would,' said the comandante, leading us from the dim corridor of cells into an office behind the front desk where relatives of the interned waited with bundles of food. He gestured for me to sit, and the guard set me down and stepped back. Then the comandante took a Ziploc bag from his bureau and asked me to check my wallet.

'It's okay,' I said.

'Please. Check.'

I opened it up. The bills were still damp from the river crossing.

'All there?'

I nodded and picked up my mobile.

'It doesn't work,' said the comandante. 'The river got inside it.'

I slipped it into my pocket.

'Your signature.'

The form was typed in Spanish, and I tried to read it to make sure I wasn't signing a confession.

'Sabes leer Español?' asked the comandante.

I shook my head.

'It's simply an inventory.'

I scored my name across the dotted line shakily, a moniker with no meaning to me whatsoever. Then I slid back the wooden chair and stood. 'I can go?'

He nodded. 'But sit for a moment.'

I hesitated, then again took the wooden chair before his desk.

'I assured them you'd be released by noon.'

I was puzzled. 'Assured whom?'

'Your benefactor, of course. They will be waiting.'

I felt my palms sweating on the arm of the chair. 'I tell you now,' I snapped. 'If he's waiting with a gun you'll have a murder on your hands. Either his or mine.'

The comandante tutted, shook his head. 'No, señor. You're mistaken. Not a man. An Englishwoman.'

My skin prickled.

'I only heard her on the telephone, but what I learned from her voice was that, yes, perhaps she's angry with you, though I doubt she will kill you.'

The door bumped open and a young officer backed in carrying a pot of tea and two cups on a metal tray.

'She has made the necessary, how shall we call it, arrangement for your release.'

Jenni? A bribe? 'I don't believe you,' I said. 'She doesn't even know I'm in Mexico.'

273

The comandante checked his watch. 'She will be landing in Monterrey.' He studied the ticking hands. 'About now. And I agreed you'd be at the bus station by nightfall.'

The officer set the tray down on the desk, and the comandante lifted the teapot lid and regarded the steaming contents. Then he looked up. 'First an American man enquiring about your health. Then an official from the British consulate returning my call, and finally a woman from London.' He put a spoonful of sugar into his empty cup. 'You lose one woman in a river, and then another comes to your rescue. I wonder if her line of questioning will be more successful than mine?'

Jenni. What did she know? And did she have any idea why her fiancé was suddenly behind bars in Mexico?

'Señor, when I first asked you about the women, you corrected my English. "Woman", you said. "Women" is the plural. And then you said nothing else. Now, I believe my grammatical error was actually correct, no?' The comandante sat back in his leather chair, briefly checked his computer screen and nodded with satisfaction. 'Muy bien.' Then he looked at me again. 'And I doubt this woman waiting for you will take silence for an answer.'

He was right. She wouldn't.

'But, well, you have no reason to talk to me now. Perhaps you should save your explanations for her.' The comandante poured tea from his pot and offered me a cup. 'You English like milk, yes?'

I declined, asked if I was free to leave. The comandante shrugged and blew on his black tea, sipped, then set down the cup with a clink.

'I'm not sure you're listening so well, but try.'

My mind, after days of nothing but four walls and thoughts of Kay, suddenly had to cope with the fact of facing Jenni, explanations.

'The first arrangement for your release was in US dollars. And considerably more than the English pounds transferred this morning.'

I clenched my fists beneath the table.

'However, the woman on the phone, seemed, well, the deserving party. Something in the sound of her voice. Her plea.'

Segur had tried to buy my flesh and blood. The comandante explained that a man interested in my welfare had volunteered to pay bail. And while the comandante considered the correct legalities, as he phrased it, Segur sat in a cantina across the road from the police station. When he slept or used the lavatory, men he'd hired from one of the local cartels kept watch for him, and only when the comandante threw his weight around and sent Segur back to the US was it safe for me to be released.

Because Jenni had begged for my life.

'This job,' said the comandante. 'This uniform. This unseemly business of murder, bribes. Funerals. It can stop a heart dead. But your Englishwoman, she . . . what's the word. Yes, revive. She revived my dead heart.'

He raised his cup, then decided what he had to say was more important than the drink and set it back down on the saucer. 'But you, señor. You still have murder in your heart.'

He was right. Segur had died a thousand times in my bare hands. His death, his last breath, was all I had left apart from my grief.

After dismissing the officer from the room, the comandante sipped at his tea. I studied his round face and thin lips, perfectly groomed fingernails, the silver Rolex.

'Listen.' He put down the cup. 'A few years ago this town was like Iraq. Not that it's a resort town now, and certainly no place for your Englishwoman. But then cartels battled in the streets with bazookas and grenades. A police chief was killed. Seven hours after the welcome ceremony for his replacement, he was killed, too. I knew this man most of my life. The evening before he was gunned down I went to a party at his house, played soccer in the yard with his sons. The next day we lay him in the ground. A mother watches her son into the earth. When I pay my respects to her at the wake, I promise vengeance, that the men who murdered her boy would be cut down. She said to me, "And bloody your memory of Raul? So instead of remembering him with the good food his wife cooked and the company of his children, his friendship, you have more dead men?"'

Again, in a slightly effeminate gesture, he filled his cup before continuing. 'In the movies, when the wronged man seeks out the destroyer of his dreams, we call him our hero. In his revenge we have justice. And this is Hollywood, you might think. But in Mexico we know the difference between the real world and the movies. Not that we think the movie is false, just that we know life is a show, too. A wronged man here must act, play the part of the avenger or leave the story. So the crime of passion is a show, yes, but the show is all there is.'

'You didn't want me to kill someone in your town.'

The comandante muttered something in Spanish, tutted. 'Neither did I want someone to kill you in my town.'

'Who would want to do that?' I asked, not wanting to tell what I knew, fearful of subterfuge if Segur and the comandante had been talking.

'Please, señor. A man is seen firing shots across the Rio Grande. Men only fire guns at each other if money . . .' he paused to finish his tea, 'or a woman is involved.'

'Can I go now?'

'You can. Not that I'm looking for thank yous, but you should know it's only safe for you to venture beyond these walls with my permission. Because under this uniform is a beating heart.'

Jenni. All I'd done to her and she'd come to my rescue. I was crushed by the thought of what she must be feeling.

'My last question. Not that I expect you to answer this one either, but still.' The comandante leant forward in his seat and looked hard into my eyes. 'Certainly a man can be destroyed by the love of a woman, of this much I'm sure. But do you really believe a man can be saved by this love?'

The ceiling fan whirred, a lost propeller come free of its wings. On the wall above his desk hung a map of Mexico. Beyond the northern borderline the US was a blank country without names of towns or states.

'Yes,' I answered, because it was all that remained of who I was. 'I have to.'

The comandante sighed. 'The memory of this love? Or what you hope is waiting?'

I didn't know, and while wondering if I could survive both without being torn apart I stood to leave without asking for permission.

The comandante nodded to himself, stared into his empty cup and pointed to the young officer who opened the door. He asked if I needed an escort to show me to the bus station, but I said I'd rather find it myself. And with a wave of his hand the comandante gestured for me to go. Before I did he casually remarked, 'Two dozen witnesses saw her drift under the International Bridge.'

I froze. 'It was dark. How could they see anything?'

'She wore a white dress.'

Right then, I saw her. Floating in the room.

'They say it was glowing.'

Then I turned and walked from the office. Another policeman lifted the counter so I could pass through the crowded reception area and out of the doors, into the Nuevo Laredo sunshine, bewildered.

For a few minutes I waited on the steps, somehow expecting Kay to walk over and collect me from jail, simply pull up in an open-topped sports car and hit the horn.

Or Jenni.

But no one was there to greet my freedom. My shame. I drifted busy streets, with no more idea of what day of the week it was than what year. Children saw me and begged, others hawked necklaces, candy. I asked a man at a news-stand for directions to the bus station. He pointed in a general easterly direction, then saw my bloodstained shirt and focused back on his till.

'This world,' I said to him.

He looked up. 'Qué?'

I opened my empty hands to the road, the busy sidewalk. 'Unless you have someone.'

He waved me away, spat on the paving stone before my feet.

I tried my phone again. No life. I walked. I couldn't remember when I stopped walking, but I must have done because I was curled in a doorway and only knew I was when I caught a boy of no more than eleven or twelve trying to steal the watch from my wrist.

On the edge of a plaza, where old men sat and played chess, miniature birds swooped and dipped, snatching insects from the morning air.

Swallows, not hummingbirds.

For three days in a stone room I'd thought of nothing but her. Nothing. The first morning they stripped me, the comandante had looked at my naked body and asked, 'Who was the man firing the gun at? You, or the woman?'

I had no answer.

'You were with a woman,' he would state. 'Where is she?'

'Why the fuck do you keep asking? I screamed. 'What does it matter now?'

I sat handcuffed to his chair and thought they might torture me. I couldn't imagine what they could do that would be any more painful than being alive.

And what could I have told him that would make sense? That a man from England had left his loving fiancée to come to the US to see another woman. A woman he took from another man. A woman he talked into running from her life. Though she'd say I'd run from my life to hers. That wasn't a lie. I had.

'Why would two people swim from the US to Mexico?'

I shook my head again. For the first two days I was catatonic, unable to produce a sound. And if I could, would I have told him how we ran through the reeds like the figures from my dream, how we dived into the Rio Grande?

'I love you,' is what Segur had shouted from the riverbank. '*I love you*.' Then I heard the shots, the flat reports. I screamed at Kay to swim, then goaded Segur to shoot at me.

He didn't. He stood very still and aimed at Kay, the white muzzle flashing. I tried to swim between him and her but the current had pushed her ahead. Fountained water from the bullets that missed sprayed about her, until the flesh and bone thud of lead striking her body, the last shot he fired.

She was struggling to stay afloat when I grabbed hold of her.

'Nearly there,' I kept saying to her. 'Nearly there.'

I kicked hard and didn't look back, my arm hooked under her shoulders. 'It's okay,' I told her, 'it's okay.'

Carrying Kay, swimming in a pair of shoes, I fought the river to keep us afloat. After finding my feet on a sandbank, I pulled her through a stand of reeds on to the shore. Her legs loose. Her head heavy in my arms. She coughed, and blood seeped from the corner of her mouth. I laid her on the ground, and when she asked if we were in Mexico I told her not to speak.

'We made it,' she said. 'We're here.'

She lifted her head to kiss me. I tasted the blood on her lips. 'I have to see how bad it is,' I told her. 'I need to turn you over.'

I rolled her on to her side. There was a small rip in her dress beneath her left shoulder blade. She coughed again. The sound of something awry in her lungs. I tore the dress open and inspected the puncture, a neat, dark hole. I was sure she'd be okay, that the wound was too small to kill. Then I eased her on to her side and saw the blood. A red flow spreading. I could hear traffic on the road above the tree line. 'I'm going to run and get help,' I told her, cupping her head.

'Stay,' she said. 'You stay here now. With me.'

WHEN I LOOKED BACK to the plaza, saw the men still playing chess, the birds in the trees, I noticed that I'd been holding a stone so hard I'd opened up the cut in my palm. I let it fall, bloodied, into the gutter.

Then I stood again and walked. If Jenni had arranged with the comandante that I get on the bus to Monterrey, then that was what I must do. All I could do. I thought of going down to the river, as if Kay would be sitting on the bank, waiting.

I could see her flashing smile, that bright flaw in the dark of her iris.

As I walked I passed people who looked at my face in such a way that I wondered what they must see for such a crease of sorrow to suddenly appear on theirs.

Finally I found the terminal and bought a ticket. I wandered the concourse with the stub in my hand until a gaudy red and green contraption pulled into the bay. The young guard from the police station, who must have been following me from the moment I stepped on to the street, gave me his pack of cigarettes and gestured for me to board. He spoke softly and gravely to me in Spanish, then walked away. I let the women on first then stepped up. I took a bench seat, my only thought apart from Kay's face that I was about to ride a converted US school bus.

From the suburbs of Nuevo Laredo and on to highways skimming farmland and mountain ranges and villages I didn't know the name of and never would. Villages where women swept dust from their steps and boys kicked footballs across dirt pitches.

I sat and stared at the space beside me. It seemed an impossible illusion that Kay wasn't with me.

Then, as if my brain forced me to sleep to protect itself from my thoughts, I dozed, fluttering in and out of consciousness. Woken by jarring potholes and blaring near misses with oncoming rigs, I once reached over to check that she wasn't there.

An hour or so later the bus swung into a garage, a rest stop. Children offered peanuts and sweets as I stepped down to the forecourt. I walked to the toilet block watching the sky, wisps of cotton on the vault of blue.

I pissed dark yellow. Something was wrong. But what ailed my body seemed irrelevant to my life.

Turning from the filthy pan I noticed a rat sitting in one of the urinals. A tall, brown rat. Watching me walk back out to the sunlit gas station.

Foil bunting rippled from the fence. I thought I should drink something and stood in line with a truckload of Mexican soldiers who bought plastic bags of Fanta which had been decanted from the glass bottles by the stall holder. I sucked up two bags through a straw.

The bus sounded the horn. The passengers headed back to the same seats that they'd arrived here on, myself included, again sliding along the bench to stare from the window at the soldiers clambering aboard their truck, the barefoot children making last attempts to sell their sweets and nuts.

A few miles on the bus shuddered to another halt by a field of maize. And when three policemen boarded in bright baize uniforms, I had no fear. I knew the police robbed tourists in northern Mexico, took watches and money from foreigners. But what could they take from me that I hadn't already lost?

Armed with automatic weapons they nodded to the driver and slowly walked the aisle. None of the passengers caught their eyes. A baby-faced cadet with the fluff of a first moustache and an Uzi with a butt extension took the seat beside me. I shuffled over. The boy immediately fell asleep with his head rocked back and mouth open. The gun was aimed at my gut.

And the boy had fallen asleep with his hand on the trigger. When I saw that the safety was off I stared at the dark hole of the muzzle as if looking into the black heart of a dying star, waiting to be taken with the light.

But an old man with tobacco-stained hands and a beaten fedora saw the gun and carefully nudged the cadet.

The boy looked at me. Then he looked at the safety and flicked it on with his thumb and slept again.

Dust hung above the highway. Fields and fallen-down shacks of corrugated and rusting steel. A lizard scuttled along the window of the bus. What did it make of the rushing scene beyond the glass? What did it think when the bus stopped on a road absent of houses or people and the three policemen got out and waded into another field of maize?

I watched them as we pulled away. The empty seat.

Above a mountain range to the west, the bruised cloud gathered. Rain flashed in the setting sun. And I thought of Kay, what she said about a river floating a body out to sea.

'Am I in you?' she'd asked, on her back, the blood blooming through the front of her dress.

'Yes,' I'd answered. 'Yes.'

She'd smiled, lifted her head to kiss me, before her body went limp in my arms.

I sat holding her until the dusk burned itself out, until the world was more shadow than light. I kissed her lips till they went cold. Her cheeks and the ridges of her eyebrows. I ran my hands through her hair and brushed it from her face and spoke softly to her and told her that she couldn't leave me because I wanted to live with her in a house by the ocean where the wind sang in the palm trees and waves thudded the shore at night like a beating heart.

Then I said that I loved her and that the word was feeble against the depth of what I felt.

And before the men in uniform came down the bank, guns drawn, lights and sirens wailing, I pushed her into the river.

The white dress billowing around her, glowing.

IT WAS DARK WHEN the bus pulled into Monterrey. Shuttered shops and wide boulevards. Palm trees growing around streetlights, like clawed hands closing on a candle flame. Before we neared the manicured gardens of the lit suburbs the overcast night had pulled a starless blanket over the world. Only the driver, reflected on the windscreen in the glow of the speedo, or the flashes of passing car beams, was proof that he wasn't the ferryman taking us across the river to Hades.

Then the station, bright and busy, people shuttling through the terminal, families waving at departing relatives, welcoming loved ones. I was the last to file from the bus, watching the other passengers carry off bags, the last of the food they'd cooked for the journey. I had no luggage, no change of clothes for my bloodstained shirt.

Coming down from the steps on to the station concourse, stepping round a husband hugging and kissing his wife, I was hit so hard that new blood splashed upon the old.

'Y OU FUCKER,' SHE SAID, hitting me again. 'Fucker, fucker.' On the third blow I realized it was her. I never guessed that a fist striking my face could feel so vital.

'You stupid, stupid man.'

She only stopped hitting me when the Mexican husband who before had been holding his wife's hands now held hers.

'Please, señor,' he said to me.

WHEN I HUGGED JENNI she kept her arms by her side. Rigid and taut. But there and then, I was grateful for that much contact.

And we were a garish sideshow to the audience of the bus station. On the bright concourse, Jenni, immaculate as I'd ever seen her, and me, the dishevelled man, the dirty bandage on my hand, new blood leaking from a cut lip. Not one soul who set eyes on that scene didn't know that another woman was involved.

'Thank God you're here,' I remember saying. And 'Sorry', a hundred times. A thousand. And each utterance of the word as useless as the one before, the one after.

Before the station security guards came over and ushered us towards the exit, Jenni lifted her chin and walked away, with me following, the slinking dog. I asked her a banal question about how she got here, but she simply shook her head in disgust and strode ahead.

As we climbed into a taxi a beggar unwisely approached us with his hand out. Jenni cursed. 'One is enough,' she spat before I sat on the seat beside her.

S HE LOOKED OUT OF the taxi window, not at me. City lights shone through her hair and across her face, the first, gleaming, silent tears. When I reached out to put my hand on hers she snatched it away. 'Please don't touch me.'

So instead of another useless sorry I said, 'Thank you.'

'For what?' she said, darting a look at my eyes with a flash an anger that could either set fire to whatever was left of me, or rekindle it.

I told her she'd probably saved my life.

When the taxi slowed for red signals I was terrified of the silence. I had the sensation of shrinking, getting smaller and smaller on the wide leather seats, sitting beside a woman who suddenly seemed to tower over me.

'Just imagine,' she began, staring through the wind-screen at the traffic, 'for one second, for one split fucking second, that this had happened the other way round.'

I started a reply, but again she turned and blazed a look, shouting, 'I'm fucking talking right now. Not you. *Imagine*, I said. Imagine you're asleep in our bed while I'm, as far as you fucking know, rushed off my feet on some urgent project, when you're woken by a phone call at four o'clock in the morning, a serious and concerned man announcing that he's from the British Consulate in Mexico. Mexico? The last

288

thing I heard, well, read, in what turns out to be a lying gutless text, was that you were needed in New York for another week.'

Then she paused, seemed to fight the air for her breath, rapidly inhaling, exhaling. When I asked if she was okay, if she wanted me to open the window, she screamed again, 'Fucking imagine it. From when you actually loved me. Imagine that call. A voice on the phone in the dead of night telling you I was in prison in a country you had no idea I was going to.'

Before I even formed the word with my mouth she warned me not to apologize.

'Because the next man I get on the phone, this fucking comandante, is telling me that yes he could let you go, but that I should know another man had a vested interest in your release. He said the security arrangements would be an additional cost. A fucking bribe.'

Jenni had told the comandante where to go, that she'd be speaking to the British Embassy and that they'd pay him a visit. Before she hung up the comandante had subtly asked her if she knew about the 'other woman'.

'*Other fucking woman*. Oh, he had my attention then.'

The comandante, as he had done to me, spun her tales from the information he left out. The glowing dress, the reasons one man fires a gun at another. And that if he looked from the police station window he could see a man sitting across the road on his third coffee, the same man who'd already offered to pay for my release. Jenni didn't hang up the phone. Because she cared about me, because *she loved me*, she put aside the thoughts of why I was swimming across a river with a woman not her, paid the bribe, then flew out on the first flight she could get to make sure I really was safe.

'I'm ready to spend my life with you, my whole fucking life. Then this.'

And that was the full stop to all she wanted to say right then. Next she turned to the window and cried. The entire way back to the hotel the taxi driver and I listened to her sobbing. All I could do to punctuate her tears was say her name over and over.

I sat on the floor in the hotel room. Knees pulled to my chest, back against the wall. On the bed rested Jenni's suitcase, yet to be unpacked. She was standing at the window, looking out on the lights of Monterrey, a frame of black and neon.

'How,' she said, splitting the chrysalis of silence growing since we'd walked from the taxi and into the reception where she'd clinically booked me in with the concierge as if I were a visiting conference guest.

'How did I get here?'

Finally, when she turned from the city to the room, to me, I presumed she wanted me to tell her.

'Can you do it without lying?'

I told her I could and she shook her head. 'Bullshit.'

When I started talking about the wedding she said, 'Stop.' She was again looking at the Monterrey rooftops, the wavering lights. I was an unbearable sight. And not until she moved from the window to open her suitcase was I again physically present, tolerated in her space.

'Stupid fucking thing.'

Because the zip jammed I had a reason to stand up. For a few brief seconds, as I pulled out the strip of material snagged in the teeth, we occupied the present, together. Not the unbearable weight of the recent past, pressing so hard against the future it had broken it into pieces.

'You stink,' she said.

I did. Of river and prison. I suggested I should run a bath. She didn't answer. She just sat on the bed and twisted and untwisted an elasticated hair tie round her fingers.

I said, 'I do love you, you know.'

She shook her head again. Told me to wash.

In the bathroom I avoided the mirror, dared not look at myself. Every act took a monumental effort. Pushing in the plug, turning the taps. Taking off my tired and bloodied clothes. I sat on the toilet seat and rolled off my socks, unbuckled my trousers and let them fall when I stood up and removed my underwear.

Then I sat in the bath and cried. Felt my face contort like an inconsolable child's. I curled into a ball and put my head in my arms, eyes scrunched closed, and once more saw the red blood flower through the front of her dress, the fear behind her dying smile.

When the water went cold I sat up and realized Jenni had been watching me weep, sitting on the tiled floor against the door frame. And for the first time since hitting me at the bus station, *she looked at me*. With more pity than malice.

WITH A TOWEL WRAPPED round my waist I sat on the very corner of the bed and told her what she didn't want to hear, reciting the story backwards, from the bus to the prison. The river. Segur and a gun. And when Jenni wept for Kay, I did too.

She was lying on the bed, cold in the air-conditioning I couldn't work out how to adjust for her. Fully dressed under the covers. First crying into the pillow, then head back staring at the ceiling, blankly listening to me confess.

Soon she was demanding details. The trip to the Catskills, New York. When I got to that day in August she suddenly said, 'If the other woman weren't me, and I were just hearing about people I didn't know, I might be sympathetic. If that's the right word, the right feeling for two adulterers.' She paused and sat up on her elbows. 'But I'm the one who was supposed to be left behind.'

I said something nebulous about fate, that I was here in a room with her. Not Kay.

'Oh how fucking poetic. And if she'd made it across the river with you? Then what?'

Before I defended myself she said, 'Poor Kay.'

I stood from my corner of the bed and walked over to the window. My pale, nearly naked phantom reflected on the black glass, the city neon pulsing through my transparent flesh.

No comfort in the blue dawn. Craggy mountains emerged from a wash of pale sky in the hotel window, the jagged range touching sunrise hours before the plains. I'd tried again to sit with Jenni, to feel the warmth of another body. But she turned on to her side and tensed up, a back as hard as stone when I put my hand on her.

I looked out of the window, saw the mountaintops glow as if beacons had been lit on the barren peaks.

I dared not sleep. Fearful of whom I might dream, whether I'd wake from a world with Kay, conjured or not.

But Jenni slept, maybe an hour. Or she simply closed her eyes and could no longer hear what I was saying. Then she sat up and told me to get off the floor and dress. 'Fuck if I'm sitting in this room any longer.'

When I went to put on my tired, stained clothes, she threw a shirt from her case on to the bed. A pair of socks.

'Thank you,' I said, both of us knowing I was thanking her for a lot more than my clothes. I was thanking her for at least my freedom, and quite possibly my life. I asked her if she knew this.

'I know what you told me.' She was rifling through her case for something. 'But that and reality can be two very different things.'

I told her that she must believe me.

'Or what?'

'I have nothing left.'

She stopped looking for whatever she'd lost. When I said it might have been better if I'd died in the river, or been shot by Segur outside the prison, she called me a selfish cunt. 'If you think about killing yourself, and maybe you have, then you're a coward.'

I was stunned, had nothing to reply to her with. Because I had.

'And of all the names under the sun I could call you right now, I never believed I'd call you that.' She rummaged some more in her case before turning the whole thing upside down, emptying clothes, the detritus of make-up and toiletries. 'Are you?'

I shook my head. 'Not if I have something to be brave for. A reason.'

'Me?'

I answered yes.

A T SOME POINT IN the night I'd called her my rock. In response she'd said, 'Well every word you say is chipping part of me away.'

In an attempt to parry the blows of intensity, the telling of what had happened, we walked from the hotel room down to the breakfast area, both of us leaving plates of food untouched before stepping out of the hotel foyer and on to the streets of another country, one that neither of us had planned to be in until a few days ago.

'You should buy more clothes,' Jenni remarked flatly.

We caught a taxi to a huge shopping mall. 'I haven't told my parents I'm even here,' was the only thing she said on the short journey.

While I bought new clothes from a department store Jenni sat on the edge of a fountain, tossing in coins. I walked over, but she didn't even raise her head when I stood next to her, instead she just said, 'And what would you wish on a coin thrown into a fountain?'

On the way out we went past a row of call boxes and I said I needed to do something.

'Who?'

'Please listen,' I begged. 'No matter how hard it is to hear.'

With my phone broken, and Jenni's not connecting to a Mexican network, I bought an international dialling card from a kiosk and finally got the number of the Laredo police department. I told them what had happened, from Segur breaking into the motel room in Corpus Christi to the shooting. Whilst the sheriff I spoke to offered to investigate further, he would only confirm that a Mrs Kay Segur had been registered as a missing person on 29 November, and that until a body was found, or further witnesses came forward, there could be no formal case. He also questioned me, in some detail, as to my relationship with the missing woman. When I swore at him that she was dead, murdered, not simply missing, and that I'd just given him the name of her killer, the sheriff's tone became suspicious, asking me why I'd left the US illegally, why I was on the riverbank with her in the first place.

I slammed the phone down, furious, leaving him with the words that her murderer was walking free.

Jenni was sitting on the floor of the shopping centre, legs oddly askew.

And I realized Segur was as free as a man could be when he's responsible for the death of a woman who once loved him.

THERE WAS A PINK palace, old colonial buildings mirrored in the platinum glass of bold new statements of business centres and office blocks. I saw much of Monterrey in the reflections from Jenni's sunglasses. A grand plaza and another fountain. And always hovering above the city a peak called Saddle Mountain, an empty seat of rock waiting for a sky-sized rider.

When she went to the lavatory in a tourist information office I ate three Mexican doughnuts from a street stand, the first food I'd eaten in nearly two days.

Then we walked the wide avenues, drifted the city as if floating. Occasionally running aground in a park, on a slatted bench.

'I'm so beyond feeling anything, now.' She shook her head, looked to that scooped-out peak, the cable cars strung along its green slopes. 'Maybe guilt. Yes, guilt. Because I compete for your attention when you should be grieving.'

If the numbness of life against death is grieving, then yes, I was.

She smoothed her skirt, picked up a fallen leaf that twirled from a branch to her feet. 'And what, so your way of coping is wait twenty years, see another woman who sparks something, and then think by sleeping with her you can resurrect the dead.'

I didn't know what she meant.

'Really?' She took off her sunglasses. Her bloodshot, pale blue eyes. 'You have this mother-shaped hole in your universe, and for a while, when you were buying houses and cats, planning a wedding for God's sake, I thought I might have actually filled it.'

She folded her sunglasses. She said, 'Sam.'

Then she finally reached out and put her hand on mine.

J ENNI GOT ON A plane without me. After the touch in the park, almost a holy laying on of hands, she said she was going. Before the steps of a museum where huge wooden doors opened on to hallways lined with the silver breast-plates of conquistadors, she told me that she'd done all she could and that whatever happened next I had to bear alone.

'I can't stay here,' she said, gesturing at me, the sky. 'In this. I'm being overwhelmed. I thought I'd be stronger.'

I told her she'd saved my life.

She shook her head. 'You have to do that, not me.'

She was right.

We walked back, miles across town through an orange, powdery dusk hanging in the glowing streets. At times on that walk I thought I might not see the morning if she left that night. Then I thought about what she said about me being a coward. And I thought of her, living on should I die.

That evening Jenni packed her case and allowed me to carry it for her from the hotel to the taxi. 'Not the airport,' she'd said. 'Not that far.' Her eyes watering at the thought of me driving Kay to Heathrow, the crash which started a chain of events that led from a wedding in the Cotswolds to a hotel foyer in Monterrey, the woman I'd proposed to flying home without me.

Then she was a face in a car window.

Like a stranger's face on a painting carried from a house.

I returned to the empty hotel room, picked up the spare clothes I'd bought from the department store, put them in a plastic bag and checked out. Half a life on from wandering the streets as a teenager, here I was again. Watched by a mountain shaped like a saddle.

On a map in the station I saw a coastline, and took a bus to Veracruz for no better reason than that it was by the sea. Beaches of black volcanic sand, hotels facing the Gulf of Mexico. I waved the driver past the air-conditioned foyers of plusher accommodation and took a room in a crumbling guest house. For the first few days I couldn't sleep, and instead climbed the fire escape on to the roof and sat wrapped in a blanket until the morning sun came hard and bright. By looking at the mass of stars wheeling across the sky I tried to console myself by feeling small, insignificant. If I slept I dreamed I was on the surface of a barren moon. And if I was awake this was what I tried to imagine, that I was the lone being on a pockmarked satellite, hoping that the theory of infinity was true. Because that would mean I hadn't done what I had in a different life. On another earth Kay was still alive, and I was now at home in bed with Jenni because I had, in this version of who I was, the sense and wisdom to know that what we had was so very precious. A love to be treasured, not discarded, abused.

But then the morning, the world and all its drama. Dashing taxis and honking horns, gaggles of laughing children walking to school.

If I stayed in the room my mind would play tricks. I'd turn and see her in the corner. Right there. Sitting on the wooden chair with her legs crossed. Standing naked in the bathroom, the gleam of light on her wet black hair.

Then gone.

I walked. I drank cans of Coke from vendors riding tricycles pulling ice boxes. Then I walked some more, along the black sandy beaches for miles. Lost my body in the pounding surf. Lost thought. I sat and studied shell fragments, fans of ceramic pink. Cold to the touch. Not a body, the warmth of another.

There was a night I went from bar to bar knocking back doubles. In a marble-tiled square women danced and sang. Men smoked cigars. But the tequila jumbled my thoughts of Kay, made me angry. And made me think of him. Death and murder. Drunk enough to ring his office in New York and leave blood-curdling threats with a polite secretary.

Pain, like a scalding, searing the back of my head.

One grey dawn I sat on the swings in an empty playground watching the sun rise, a cold white pearl in the morning haze.

I swam in the sea until I was exhausted, let myself sink and look back at the refracted surface. I tried very hard to kill myself. Then each time I came up for air, the gasping breaths.

If I closed my eyes I could smell her, the scent that had lifted me from my bones. I had flashbacks of tiny, forgotten moments. The way she turned her collar against the cold in Central Park, picking up a pine cone in the Catskills.

And scenes we hadn't lived. Walking a kitchen in a robe, her bare feet on a stone floor. Opening French doors on to a verdant garden. Pure fantasy.

Kay is dead, gone. I spoke the words aloud. An attempt to accept the bare truth, the plain fact. While I didn't kill her I must be responsible. Added to the blame of her murder is my betrayal of Jenni. I'd told her, as if it made an iota of difference to how she felt about what we did, that Kay too had spoken of her guilt over the affair.

But not over Segur. A killer. An unhinged man. Though to call another man that after what I did felt hypocritical.

The odd thing was that Jenni knew before I did that a man had been sitting and plotting my death. And she knew that a woman was involved, a body floating down a river. Yet she still paid a bribe and flew across an ocean to make sure I was okay.

If I'd had a call about Jenni and another lover I doubt I'd have reacted as nobly as she did on hearing where I was, days after I'd been too cowardly to call her and admit what I was doing.

And perhaps this was the flaw. No, not *the* flaw, but one of the flaws. That she was too good for me.

A 'mother-shaped hole in your universe', she'd said.

Was this the reason Kay and I were compelled towards each other from the beginning? Two people with black holes at the core of who they were, two stars swirling until one finally devoured the other.

Again, Jenni was probably right. A daughter, secure in the love of her family, certain that love was something good. Not a twisted fiery emotion that could burn whatever it touched.

With a sense of true grief I thought about her mother and father, people I came to love, then cut from my life. I hoped that when Jenni was ready to see me again, Philip and Freya and I could at least meet and talk. Though perhaps that was wishful thinking. I wouldn't blame her parents for never wanting to lay eyes on me again. I was the man who betrayed the love and trust of their precious daughter. Her father joked that I was the son he'd always wanted, and the pride he showed when I announced promotions or performed well on the cricket pitch was genuinely paternal. I imagine he felt my actions as a slur against all the family.

I had never doubted how Jenni felt about me, but I had doubted whether it was truly for the man I was, I am. I was wrong. She knew my darkest corners. And she knew I kept those places hidden from myself, so she in turn kept them hidden from me. Like the caretaker of a building upon a labyrinth of secret passages known only to her.

Why did I keep them hidden? Fear? Because I'd never escaped the death of my mother, the memory of her kisses on my head before I went to school, the softness of her touch, my hand in her palm?

But this was no excuse. A reason, maybe. But not an excuse for abandoning what Jenni and I had.

I put all this down in a letter to her. Pen on paper. An attempt to say what I couldn't in Monterrey, when emotions tangled with the words. When I read back my crooked writing I hoped it would explain me, make everything okay. However, I could only fail if I tried, and that trying, I'm afraid, was the best I could do.

The day after I posted the letter to Jenni I watched the fishermen fixing nets, sanding down boats and drinking coffee before sailing their puttering trawlers into the fiery dusk, returning only in the morning light when sagging catches of wriggling silver were hoisted on to the wharf, packed in ice and trucked over to the seafood market. Once I stopped sleeping on the roof and watching the stars I took some comfort in being part of something bigger than myself by following the comings and goings of the fish market, the plumbed depths brought to shore and unpacked by men listening to tinny radios pumping out rumba and old mariachi tunes as they wheeled barrows full of shrimp and lobster and brightly coloured fish alongside octopus and squid to the wooden trestles of the stalls. And behind the array of gleaming scales the salesmen and women stood. Boning fillets with flashing knives, weighing up the price then wrapping the cuts in paper to exchange for a few pesos. This greater rhythm of life that has thrummed along for billions of years without me, Kay or Jenni, the thought that our very minds and bodies have blossomed from organic molecules that rained on to the oceans before evolving beyond the haphazard drift of a single cell into beings capable of such profound grief, joy and *love*, seemed once again utterly remarkable.

Up until that night I'd kept the shutters in my room closed. I couldn't bear watching the cats step across the tiled roofs, the mother and her daughter in the apartment opposite sitting and chopping onions together, laughing at the TV, before welcoming home a husband, a father, with a glass of cold beer and a kiss.

When I opened up the shutters I believed I took a step back into the world, towards feeling again.

Believing I could be a better man. Not redeemed or saved. Just better.

In the last phone call Jenni said that she may one day forgive, but what does it matter if she can't forget. The truth is that I don't want to forget. I promised Kay I wouldn't.

I think back to the day in Central Park, when she showed me the lifeline on her palm, the abrupt end. I'd told her it was nonsense, superstition. I try to picture her hands, but I can't. When I imagine her now I feel so close to her that I can barely see her. Because she is in me, part of who I was, who I am. That I can't escape. No more than someone can escape the bones of their ancestors. From when I first saw her at the wedding I knew she always would be. And if I'm looking for a definition of love then perhaps this is it. That another person can help fill the empty space inside us. Even when they're gone.

# EPILOGUE

A STORM BLEW IN off the Gulf, and the trees that line this quiet street thrashed in the thunder and lightning as if tormented and flayed by an invisible hand. The rain came hard in stinging drops, soaking my shirt to my skin, flooding the narrow alleys where water streamed down the steps.

For days a humid air had hung upon the coast like a damp and fetid cloth draped over the city. The palm leaves flopped with a pallid languor, and the flies buzzed about with a pestering vim, perhaps aware that the oncoming weather was about to wash them from the sky.

First the wind picked up, a heated draught of oven-baked air slamming shutters and chasing plastic bottles along the cobbled streets, blowing hats off the younger men and leaving them clutching at nothing. The older men, long ago knowing what wind would steal their straw crowns, hung on tight to the wide brims.

Just as the rain came down in pellets, fired from the black clouds that tumbled off the ocean to the shore, I was walking along the wharf. And instead of running back to my hotel I stood for a while and watched the fishing boats rock on the choppy water, the harbour wall flare with the white of breaking waves. Gulls arrowed with the gale or beat their wings against the rain, heading out to the seamless horizon where sky and sea drew no lines but for the cracks of lightning.

I returned to my room, opened up the shutters and watched the veins of electricity illuminate the dark. When the storm finally abated I slept through till the morning, for the first time.

After a night of rain the streets gleam as if freshly painted. Monochrome into colour. But this may have more to do with my dream of Kay. A dream so vivid that to call it one seems wrong. Even though I leave this continent, I'm not leaving her.

Two days ago I booked a flight to London, departing from Veracruz this afternoon. By now Jenni will have read my letter. Though it's with more fear than relief that I will board the plane. It's all well and good for me to sit and grieve alone, to counsel myself, but she will be my judge, juror and jailer when I return. I do not say return home. She's taken the kittens and moved in with her friend, calling our flat as cramped as a coffin.

My final task is to pack the cheap suitcase I bought at the market. Not that I have anything but a few pairs of underwear, a couple of shirts and a razor. I bought the case because I need the act of carrying luggage, a semblance of normality.

After zipping it closed I open the shutters to the incandescent blaze of morning sun. A stark negative of a bare room. The wooden bed and dresser. A cracked mirror and a wardrobe full of wire hangers. I make sure I have my passport, still wrinkled from the river. I turn to the photo, the stranger in a shirt and tie. Then I check the bedside drawers one last time. Outside my window, past the rusting iron balcony, a cat walks the rooftops.

As I turn to pull the door shut the phone rings. An old-fashioned dialler and receiver, rattling with the call.

I pick up, say hello. No answer. I say hello again. Crackle and static, the faint murmur of a city in the background, traffic. Then nothing.

I put the phone down, grab my case and walk downstairs to the reception, a square-cut hatch in what looks like the family's living room wall. I can see the clerk, possibly the manager's son, watching a football game on a portable TV. He sees me at the counter and saunters over. I point at the phone on the desk, ask if he called my room. He shrugs his shoulders and shakes his head, then looks past me to the entrance of the guest house and says, 'You taxi?'

A white sedan is parked out front. I thank the clerk in Spanish, and have the thought that I've been here before. A man clicking across the marble floor of a hotel foyer, the night in New Orleans, the flowers on the table, Kay, the weight of her in my arms as I carried her along the corridor.

'Mr Sam, yes?'

The driver is slim and tall, well dressed, a white open-necked shirt and a dark blazer. I see my emaciated reflection in his mirrored sunglasses, the pounds I've lost. He takes my case and fiddles with the keys to the boot. 'Momentito.' He leans back inside the driver's door and flicks it open. I go through the charade of securing my nearly empty case, then walk round to the front passenger door.

'Please, señor.' The driver quickly opens the back door and says, 'More comfort.' He smiles, pats me on the back as I climb inside.

I take a last look at the guest house. The neighbour's cat on my balcony, watching us leave.

The driver smells of cheap cologne masking something else, maybe fire smoke. He pulls on to the highway, switches lanes by sticking his hand from the open window and waving with his palm inward and fingers to the sky, as if he were the president or the pope. At a bus stand he swings over and stops, turns and says, 'My brother,' then points through the windscreen at another man approaching the car. He's a little portly, squeezed into a shirt too small. I hope he doesn't want conversation.

He doesn't. The men barely nod at each other before the portly brother turns to me and briefly grins.

We pull away. The driver flicks the wipers on instead of the indicator. The blades judder on the dirty glass, and he mutters something in Spanish. When he misses the slip road back on to the highway I lean forward and say, 'We are going to the airport?'

The driver turns. 'Si, si. No problem.'

'Short cut,' says the portly passenger, a gold tooth flashing.

We take another highway, still under construction, the opposing lane coned off to traffic. Then another road, unpaved, veering from the elevated highway. The men talk quietly, nod to each other. I know the stories of kidnappings and extortion, the robberies. But this is something else.

By my feet is the driver's ID card. I pick it off the floor, and before I hand it over I see the smear of blood. The wet thumbprint. Then the mugshot, neither of the men in the front seats.

And when the driver crunches gears, again, I realize it's the unfamiliar gearbox, not a mechanical fault.

We head further from the highway, past a warehouse and a landfill. Dumper trucks filled with rubble. Beyond this spit of land is the sea, a band of electric blue. When I lean back from checking if the central locking is activated the portly man has already turned, the snub-nosed muzzle of a pistol jutting from his fist.

Segur has not let go of her. He never would.

But the final thought is mine.

I say, 'Tell him this.'

That last night I dreamed I was walking beside a river where great boulders had been washed down a mountainside. Stones from a different millennium shaped by seas and rain and the scouring wind. I hopped over the rocks then followed a dirt path across roots and pebbled shores towards the roaring sound of crashing water.

Like a long white ribbon dangled from the sky, a river fell from a cliff at the height of clouds. Mist swirled and smoked, rose from a pool of such clarity that she looked as if she were swimming in air.

## ACKNOWLEDGEMENTS

*The Hummingbird and the Bear* would not have its wings without James Gurbutt, David Miller and Alex Goodwin, whose input and editorial verve proved vital to publication. A special thanks, too, to Amy Montminy, not only for her fine work on the US side of the narrative, but also for sharing her drive and focus to ensure I finished the manuscript with the attention it deserved. I am also indebted to the sharp eyes of Nancy Webber and Jo Stansall for their expert help in preparing my words for the printer, and to the trustees of the K Blundell Award.

Where the novel heads south of the border I owe a muchas gracias to Christine Scott and David Maung for help with language and location, as well as to John Need for sharing his tales of rattling bus rides across the Mexican countryside.

A hearty thank you also for the feedback and encouragement from readers of earlier drafts: Nick Brown, Wes Brown, Amanda Elend, Michael Jones, Valeria Melchioretto, Wayne Milstead, Agustina Savini, Barrie Sherwood and Daniel Warriner. Your critique was always welcomed, and key to the polishing of script and story. Metaphors on mortgage selling akin to drug pushing must be attributed to the Graham Rayman article, 'Wall Street Walkers' in the 5 November 2008 *Village Voice*. The scenes of swimming seahorses to the aquarium of J. T. Boehm, and escapades in the Cotswolds to Jonathan Gibbard. For his continued dedication to my website I am very lucky to have the talents of David Cook. And I must also acknowledge the exemplary institutions of both the British Library in London and the New York Public Library in Manhattan, for providing the facilities and calm to write a novel when certain bars in Brooklyn, or the cafe in Foyles bookshop, were either busy, closed, or sick of me taking up their space writing.

I am especially indebted to those who shared personal stories and private histories that might have been painful to revisit, and hope I have been faithful to the essence of their original telling.

And finally, not forgetting a special thanks to Salena Godden for wearing a yellow dress in a sunlit field, the spark to a flame, a novel.